The Purrfect Arrangement

REGINA BROWNELL

HALF FATE PUBLISHING

Chapter 1

PENNY

I stare into the intimate crowd of adoring fans cheering me on. What once gave me peace now leaves me anxious. It's been that way since my parents passed away and I can't shake it. I'm about to play the final song on my tour. I used to be upset when it all came to an end, but between my parents and my breakup last year, I just want some time to myself.

"We love you, Penelope!"

I wave at the girls screaming in the front row. One of them covers her mouth as tears stream down her face. It's the one thing that keeps me going. I made a difference to her. My heart fills with happiness once more as I lift the mic to my mouth.

It's hot under the stage lights and a stubborn piece of auburn hair that fell loose from my ponytail is sticking to the side of my face. The round stage I'm on in the middle of the crowd is lit up white, casting a soft glow on the front few rows.

Life has been a whirlwind. I've been touring nonstop and released three albums since I won Talent in America at seventeen. It was a ride I never wanted to get off of until my life changed forever at twenty-two.

I place a hand on my chest and run my thumb over the bumpy design of butterflies on my locket. I always make sure it's there, safe and sound.

"Okay, Los Angeles! Are you ready for the last song?"

The roar from the crowd is a feeling I'll always love.

"This one is called "Forgetting You" and it's on my last album, *After*. Thank you so much for being here tonight."

I count off and lose myself in the music and the love.

※ ※ ※ ※

My manager, Tanner, who also worked with my late father, is ready and waiting in the wings. As usual she's dressed in all business attire, gray hair slicked back in a tight bun. Over her arm is my denim jacket and purse.

I can't wait to get back to the house and shower the sweat off my body. Maybe I'll take a bath and order some takeout. I hand my guitar off to a stagehand to put away. The area turns into total chaos as men and women in all black pass by to get to the stage and break things down.

"Great show," Tanner says, voice raspy as she steps into the dim lighting and wraps an arm around me.

I lean into her, my muscles feeling weak. "Thanks. I'm ready to crash."

"Let's get you home."

2

Oddly enough the word home gives me pause. I've lived in L.A. my whole life, but it never truly felt like the proper name for it. There's something missing, but I'm not sure what.

How can the girl who has everything feel incomplete?

She hands me my bag and denim jacket. Inside the pocket my phone starts vibrating. I pick it up as we navigate through the hallways. It's my sister, Sarina. I don't hesitate to answer. She lives in New York, so we don't see each other often. If I'm lucky enough to catch one of her calls, I always answer.

"Hey, Pen. How did the last night go?" she asks.

"I think it was my best night on tour. The fans were really into it and the meet and greet was probably the most fun. A lot of familiar faces. I'm so done though." I laugh but it comes out with tension as a lump forms in my throat.

"I'm so glad it went okay. Hopefully the media will—" I pause as the security guard at the end of the hallway opens the door. The January night air cools me off. My driver, Charles, is waiting beside the black stretch limo with the door open. I'm halfway there when flashes go off in my face. From around the corner of the brick building a crowd of media starts heading for me. My stomach knots. Tonight was not about interviews; it was about connecting with my fans through music.

"Penny, we'd like to ask you some questions!" a male voice in the crowd shouts.

"We aren't taking any questions at this time," Tanner says, placing an arm over my shoulder. She guides me to the limo through the chaos.

A rough booming voice yells at them to get back. They don't listen and my heart rate spikes.

"How does it feel now that the world knows that your whole career has been a lie?"

God, these vultures are everywhere.

"Miss Clarke." There's a mic shoved in my face. The woman's voice is smooth like glass. "It has come to my attention that a close friend of your fathers, Lance Greenfield, and your ex-boyfriend, Erick Platt, are releasing a documentary this April to address how your father played a huge part in your career. Do you have any comments on that?"

"Is it true your father paid producers of Talent in America so you would be the winner?" another man interrupts.

Heat surges through me. I don't know where to look because of the bright lights and chaos. Tanner's hand and my sister's faint voice in my ear are the only thing keeping me from breaking down in front of them.

"Penelope, do you admit to lip syncing live? And not writing your own music? Erick stated those in the leaked interviews," a third guy says.

"Penelope—"

They don't take turns, each one talking over the next. I can't get my thoughts in check with the chatter. I lock eyes with his deep brown ones. Charles. Tanner steps behind me so I can get in first. Beside us, a few guards stand between us and the media. I slide inside the limo.

"Close the door," Tanner says, while she's still standing outside.

I stare out at her.

"I'll take care of this," she says as I'm cut off from the mob.

I gasp for air as if it's being sucked out of the limo and I'm trying to hold onto the last of it. Voices and camera flashes seep through the tinted windows. I rest my head back against the seat and inhale for a few seconds, hold it, then let go.

"Pen? Penny? Everything alright? What happened?"

My sister's voice on the other end of the line sounds far away, unable to cut through the ringing in my ears.

Deep breaths, Pen. Deep breaths. My chest aches. Angry tears fill my eyes. *In and out. Come on. Snap the fuck out of it.* Was this how my parents felt the day of the accident? They were rekindling their love, and these vultures were the reason for their early departure from this earth.

"Penny? Do I have to get on a plane to come and get you? Damn it, Pen."

The knot in my throat is unbearable and painful. I can't do this anymore. It's been five years since my parents' accident, three years since I thought I found love, over a year since shit hit the fan and ended in a messy break up, and now all I want to do is go silent.

"Penelope Grace Clarke! Answer me right this second."

That snaps me out of it. My fingers graze over my locket. Inside holds a picture of a memory I don't ever want to forget.

"I'm here." My voice is barely above a whisper.

"What happened?"

I blow out of breath. "I don't know. There was so much commotion. Something about a documentary. I'm a fraud? I—I —"

"Pen. Hey. Breathe. Okay? Why don't you come to stay at my house. It's three thousand miles from the chaos."

I try to relax my body. Sarina stays quiet as I inhale and exhale slowly.

"Oh, I have an idea! Why don't you cat sit for me?"

"Cat sitting?" I ask into the phone, holding it between my shoulder and ear. "Sarina, have you lost your ever-loving mind?"

Sarina laughs like the hyenas in *The Lion King*. I miss her so much. When my singing career took off, I began to see less and less of her. We are eight years apart. I was ten when she moved to Long Island for college. Now, her career, her home, and her friends are there—her entire life. Except for me.

"Well, cat, axolotl, and a grumpy roommate," Sarina clarifies.

Leaning forward, I grab a bottle of something strong in the limo bar. The hem of my shorts rides up and the bare part of my leg sticks to the leather seat. Charles breaks hard and instead of me, my phone tumbles to the floor. Sarina's voice screeches through the speakers as I reach for it.

"Hey now, don't dismiss—"

"Sarina, chill. I dropped the phone."

I grab it, set it beside me, putting it on speaker. I pop open the bottle of Disaronno and down some of it. The smell reminds me of cake frosting for some strange reason.

"What makes you think this will keep the paparazzi off my back? I might be able to escape them, but what about all the things they said?" I ask curiously.

I've done my best to keep a low profile, but they just keep coming at me.

She scoffs. "You know half of it is probably a lie, right?"

Is singing even worth it anymore? I miss when it used to be me and my guitar. Now, it's all about tearing someone down.

I cap the bottle and put it back.

"Firstly, I need someone to take care of my pets because grumpy roommate and grumpy cat don't get along. He and the cat had a standoff yesterday," she says dryly, and I can practically hear the eye roll through the phone.

I snort. "He sounds like a winner."

"Zach's not bad. I was joking about the grumpy part. We have a weird friendship. He and I get each other. He's a good friend and roommate—pays me on time. He works late mostly, so he's not around much."

It's been a while since I've laughed. It was like after my parents passed, life decided to take a turn. One I was not prepared for.

"I miss you," she adds.

"I miss you too, but I don't know."

"I'll be gone three weeks tops. Zach is not going to take care of Larry and Petunia. Larry despises him and any time he gets near he growls and attacks."

"Are you sure this guy is safe to be living with? Even the cat and axolotl don't like him."

"Oh, no. Petunia, that sassy little pink amphibian, adores him. When he goes up to her tank, she's all gaga eyes."

"Sarina, she's a freaking axolotl. They have bad vision."

She giggles and a pang of longing hits my heart. Talking to her always makes me feel better.

"Believe what you want but I think she's got a crush. Anyway, he's not going to make sure she's fed, and her tank is clean. Then there is Larry. His litter box needs to be done. I leave at the end of the week. I was going to have a friend take care of them, but this is perfect. You can get out of the chaos of the city. Long Island isn't the middle of nowhere, but this neighborhood is quiet. You don't even have to go out. Think of it like a vacation. You can hide from the media even more than you have been. At least they won't be camped out on my lawn. They gave up on the offspring of Christopher Clarke who became a retail merchandiser years ago."

I pick at my nails. "A vacation where I have to clean litter boxes and tanks?"

"Please. I'm not below begging. I'm on my knees. Pretty please . . ."

She's not wrong. The media hasn't paid any attention to her or her whereabouts in years. The last time was for our parents' funeral. I have nothing coming up until spring when I record my next album. I can't remember the last time I was free of the media or had a break.

"Okay." I pause to take a breath. "I'll cat, axolotl, and grumpy roommate sit for you. Question . . ."

"Answer . . ."

I smile through the tears.

"I don't have to clean and feed grumpy roommate too, do I?"

Chapter 2

ZACH

Wingmans pub and grill has been my home since I was eighteen. There's something comforting about the random music playing, the clinking of glasses, muffled sounds of voices with the occasional cheer when their team scores a goal, and the aroma of chicken wings and alcohol.

I started out as a waiter the summer after high school. It was meant to be a job to get me through community college, but it turned into a full-time gig with slightly more pay.

"Yo, Zach! Can I get another beer?" Miles, one of our regulars, asks as I pass by his table.

At the center of it all between the bar at the front and the unused stage at the rear, there are round wooden tables. On the left wall are the TVs and where the sports fanatics, like Miles, hang out. They're a fun crowd.

"Gotcha, man. Give me five?"

"Yes, sir." He returns his attention to the game.

"C'mon, did you see him miss that?" his friend yells.

Their rowdy voices fade as I push through the doors beside the bar to enter the kitchen.

"Zach, table seven is ready," Danny, one of the cooks, calls out to me.

"Perfect, thanks."

The kitchen is in full swing with cooks and servers. It's not the most pristine-looking place, but it's as clean as you can get for an older building. We flawlessly pass each inspection.

I push back through the tan swinging doors. The Penguins scored. Everyone is hyped up. I serve table seven their food and in record time I'm handing Miles his beer.

"Damn it, hit him," Miles yells.

"This fucking guy. Shoot the puck!" His blonde friend joins in.

Miles stands, running a hand through his dark shaggy hair, making the bar stool he was sitting on wobble. "Pull the damn goalie!"

I stop at their table and check out the game. Islanders are so far behind it hurts. I watch hockey on occasion but never get fully invested like these guys.

"Bad news?" I ask.

"Playing like shit tonight," Miles grumbles.

"Can I get you guys anything else?"

"A new goalie?" an older gentleman deadpans.

"Wish I had the power."

I walk around to check my tables. The game cuts to commercial. A female anchor's serious voice comes from the speaker. "Christopher Clarke's documentary. How will this affect his daughters' career? Can she come back from this? Story coming up at eleven."

The name sounds familiar, but I ignore it as I see Clarice at her usual table near the stage. She's my late grandma's younger friend. She wasn't in my life until my early teens. There were times when she'd treat me better than my grandma, who was my primary guardian. I never knew who my mom was. My grandma refused to tell me. Clarice was more like a mother than my grandma ever was.

"Hey there, son. How are you?"

Her black hair, streaked through with gray, is up in a bun. As always during hockey season, she's wearing her favorite Islanders jersey. In her hand is a knitting needle. A smile lights up her eyes. They're a similar golden brown like mine. I pause at the sight of them. I've always felt this connection between us like she was there in my life for a reason. On the holidays, her gifts would always be thoughtful and things that I spoke about months prior would wind up under the tree.

"Not bad. Nice to have some noise in here again. Been quiet this winter," I say.

She pauses her knitting. Her favorite thing to do is make little things for the Wingmans team. Tonight, she's got the start of a clover going. She gave me one a few years ago. When the owner Mark and his wife Cynthia were expecting, she knitted them cute little sea creatures.

"Well, you know you always have my business."

"We should start one of those punch cards and when you get to the last one, we offer a free meal," I joke.

She waggles her pointer at me. "You were always one to think outside the box, Zach. Should bring it up to Mark. I could use a free roast beef sandwich."

Our laughter reaches the next table over to where some more of our regulars sit. A couple in their early thirties just married. They came back from their honeymoon last week and the first place they stopped was Wingmans. Clarice gives them a wave. Most of the people who normally come in know each other.

"How's Sarina doing? I haven't seen her around much," she asks. Sarina is my friend and roommate.

"She's been working a lot. Thankfully she hasn't gone out of state since I've moved in. Larry the cat has a vendetta against me."

Clarice laughs. "He's not the man of the house anymore. Give him time."

I shake my head in amusement. "Time? I've been there for almost a year."

She smiles. "Well, give her a hello from me, will ya? That girl never takes a break."

"I keep telling her to, but she won't listen. Is there anything else I can get for you tonight before I head up to the office?"

I have a meeting with Mark. I've been going over in my head all day what it could be. I've heard rumors from customer questions about layoffs due to some financial troubles, but I won't believe anything until I hear it from his mouth.

My shoulders stiffen at the unimaginable happening to this place. I stare off for a moment or two before Clarice's touch pulls me from my thoughts. She squeezes my hand, and I peer down. I get lost in the comfort of it. It's completely unlike my grandma, who pretty much left me to fend for myself and never once hugged or appreciated anything I had done around the house for her.

"I'm good, Zach. Thanks. I see the worry in your eyes, son. Keep your chin up."

I charm her with another grin before letting go. I climb the stairs to the office and glance out at our mostly full pub. I'm probably worrying over nothing, but losing this job would mean another setback for me. Despite living with one of my good friends, I still am paying her rent because I'm not there to live off her livelihood—I'm there to get back on my feet.

I'm the only one in the office as the heavy wooden door shuts behind me. It's a small square room with an attached bathroom. Along the same wall as the bathroom at the far side of the room are tan lockers for employees. Directly across are black filing cabinets. We don't normally hold full staff meetings here due to the size.

I take a seat in the chair behind the desk for a breather. I stare at all the awards hanging throughout the room. Long Island's Best and all the others give me hope this meeting has nothing to do with the downfall of this place.

The door opens and my body tenses at the possibility of what's to come. The sounds of "Austin (Boots Stop Work'n)" by Dasha filters in along with Maddie, one of my good friends and the bartender here.

Madeline gives off a biker girl vibe with her leather jacket and raven black hair. Underneath the persona she's the exact opposite. She's well loved by our guests. Our eyes meet and despite her carefree singing, her usual vibrant, hazel ones appear heavy.

"Oh, hey Zach." She greets me cheerfully, but behind it her voice wavers.

"You know one day you better take Sarina up on her offer to take you to a karaoke bar with those pipes of yours," I tease.

"You won't catch me on any karaoke stage, but I could say the same about you! With those pipes of yours, you'll blow people away."

Only very few know about my ability to sing.

"These pipes are for the shower only."

Her laughter isn't full, but her spark is still there buried under the sadness. I don't dare ask what's going on. Her wedding ring keeps disappearing and returning. Tonight, it's gone. I know there are troubles, but Madeline is one of those I'll come to you when I'm ready kind of people. I'm not her first choice and I'd probably give shit advice anyway. She has a person. It's Sarina.

The door to the office swings open and the owner of Wingmans, Mark Rosendale, stands tall at a jarring six foot three. He crowds the doorway, gaze sweeping across the room.

"Hey guys, I'll make this quick."

Maddie leans on the front of the desk and as I get out of Mark's chair, she and I exchange a look. I think we're both wondering the same thing. I walk around and stand beside her.

Mark inhales deeply before speaking. "The last two winters have been a bit rough in regard to making enough to get out of the red. Our summer rush for the year wasn't enough to help us with our recent lull. I've been trying to come up with ways to get more bodies in here, but I'll be honest, I'm burnt out. With my wife pursuing the next stage of her career and childcare . . . it's been rough."

The color in his face drains. The man I've looked up to is crumbling before me. There's no anger behind his voice—only sadness. He stares at the floor. Mark opened the pub the summer he graduated college with the help of the professor who believed in him. It's had its ups and downs but ultimately survived.

Madeline grabs hold of the desk, knuckles white. "What can we do to help?"

The words were on the tip of my tongue, but I'm speechless. I tried to deny the rumors I heard.

He lifts his head, rubbing the dark scruff on his chin.

"Yeah, man. Anything. Just say the word," I offer.

His cheeks puff with his next exhale. "For now, keep up your A game as usual. I'm not sure there is much we can do. I'm all for ideas and I'm trying to keep a positive mind about this. I'm going to meet with my lawyer soon to go over things, but I just wanted you to be prepared."

"Does anyone else know?" Maddie's voice is small.

"I told Pat, Danny, and Ryan since they were on shift last night. The rest I'll do as they are in. I wanted to wait but I also want to be transparent. My staff's wellbeing comes first and it's not fair for me to spring it on anyone at the last minute. I'm trying to look at things logically and I'm taking one step at a time. It's a lot, but I'm hoping all the worry is for nothing."

I rest my hand over Maddie's, and she loosens her grip on the desk. I do it more to comfort her but also to calm my erratic heart.

"We're here for you, Mark," I say. "You've been there for me and now it's my turn to step up for you." The words and what I'm feeling deep down do not match. I want to be there for him and help but the fear has my brain frozen. Not a single idea comes to mind.

"Thank you both so much. We'll take it as it comes. Alright?"

We talk for a few more minutes about the night ahead before leaving. Mark stays in the office. The music and noise hits us as the door to the office closes. Maddie and I stare out at the hustle and bustle below. Laughter and cheers ricochet from the far side of the pub as one of the teams scores a goal. I take it all in, in case one day it all disappears.

"We'll be okay," Maddie says. "I just know it."

Chapter 3

ZACH

I groan as the sunlight pierces through the annoying white curtains across the room. It dances over the wood flooring in a streak. I'd like to get around to changing them to the blackout ones. It's not going to match the royal blue paneled walls, but I—shit, well I wasn't planning on taking up space in Sarina's house forever, but after last night I don't know what is going to happen.

"Oh, Zachary!" Sarina calls in a sing song voice, banging on the door.

Speak of the devil.

I run a hand through my sleep disheveled brown waves of hair. It's just long enough to tug on the ends. I'm a mess over the situation I'm in.

"Zach Efron," she teases.

"Zach Cullen," I correct, in a voice that matches hers.

I didn't get home until almost four in the morning from my shift. My hours don't give me the best quality of sleep and it's only . . . oh, shit, it's three in the afternoon.

"Can I come in? You're not walking around naked again, are you? Not like it matters—ding lings don't exactly get me all hot and bothered."

This woman has no filter. I chuckle. "I'm good, come in."

The door flies open. Her hand and wrist with a silver chain bracelet is the first thing I see poking through the opening. She waves it around, the charms on the bracelet jingling. With one hand covering her eyes, she steps in. She peeks between her fingers.

"I thought you said it didn't matter?" I pretend to pull off the sheets and she screams.

"I can raise your rent, you do realize this, Mr. Efron."

I huff a laugh. "Yeah, but you won't."

"I won't if you do me a favor."

I sit up, lean against the headboard and cross my arms over my bare chest. She removes her hand, uncovering her brown eyes. Sarina is a good-looking woman. I flirted with her when we met, but then she straight up told me men weren't her thing. That was years ago and now we have this friendship filled with sarcasm and humor.

"So, my next job is out of state, and I'll be gone a couple of weeks. That doesn't mean you can invite women over to play."

"Sarina, you know not a single woman has made it to this bed. You would have heard it through the thin walls."

She places an index finger on her chin and looks up. "Point taken."

I haven't felt much like dating since my ex, Macy. Before her, relationships were carefree and easy, but when you buy a ring for someone and they break up with you on the same day, it hits a little differently. What's even better is finding out she's engaged to the doctor she left you for the morning you lose your apartment because of a mold infestation. Last year was not my best.

"I have a big ask, but I trust you'll be okay with it." She tugs a hair tie off her wrist and throws her golden-brown waves up into a messy thing on top of her head. Like she's preparing for a battle.

She has an 'I wore Abercrombie and Uggs in high school vibe'. Today, she's in a flannel shirt, unbuttoned so her bra is nearly showing.

"Shit, I have to take care of your evil cat, don't I?"

"Hush and listen. My sister needs a getaway."

"The famous sister?"

"My only sister."

"Right. Proceed." I twirl my hand in a keep going gesture.

"She's struggling. The press is so far up her ass it worries me. Our dad did something stupid in his past and now we're paying for the consequences. She's safer here as my cat and axolotl sitter."

"How does one axolotl sit?"

"Zachary, you're wearing my patience thin."

I raise a brow at her.

She sighs. "She was hesitant, but I convinced her it's her best option. Do I need to draft up an NDA? You cannot, for any reason, leak where she is. No matter what. Even if a pap comes up to you with ten zillion dollars. She's my baby sister and I need her to be safe."

Is her sister fluent in sarcasm like she is? If so, we will get along fine. I honestly don't care to out her to anyone. I don't have time for drama of that persuasion, and I prefer to live life under the radar.

I'd do almost anything Sarina asked me to do. She gave me a place to stay when I was living out of my car.

"I'll keep an eye on her. I don't want chaos. I like living my quiet life here with you."

"Rule number two: don't be a dick. You need to be nice."

"I'm always nice."

She purses her lips, and I chuckle.

"Also, don't flash her your adorable little grin."

My lip curves into a smile.

"There it is—please, don't do that. You have this little dimple. Even under the reddish brown thing you call scruff on your handsome face, you can still see it."

"So, I'm handsome now."

"Zachary Efron, please listen to me. Another thing is don't get me started with your hair. Women love men with wavy hair they can run their hands through."

I snort. "Are you a hair expert?"

She ignores me.

"No flirting. Got it," I say.

"I won't be here when she comes so can you kind of show her the ropes and everything?"

"When is she coming?"

"She'll be here on Friday. Three days from now. Her plane gets in at noon, so maybe around two or three?"

"Okay, I'll be here. I have work at six."

"Perfect. Thanks, Zach. I appreciate it. Oh . . ." Her voice softens. Worried lines wrinkle her forehead. "Do you mind if I check in with you occasionally? I know it sounds crazy, but I need to know from an outside perspective how she's doing."

I don't use social media, but I might need to check in to see what is causing the media frenzy.

"Yeah. Sure. Anything you need."

"Thanks." She whirls for the door but stops and points a finger. "And rule number . . . I can't remember. No sleeping with my sister."

"Well, now you're—"

"Eh!" Her eyes widen as she tilts her head.

"But I—"

"Neh!"

I laugh. "Joking, Sarina. I promise to be good."

She grins. "Good boy. Now I've got some packing to do." She takes another step, but again doesn't get far. "Thank you. Truly. She's . . ."

Sarina's cool demeanor falls. She glances at the hardwood floor and takes a few deep breaths. Since I've moved in, I have never seen her so distraught. I remove the blankets and pad over to her.

"Sarina?" I place a hand on her shoulder.

She inhales and exhales. "She's been through a lot the last few months. I'm worried about her. I say the sleeping thing not because I don't trust you if something did happen." She narrows her eyes. "Her ex used her, and it didn't end well. There's a documentary about my family. It's not good. She's here to get away. Love is the last thing on her mind. Be nice? Okay?"

"So, no walking around naked, huh?"

She glares at me, a tiny hint of a smile on her lips. "No. Absolutely not. And she's not an asshole like me, so maybe a little less sarcasm. Although, she's used to my ass so . . ."

Laughter bellows up inside of me. "Got it. Be half an asshole."

She smacks me playfully on the shoulder, and I pull her into a one-armed hug.

"Are you hugging me right now?" she asks.

"Thought you could use one."

She pushes me away and grins. "Yeah, I think I did. Oh, can you feed Larry for me tonight? I have to run out around dinner time."

Larry must know he's been summoned because the tiger striped demon cat glares at me from the hallway.

"It's watching me."

She laughs. "It knows you're afraid of it—him. I'm only asking this once? Okay?"

"Sure, sure."

I step forward to shut my door. She's already down the hall when demon cat starts swatting at the air as if I'm going to attack it.

"Larry, psst, psst," Sarina calls and he follows.

Chapter 4

PENNY

The private jet into Islip was a relaxing ride. I never liked planes. The first time I flew by myself I was sixteen. Dad invited me on his summer tour in Europe. I thought I was going to die on one because the turbulence was so bad. The hardest part for me and my sensitive stomach is the takeoff and landing. Thank God for those anti-nausea bracelets or I'd be fucked.

Memories flicker before me on my phone. A soft smile grazes my lips as my eyes fill with emotion. When I'm feeling anxious, I sometimes replay an old home video I found after my parents passed. While the hard copy is at my home in L.A. I recorded a bit of it to have with me.

The Great American Music Awards in 1994. It's a night I'll never forget even though I wasn't born yet. It was the year Dad won the Artist of The Year award. When I was little, I always asked Mom to put on the tape with the footage from the red carpet. To me she looked like a princess in her long golden dress. Her sandy blonde hair was pinned up in a stunning updo. It curled a little on top, and in the front, she had two thick curled strands. Camera's flashed and the dress sparkled when she moved. It hugged every inch of her so beautifully.

Dad walks up to her left side, his dark eyes focused only on her. He's in an all-black tux with the button not fully done. His shoes shine from the lights and his dark hair is slicked back with a ton of gel. Mom's face lights up with joy and pride as she holds Dad's arm. He takes her all in before she glances up and the two lock eyes. My heart is full yet so broken at the same time. I sniffle and wipe my tears. They turn to the cameras. I'm in awe. The King and Queen of rock hold a special place in my heart.

I stop the video and peer out the window. The limo pulls up to the curb in front of a small, yet spacious, light gray sided colonial home. The lawn is well kept but is more of a faded green from the winter months. My favorite part is the front porch. I'm sure it's Sarina's too, as she loved the one from our childhood home. The pictures of the place don't do it justice.

> Hey, I've arrived. I'll let you know when I'm settled. Hopefully Larry hasn't murdered your roommate yet. I'm sure if he did, he'd plot something evil with Petunia.

My sister responds within seconds. It's funny—my inbox is completely silent other than Sarina. The moment the documentary was announced, the people who I thought were my friends stopped talking to me. I release a shaky breath and try and hold it together. I've got to move on and get my head on straight.

> *Sarina: Shit! I didn't even think about that. I kind of like Zach. Hopefully he's still in one piece. Oh . . . and Pen?*

> *Yeah?*

The trunk of the limousine opens. There's some commotion as Charles grabs the luggage and places it on the sidewalk. He didn't park in the long driveway. There's only one car. It's a gray Nissan. I'm assuming it's Zach's.

> *Sarina: Never mind. Be good, okay?*

I narrow my eyes at the phone as if my sister was standing right in front of me.

> *Sarina: Mom and Dad would have been proud of you for taking a step back, and for being strong when it got to be too much. I know I am. Love you lots. XOXO.*

I swipe out of the messaging app and staring back at me is a family photo. Dad's hair was a lot messier than it was at the award show. He was the tallest of the bunch at six feet. Mom's hair falls in waves at her shoulders. We share the same rounded nose, while she and Sarina have brown eyes. Sarina was ten and me only a tiny tot with pig tails in my father's grasp. The photo screams cheesy department store portraits but it's one I keep close.

What would Dad think about this documentary? What would I say to him? He paid my way to the top. I can't believe I won the show *Talent in America*, not from votes, but from power. My heart sinks.

The door to the limo opens. A cool Long Island winter breeze flitters through. I forgot to dress more appropriately for New York weather. This light black sweatshirt is not enough.

"Miss, we're here," Charles says.

I step onto the sidewalk of a quiet neighborhood. I breathe in and out, allowing the air to infiltrate my nose. Birds sing and some children laugh in the distance, but it's mostly calm. A car drives by. The one thing missing is the click of cameras and the voices asking questions.

I exhale and open my eyes.

Charles smiles at me. "Can I help you get inside?"

"Thank you, but I think I've got it."

I grab the handle of my rolling suitcase beside him. The matching black carry-on bag is situated on top. I don't know why I'm so nervous. It's time for me to relax. I don't have to leave the house if I don't want to. There are so many things I can do and not get noticed. I've got my hat and glasses. A mask to be safe. It will have to do for now.

The suitcase bumps over the two steps of the porch and I roll it across the creaky old flooring. I go to knock when there's a yelp from inside.

"Larry! Larry, don't you dare. I'm—stand down you raging ball of fur!"

A laugh that felt like it could be heard for miles tumbles from my mouth. I should probably save him.

"Uh . . .Zachary?" I knock on the door. "Hello?"

"Fucker. I got you..."

There's a crash and scream. I turn the handle and to my surprise it opens and bangs against the wall. A grown man is crouched on the back of a knocked over chair. The cat is positioned only a few feet away. His striped fur and tail are ruffled.

"Larry," I say sweetly. "Psst psst psst."

I let go of my luggage handle. It takes a few seconds for the cat to realize I'm in the room. Forgetting about Zachary, he prances towards me. Larry weaves in and out between my legs, purring and rubbing his face on me.

"That's a good boy, Larry. Yes, such a good boy," I coo.

I bend to pet him but Zachary yells out. His voice startles the cat. Instead of a nice pet I'm met with claws.

"Ow, damn it, Larry, I thought we were friends."

"That demon cat only loves Sarina," he says.

I turn my gaze from demon cat to the grumpy human. Zach's light golden-brown eyes find mine through wavy strands of his hair hanging in his face. My cheeks heat under his magnetic stare. I hate the way I inhale to combat the unsteady beat of my dumb heart. I lift my hand to my chest and tinker with my silver locket.

"Demon cat knows his aunty. We cuddled when he was a wee itty-bitty kitten."

He tilts his head to the side and runs a hand through his unruly hair. I try hard not to watch as one strand keeps falling back. He makes an annoyed little huff, and it's kind of adorable.

"Demon cat, really? A cuddler? Are you pulling my tail?" he asks, his attention focused on me as if he's forgotten the cat attack.

I snort. "I don't pull tails, Zachary. I'm serious. He and I were BFFs. Cat's might have a limited number of people and places saved in their long-term memory, but it doesn't mean they can't remember years later."

"First, love, it's Zach. And second, are you a catspert or something?"

His baritone voice on the word *love* causes goosebumps to rise on my arms. Nicknames usually irk me, but somehow, the way it rolls off his lips does something to me.

"Love?" I retort, trying to hold back a grin.

He shrugs.

"First rule, no nicknames. Okay, sunshine?" I tease.

A slow grin tugs on his lips, exposing a tiny dimple underneath the light scruff on his face.

"You've got rules like Sarina, huh?"

He's good looking and sarcastic. I laugh to myself. It's no wonder he and Sarina get along swimmingly.

I ignore him. "Second, we weren't allowed to have cats growing up because we were always on the go. Sarina and I wanted one so badly. We picked Larry out together. When I left to tour Sarina said he cried for hours."

Zach gets to his feet. He's taller than me, enough where I have to crane my neck slightly to meet his eye. He bends in his tight jeans to grab the chair. My eyes betray me, and I can't help that I focus on his ass. He resets the chair and Larry growls like a dog.

"I see you're as fluid in sarcasm as your sister."

I shrug, trying to keep cool but fail with a smile. "I dabble."

Larry hisses as I pick him up. To my left is the entryway to the den. I scratch behind his ear, and he mellows out. As I cross the threshold to the bright white, eggshell colored room, he wrestles out of my arms. He lands and trots over to a fluffy cat bed beside an old tan couch.

I turn back towards the main room.

"Shit, Penelope your hand is bleeding."

I stare down. "Huh? Oh."

He's got a battle scar too. There's blood seeping through his grey T-shirt near his chest. "You are, too. He got you good."

"Your sister will kick me out if we get blood on her white area rug."

"Don't be dramatic, Zachary."

He rolls his eyes. "Come on. Let's clean up before we both get kicked out."

The floorboards creak under our feet. He leads me down the hallway. The house has an old feel to it. My sister said her favorite part was the charm. According to her it was built in the early 1900s. It's also been renovated to keep up with the times.

He pushes on a wooden door that's small and tucked away beside a flight of stairs. There's no shower in this one.

"Our first stop on our tour is the downstairs bathroom," he says, in a tour guide kind of voice.

He rummages through the medicine cabinet above the sink and places some alcohol on the counter.

"It's best to clean the wound with soap and water a few times first. The alcohol can harm the tissue and delay healing."

With his hand still on the bottle he meets my gaze and narrows his eyes. "Alright."

"Did you try to pick him up?" I ask.

"Maybe. I'll be fine." He kneels and opens the wooden cabinet under the sink. "Here." He gives me a bar of soap.

I open the box and set it on the counter with the soap on top.

"Thanks. You should clean yours, too."

"Are you offering?" He wiggles his brows.

"Don't flirt with me, Zacha— Zach." I fidget with the ends of my hair, twirling it around my index finger.

Shit. I stop the gesture. I'm on the receiving end of another grin. My sister claims this man is grumpy. I'm not seeing the grump factor. He's just sarcastic.

He reaches for the hem of his shirt. "Oh, wait. I'm not supposed to be naked around you. Your sister's rule, not mine."

"I've seen a naked man's chest before. Keep it in your pants and we're all good."

"Yes, ma'am." He proceeds to lift his shirt up and over his head.

The scratch is above his left peck. He examines it in the mirror. It's not deep but the blood is dripping. I've completely ignored the fact that blood makes me squeamish because I can't stop staring at his chest. Light hair covers most of it and while he's in shape, and—damn it, Penny, don't look at the V—he doesn't have a six pack. To be honest, I'm more attracted to that over abs.

He swipes the soap first, turns on the sink, and cleans his hands.

"Can I touch your hand?" he asks.

"Uh. Yeah. Okay." I mutter.

He grabs hold of my hand. His touch is warm and gentle. Am I even breathing?

The water streams over the scratch letting the blood swirl around inside the basin. He runs his thumb across my skin. I keep my eyes on the sink and not him. He pats my hand dry with a sterile pad. With his other hand he grabs the antiseptic cream, puts it on the cut, and tops it off with a bandage.

"You're all set." He examines his wound. "I should hop in the shower. Thanks for offering though." He bumps his hip with mine as he walks by.

I stumble and blink. He stops in the doorway and rests his hands on top of the molding. "Come on, your room is on the way."

As if I've been daydreaming, I shake my head and follow him out of the bathroom. He grabs my luggage near the front door, then leads me to the stairs.

"What a gentleman," I mumble.

He smirks.

At the top, the bathroom door straight across is open. He moves out of the way for me.

"Your sister has the master down the hallway." He points. "Um... mine is right here." The room he's referring to is on our left. "You have two options. The one beside your sister's room or mine."

"She says the walls are thin," I say.

"Planning on having guests?" He gives a suspicious cock of his brow.

"No. You?"

"No."

"Good. We're on the same page. Should we add it to the rules? No nicknames, keep it in your pants—"

"Or shirt." He points at my chest but doesn't let his eyes stray there.

"I agree, but I'm not someone who walks around in my birthday suit to begin with," I say. "Won't all of your lady friends be sad they can't come over?"

He chuckles and scratches his scruffy cheek. "Those are few and far between."

"Sure." I look him up and down wondering how a guy as flirty as him isn't dating around. There's something about the way he stays focused on me that makes me believe him. "Okay, um . . . let me have a look and see which one I prefer."

"Be my guest. I'm gonna shower. I have to work in a few. There's enough to eat, but I do have to make a trip to the store. Oh, and I label my food, so don't take it, and I work late, so don't wait up. K?"

"Wasn't planning on it." I roll my eyes as I pass by and then disappear into the first room.

It's a decent size with light blue paint on the wall. It's simple and there isn't much in here. A full-size bed in the middle and an old oak dresser across from it. I'm not feeling it, so I head to option two.

I pass by the closed bathroom door. Over the sound of the water running, Zach's voice shines through. I press my ear against it. I won't lie. I'm shocked he's singing "Perfect" by One Direction. His range is damn good. Is this normal for him? Or is he doing it to impress me?

I'm about to walk away when he hits the chorus. He belts it out as if he were on stage. His tone kind of matches Harry's with a rasp. There's something about the carefree way he's singing that brings comfort. Like he's not doing it for attention or to be noticed but because he's having fun with it.

The door to the room I'm facing is ajar. Sunlight streams through soft white curtains. I'm in awe of the yellow walls. It's bright like summer. The full bed is covered in a yellowish green patterned quilt. There's a smaller rectangular window on the opposite side of the room beside where the ceiling comes to a weird angle.

Warmth envelopes me as I fully embrace the space. There's a desk near the weird, angled roof. It's empty. The dresser is against the wall with the door. It's smaller, but I don't mind.

I take a seat on the bed. From here, Zach's voice is easily heard. There's something comforting about it. I get a sense of home. I hold onto my locket and my phone buzzes in my pocket.

> **Sarina:** *You picked the yellow room, didn't you? I don't know why but I knew it would call to you. Love you. Was Zach in one piece?*

> *All his pieces are well intact . . . that sounds wrong. Anyway, yes, I picked the yellow room. It reminds me of our house growing up.*

> **Sarina:** *<3 <3*

I place the phone beside me and slip off my Chuck Taylor's. Laying back, I stare up at the smooth white ceiling. My mind is racing with how the next few weeks are going to play out. Zach doesn't seem too bad. He didn't ask for an autograph or picture. There were no questions about the documentary, my ex, or fame. It was like I could breathe for the first time in a month. Was there a flirty edge to his teasing? Maybe. But he wasn't flaunting what he had at me. Most men are about showing off how they spend their money to impress me. Zach was just Zach.

"Brrrrrrr," Larry purrs, jumping up onto the bed. He pushes at my arm and forces his way into my embrace, making himself comfortable.

"See, I knew you loved me." He purrs loudly as he rests his head.

I scratch behind his ear in all the places I remember he loves. We lay there for a while. I hum random songs by anyone but me.

The fresh scent of soap lingers in the air. I open my eyes and lull my head to the side. Zach is dressed in khakis and a black tee. He rests his arm against the door.

"Wow, he is capable of love after all."

I grin. "See. Absolutely no tail pulling here."

His lip twitches and he shakes his head. "Later, Pen."

I narrow my gaze. "Later, Z."

He chuckles and leaves. Once the front door shuts, I enjoy the mostly silent room. The exception being Larry's loud motor. I take a deep calming inhale, hold it, and let go, loving the sound of nothing.

I remind myself no one is waiting outside my house ready to snap a picture. I'm safe here.

The silence is perfect.

Chapter 5

PENNY

Despite not having anywhere to be, I still managed to wake up early. I was half asleep when Zachary came sneaking in at almost six in the morning. The floorboards creaked under his weighted step and it's what woke me from my slumber.

I attempted to fall back asleep but was smacked in the face by a determined paw attached to one insistent cat. Around six-thirty, I hauled my ass out of bed and went downstairs.

Now here I am thirty minutes later and the kitchen is not as clean as it was. Egg shells litter the island tile countertop. My black shirt and yoga pants didn't stand a chance against the pancake mix.

I absolutely adore the kitchen—from the wooden floors to the ornate cabinetry. The island in the center of it all is perfect to sit at or even use to prep meals, which is what I did.

I've got my phone on the island. It's playing one of my favorite New York radio stations. I had fun being on their morning show a few times. The weekend crew is on, and they're playing some banging hits for so early on a Saturday morning. I dance around the kitchen because for the first time in a while there's a feeling of freedom.

Bacon pops and sizzles in the oven. The timer goes off. I race to it, sliding in my socks across the room. It only takes me a second of pain to realize I forgot the mitts. I yelp and tug my hand.

"Shit. Ow. Fuck. Damn." I hiss.

I grab a mitt attached to one of the drawers near the sink. The bacon appears to be done. I'm not one to cook breakfast. Hell, I know it makes me look like a snobby rich princess, but I've had people making me food since before I can remember. Between that and door dash, I've only tinkered with some recipes here and there. I figure breakfast is a piece of cake.

I set the glove on the counter. My finger hurts so bad. It's throbbing and turning red. I sigh and run to the sink across the room. A large round table and chairs sit in the center of the dining area to my left. There's a matching light brown hutch filled with the nice dinnerware, the type you only use on holidays. I pause, taking in the familiar yellow design around the outside of the plate.

They're moms.

We had so many Thanksgiving dinners on those dishes. The last one is crystal clear in my mind. My parents were happy and all of us were together, including Sarina. My heart swells with emotion.

The Tate McRae song on the radio fades out and the DJ starts talking over the outro. At first his voice is drowned out by the sink, but my ears perk up as the name Erick Platt tumbles from his lips. Why did my ex have to be famous? As if the memories of his betrayal aren't enough, I have to see his face almost daily on the internet.

"If you haven't heard, a new leaked statement has been circulating social media with Erick Platt's interview from *Star Power: The Downfall of a Rockstars Daughter*. It's quite juicy, folks. Here's a short clip."

I'm stuck staring off into nothing. A stream of dust floats around in a ray of light from the window above the sink. I'm lost in it. Mom's dining set blurs into the background.

"Penelope is only hurting herself by not talking. It speaks volumes about her character."

I cringe, hating the condescension in his tone. It's one I remember well towards the end of our relationship as the distance started to rip us apart. The radio DJ cuts the clip and asks for viewers' opinions before queuing up a new song.

The sink continues to run. It's lukewarm I think, but all I have the energy to focus on are those plates and what I heard on the radio. The pancakes start smoking.

"Fuck."

It seems to be the word of the day. I shut the water. By the time I flip the pancake over, the underside is mostly brown. I sigh and pour another dollop of mixture onto the skillet. This time I'm able to cook it without burning or getting close to burned.

As I turn off the stove my phone vibrates to life on the center island. It's Tanner. I shut the radio app and swipe to answer the call.

"Hi, Tanner. Still waking up before dawn?" I try to sound unbothered.

From a business standpoint she wasn't too happy with my decision to hide, but as a friend, she understood.

I lean my elbows on the surface of the island.

"You aren't my only client, Penny." She coughs to clear her smoker's rasp.

For her it's only a little bit after four in the morning.

"Which rumor are we discussing now?"

"Sweetheart, the question is what rumor aren't we?"

I groan. "Okay. Okay. Point taken. What's going on?"

"I had some thoughts. When was the last time you wrote a new song? You still have an album to make."

I bite my lip. I know exactly how long it's been. My tour bus and hotel room wastebaskets were filled to the brim with crumpled up papers. Half written songs always strewn everywhere but ultimately left to the trash because nothing felt right. Most artists get fueled by their breakups, but not me. It only hindered my ability to write. Not like when my parents passed, and the words flowed endlessly with feelings of pain.

"Before the tour. Maybe."

"Well, while you are sitting around doing absolutely nothing, maybe I don't know, write some? I'm not trying to be an asshole."

She's the most unprofessional professional I know.

"But . . . when you come out of hiatus you are due to record a new album. We have our meeting in March to discuss the remainder of the contract."

The idea of a new album and tour used to be something I looked forward to. Dad would be part of the team during recording. He was always hands on with my career in terms of my voice, my brand, and my songs. Mom was my tour buddy. She was great with schedules and keeping track of soundchecks and interviews. When Tanner was stuck in L.A., she was the middleman. My parents played a huge role in my career and I'm beyond grateful for it.

"Pen?" Her voice softened. Still raspy, but low enough to be a whisper. "Listen to me, sweetheart. We need to crush those insecurities. Mute the voices telling you, you don't deserve this life. Out of any artist I work with, you are the hardest working one. You show up to everything. You give your time to help fans in need. Hell, you even followed in your father's footsteps and set up the program for underprivileged kids to enjoy music in their neighborhood. You are a force to be reckoned with. The gossip, as they all do, will pass. Give it time. Allow yourself to feel something good."

I try to swallow back the growing lump in my throat. The thing is people never see the good a celebrity does.

"I'll try," I manage to choke out. "I can't guarantee it will be any good. I don't have my guitar."

"Have faith. And no worries. I'll get it to you. I have to call my next client, but please keep me in the loop. Alright?"

"Ok," I say.

"Stay well, sweetheart."

After a few long, deep breaths to help center myself, I set my sights back on my breakfast. It's probably cold now, but I'm starving and don't care. I fill my plate and leave some extra's on an additional one. My stomach grumbles as I move towards the table.

"What in the hell happened in my kitchen?"

My pancakes and bacon go tumbling onto the floor. Only one remains along with a piece of bacon teetering on the edge.

I spin to face Zach. "Jesus, you scared the shit out of me."

"It's Zach, remember? But I'm flattered you'd believe I was something of a higher power."

I throw my head back and groan. "Real original," I say.

He chuckles, but it's short lived when he gets a good look at me.

"Honestly though, what happened?"

"I cooked myself breakfast."

"Oh?" He strolls over to the bacon, lifts a piece, and eats it. He hums with each bite.

"Crisp."

After I clean up the food on the floor I head back to the counter. We're facing opposite directions. Him with his back against the edge and me leaning into it with my stomach.

"Do you cook often?" he asks.

Erick used to criticize me for not cooking. I expect Zach to make the same assumption. I'm surprised when I'm met with curiosity instead of judgement.

"No. I don't. I usually have someone . . ." I stare at the floor. "I usually have someone to do it for me. Either that or take out, door dash. I mean, I can make a mean chicken nugget but . . ."

"Like throw it in the microwave for a minute and thirty kind of nugget?" A teasing yet genuine smile crosses his face.

"Nothing wrong with dino nugs."

"Didn't say there was. Have you checked out the freezer?" He winks. "Mind if I have some breakfast?"

"Help yourself. I can't guarantee the pancakes won't kill you."

Amusement dances over his features. "I'll take my chances. If your bacon is burnt to a crisp, I have faith your pancakes are, too."

"Oh, by the way I paid for a food delivery to make up for all the supplies I used up and some extra. It will come later today."

His laughter fades and the color drains from his face as his jaw ticks. The tension lasts only seconds, and he shakes it off. I don't question him, but I do wonder what it was all about. We both go for a pancake. Our hands meet in the middle. I almost forgot about the burn until he touched the sensitive spot. I hiss.

"What's wrong?"

"Burned myself on the pan."

He grabs my hand, just like last night. I stumble into him and gasp. He stares at the red area while running his thumb close to, but not over it. My breath hitches. His touch draws me in. My body easily responds with a shiver. Our eyes meet and he swallows hard, his Adam's apple bobbing. There's nothing but gentleness in his warm touch.

"Did you—"

"Run it under lukewarm water? Yeah."

"Good. You should probably put something on it to prevent scarring."

My stomach growls loud enough for him to hear. "Maybe I can eat first?"

He chuckles and whispers, "Yeah."

I tug to get my hand back.

"And you've got dry pancake mix in your hair."

I swear he's about to touch my hair but holds back. A muscle twitches in his jaw. A weird thought crosses my mind about how I'd welcome his comforting touch. It's warm and friendly.

"So, you work at a restaurant?" I ask, as we sit at the dining table.

A soft ray of morning light peeks through the window behind me. It brightens his wavy hair, showing off the reddish tint.

His mouth is already stuffed. There's syrup dripping down his lips. I snort-laugh and wait for him to finish chewing.

"It's a pub. I've been there since I was eighteen. I'm a server mostly but have my license to bartend, too."

"Cool. I was wondering why you came in so late. Are they open until the wee hours of the morning?"

"Yeah." He goes back to chewing.

After a minute or two of silence I pick up my phone to scroll on social media. I'm supposed to be here to escape, but hearing Erick's voice on the radio this morning made me uneasy. I search through some threads. It's the usual bullshit until it's not. A random wave of vertigo slams into me at the sight of the cocky blonde hair, blue eyed man who has been talking smack about me the last year and a half.

It's a thumbnail photo for a video. Underneath it says,

BREAKING: *leaked footage from Star Power: The Downfall of a Rockstars Daughter.*

"So, you're a musician, huh?" Zach interrupts.

I'm thankful for Zach's distraction. Putting the phone down, I stab a piece of bacon and bite, humming from its crispness. "I mean, my face is plastered over all of the tabloids and social media websites, so . . ."

"I don't do social media."

"Really?"

He shrugs. "I have accounts. Have had a fair share of doom scrolling in the past, but I don't know. It seems like everyone has an agenda or wants to either complain about something or cancel someone. No one can ever just be happy."

I nod. "You're telling me. I wish I could avoid it like the plague, but . . ."

He swipes my phone. "So, then avoid it."

His eyes narrow at the screen. Shit. I didn't exit out of the app. Erick's voice comes through the speakers.

"She's a fraud; it's the only explanation. Just like her no-good father. When I learned of this, I broke it off with her. I don't want to be associated with someone like—"

Zach's jaw clenches and his hand tightens around my phone, his knuckles turning white.

"Hey, what are you doing to my phone? I need that."

He pauses the video and lifts his focus to me, observing my reaction.

"What's this?" he asks.

"A stupid video. It's just a video." My voice cracks, but I don't cry, although I kind of want to.

He studies me as if I'm the most interesting thing in the room. A frown is etched in his brow.

"Delete your apps while you're here. Go off the grid."

"But what if—"

His brow rises.

"What if . . ."

"Finish your thought, Penelope."

"It's Penny. And I don't know. I should probably know what people are saying about me. Plus, I have drafts on there. Drafts that I need to post."

"Don't you have someone to manage your accounts? You are famous. I always assumed most celebrities hire people to run their socials."

"I do. I mean, I have someone who posts a lot of my videos, but sometimes I like to interact with fans."

"Okay, but answer me this: has looking at social media ever given you imposter syndrome? Or made you feel like less of a person because of something somebody who knows nothing about you or your life said?"

I can't bear to look at him. How much does he know? Everyone else is caught up, so it shouldn't come as a surprise. My eyes sting as I stare at the light brown pancake on my plate. He slides the phone across the table.

"Penny, I'm sorry. I overstepped."

"No. You're right," I say, keeping my eyes on the phone.

I type in my passcode and the home screen opens. There are so many apps, and they sit there like they are mocking me. *Breathe Penny. Just breathe.* They are only apps. It's nothing you haven't lived without before.

"You sure? I was kind of joking."

"No, you weren't." I half laugh and finally peer up at him. "The thing is you're right. I allow what people say about me on social media to affect me."

I click on the first one. The blue circle with the white *f* in the center. It takes me a second before I hit uninstall. I inhale and go for the next one. With each click and delete it gets easier.

"Done," I say, my voice is stronger than I feel.

He stands. Only half his plate is eaten. "Why don't you go and hang out." He points to the pancake mix still in my hair.

I touch the strand and laugh.

"Maybe take a shower? I'll clean up after hurricane Penelope."

"I do feel kind of gross."

"Yeah, you don't smell so pretty either."

"I hope the cat is slowly planning your demise," I say.

He grins as I stand.

"Oh, I already know he is."

I begin to walk away but pause. There's a Stitch cookie jar on the table. I take a deep breath, put my plate down, lift the Stitch head, rest my phone inside, then close it. He stares at me, a little dumbfounded. Without looking back I walk to the sink, deposit my dishes, and retreat to my room to gather my things and get this crud out of my hair.

Chapter 6

ZACH

Penny and I have something in common. Shower singing. She has grit like Miley Cyrus with the power of Kelly Clarkson. There's also a slight resemblance to Amy Lee from Evanescence. I don't know how they all mesh, but it's sexy.

I lean against the wall to the right of the bathroom door and listen. I've heard her songs on the radio before, but there's something so real about it in a private setting. She's not some popstar in a magazine. She's a real person. The video from earlier comes to mind. Erick Platt. His music sucks, so I never paid much attention to his career.

Her voice mingles with the running shower water. It pulls me from my thoughts.

"Throw it away. Lock up the key. Forget what they say. Let it go. Sing endlessly," she sings.

It's nothing I've ever heard before. To me, it's as if she's making it up as she goes.

"I throw it all away, lock up the key for another day. Let it go and sing endlessly."

She adds more words in the mix. Penny repeats them but keeps stopping on *sing endlessly*. I'm in awe of this woman. I want to stay in her orbit somehow.

"Fuck!" she cries out. There's a bang as if she's punching the shower wall.

It's wrong to listen. As I walk away, I search through my phone. With her name in the search bar, I find the video easily. I stop in front of my bedroom door.

Erick Platt is your typical Hollywood Prince. He's sporting one of those high-end sports watches and dressed in a peach polo.

I glance at the bathroom door. The shower is still running, so I press play.

"I have no doubts Penny knew about her father's plan all along. While we were dating, she made everything about him and how he used to do things before he passed away. He even wrote her music—"

The shower stops and I exit the video and close out the app. The doorbell rings at the same time, so I jog down the steps and into the main entry way. Outside on the porch are bags of groceries. A short, broad-shouldered man hops into a green and white truck still rumbling at the curb.

I run a hand through my hair. A few strands fall in front of my eyes, and I try to move them away in frustration. The stubborn part of me wants to tell her this isn't necessary. I may not make a six-figure salary, but I can buy my own groceries. I'm not ungrateful, but I wish she had asked me first.

A few hours later, I go to grab a bite before work. In the dining area a rattling sound startles me. I inspect the room attempting to figure out where the noise is coming from. It's like something is knocking against glass.

It stops. Maybe it's demon cat. He once got trapped in one of the lower kitchen cabinets and couldn't figure out how to get out. We kept hearing scratching. When I opened it to grab a box of cereal the damn thing jumped out ready to pounce.

"Larry? I swear to God, if you jump out at me, cat . . ."

I'm about to turn when it starts. The cookie jar on the table moves and I let out a laugh. Her damn phone. I told her to delete the apps, not get rid of the whole thing. I smile when I think about how she eyed me while she placed the phone inside.

She's got messages from Sarina and several missed calls from someone named Tanner. A strange sensation of 'who the fuck is Tanner?' comes over me. My body is heated like molten lava. Images of a man in a suit with an expensive gold watch comes to mind. Fancy cars, driving down Hollywood Boulevard. The type who could send her lavish gifts. I blink, attempting to rid my mind of such garbage thoughts. What am I even thinking? We literally just met.

The phone buzzes. Tanner's name flashing across the screen. Who is this dude? I start up the stairs to go to find her when her voice in the den stops me.

"Alright Petunia, here's your worm for the day. Don't miss it this time. Stepping on your food is gross. I even cleaned it for you."

I peek around the entryway. Along the far wall is Petunia, the pink axolotl's, tank. I'm honestly surprised Larry hasn't decided to have Petunia for dinner yet. He's that much of an asshole where I could see it happening.

Penny's laughter catches my attention. She holds the worm above the surface of the water of Petunia's tank. I can't help but run my eyes over her backside, a jolt of desire shooting down my spine. She's got her hair down. It's fully dry from her shower and floats in layers right below her shoulder line.

Petunia swims up to where the worm dangles, her short little legs kicking in the water.

"Okay, ready? One, two, three . . ."

Penny bends to get eye level with the tank as the pink creature floats back down and the worm follows. It falls against the tiny stones at the bottom of the tank.

"You stepped on it again. It's right there. Come on, Petunia."

The axolotl stares in my direction as if it sees me eavesdropping on this moment. There's a tug at my lips when Penny cheers for the axolotl when it finally eats the worm.

"I hope the choking is normal. Oh. Ew. Okay, Petunia, swallow."

I'm about to make her aware of my presence but Larry does it for me. He growls, like a dog. I've never known cats to growl but this one surprises me every day. Penny whirls around. I don't miss the way her neck and cheeks fill with a light pink.

"What are you doing?"

I hold up the phone in defense. She narrows her eyes.

"It's been going off nonstop. Some dude named Tanner keeps calling."

She snort laughs. "Oh. Tanner. Well then, may I have my phone?"

Her lashes flutter as if she's teasing me. I may not know Penny enough, but I almost think she's mocking me.

"I better call Tanner back. It might be important."

I close the space between us and hesitantly drop the phone in her hand.

"Is he your boyfriend?"

I've concluded my mouth has a mind of its own, especially around her. I've only known Penny for a little less than twenty-four hours. I would normally never ask a question like this. She's failing at keeping a straight face. Maybe it's best she's a singer and not an actress because seconds later she releases a giggle.

"You should have seen your face." She's full-on cackling. "Tanner is my manager, who just so happens to be a woman."

She shakes her head and grins. It's teasing but not in a mean way. The phone goes off again.

"Tanner? What's with all the phone calls?" she asks, putting the phone up to her ear.

She mouths thank you to me before spinning back to Petunia. For some reason, I can't force myself to leave. Penny is answering with a lot of noncommittal responses, but then there's a gasp.

"What are people saying? No. I have to . . . I can't. I uh— I deleted all my apps."

She continues to face the tank. Her shoulders fall and she stares down at the ground. The quick change in her demeanor keeps me rooted in place.

"It was for my own well-being. I wish I'd done it sooner. I need—"
Her voice breaks.

Some irrational part of me wants to go to her. I don't. She didn't
ask me to.

"What was the big news?"

She goes quiet and then still.

"Oh my God." Her hand flies to her mouth, muffling her words.
"I—me? Are you sure? I"—her breathing becomes erratic—"me?"
She squeaks again. "Okay. Yeah, yeah. Keep me . . . keep me in the
loop."

She says goodbye. Her voice is a little rough around the edges.
Tears stream down her face, but underneath is a smile. She touches
her chest and fiddles with the silver locket.

"I—I was nominated f-for for the G-great American Music
Awards. My dad won artist of the year, thirty years ago for the first
time. I wasn't born yet, but Sarina was five . . ." A smile breaks
through.

The happiness radiating from her is infectious, filling my own
chest with pride. Her cheeks turn a deep shade of pink. For someone
who has been through it, by the looks of it with the social media chit
chat, she still finds the beauty in little things.

"I was nominated." She speaks fast. "Me. And I get to perform."
She places a hand on her chest, then waves it in the air. "Oh my God,
you must think I'm such a . . ."

I cross the room out of sheer, I don't know, stupidity? Craving? I
stand before her.

"You look like you could use a hug, but I didn't want to—"

She wraps her arms around my midsection and sobs. I inhale her
delicate scent. It's sweet orange and reminds me of those popsicles

I used to devour when I was a kid. It fills me with a familiar, warm feeling of summer. I don't know when my brain decided to describe her scent as if I were stuck in some ridiculous romance book.

She holds on tighter and I reciprocate the gesture. She melts into me, grasping the fabric of my black t-shirt. There's a heavy silence in the air around us. I'm confused by the warmth running through my body, but it continues to grow with her in my arms. The only noise is her light sniffles as she attempts to bring herself down from the plethora of feelings bombarding her all at once.

"Thanks, Zach."

She rests her hand right over my rapidly beating heart and looks up. My eyes meet hers and I can't fucking move.

"I'm sorry. It was a lot longer than I—"

I wipe the remaining tears with my thumb. She inhales sharply. My hand holds steady, barely touching her skin.

"I don't mind. Take all the time you need," I say.

I feel like there is something more she's upset about it. The excitement is there but there's more than fear behind her eyes—there's sadness lingering in her misty gaze. I drop my hand.

"Tanner says the media and the keyboard warriors are going to town. I've heard it all before. *If she's so qualified for this award, why did she run away? Where is she? She wanted attention. She should get over it. Why is she in hiding? She probably lip syncs and is afraid to—*"

"Penelope," I say sternly, cutting her off. "This is why we deleted the app. None of it is true. You should be celebrating this victory. You did this! You. Not them. I know you've been torn down. I get its easier said than done but ignore it. You do you."

She takes one more inhale then backs away, leaving a cold space between us. She wipes the tears and touches the locket, running her thumb over the design, digging in like it helps her to feel something.

"I wish my parents were alive to see this," she whispers.

There it is.

"I have no doubt you made them proud."

A sad smile grazes her face. "You're so right. Wow. I did it, Zach."

"Oh my God."

The return of her smile is slow through her tears. Then when she looks at me something in the air shifts.

"Thank you again, Zach. I have to call Sarina."

She closes the space between us, gets on her tiptoes, and kisses my cheek. It's short, simple, and sweet. I'd be lying if I said it didn't spark something inside me. I open my mouth to say, you're welcome, but in a flash she's gone. I stare at Petunia and listen to Penny's footsteps pound up the stairs. What in the hell just happened?

Chapter 7

ZACH

When I left for work a few hours ago Penny was still on the phone with Sarina. Her excited squeals leaked through the cracks of the door. Leaving her in good spirits made it easier to leave.

I've spent most of my fifteen-minute break playing solitaire on my phone and snacking on some nachos. It's been hectic. It's a weekend, so it's expected. It's as if what Mark told us the other day was a bad dream. All the staff is aware at this point, and we are all just trying to put our game faces on for our guests.

My phone vibrates and Sarina's name flashes across the screen.

> Sarina: Hope you were well-behaved!

I chuckle and shake my head.

> She's cute.

Sarina: Don't you dare! She's going through shit. Your grumpy ass has become like a brother to me, don't make me regret saying that.

Despite finding Penny attractive and how strangely intimate it was when she hugged me, I know better than to pursue the sister of my roommate. Could I find myself fantasizing about her? Sure. It's all it can be. She's a celebrity and not interested in a regular old Joe like me. She dates guys with fancy cars, lots of money, and big dick energy. While my size could compare, I could never pamper her the way she's used to.

I run a hand over my face, frustrated with myself for even feeling this way. I've never let Sarina's income bother me and we're friends. I barely know Penny yet here I am talking about not being the right kind of guy for her. I blame being on edge of the possibility of losing this place I call home. That's all it is. It has to be.

You have nothing to worry about. I'm not her type anyway. We've already made rules: no shirt, no shoes, no service.

Sarina: Funny. I'll let you get back to work.

I grab the empty container of nachos and head down for the rest of my shift. The vibe around me is filled with excitement. There's a game going on. A crowd is gathered by the tables closest to the television. Below me "Sex on Fire" is playing from the jukebox. A group of women stand around it singing along and dancing.

I pass by the bar and Maddie, who's laughing with Clarice. It's nice to see her smiling. She and Pat are on the bar crew tonight. The ladies love him. He's tall with long blonde hair and skinny jeans and is currently bending over to pick something up while what looks like a bachelorette party whistles at his antics.

I stand beside Clarice, she's about half an inch shorter than me.

"Evening, ladies."

"There's my boy," Clarice says, throwing an arm over my shoulder.

Something in her tone when she says *my boy* pulls an old memory from my mind. It was the first birthday she was around for. The summer of 2001. Clarice caught me crying on my front stoop with a scraped knee and a busted bike tire. My grandma had told me it was my fault for doing tricks. I remember the day so clearly. The summer sun beating down on me, the sting of my scraped knee and palms, her arm around me. To me her hugs always felt maternal. She had this way of making all the bad vanish.

"So, are you going to throw a party while Sarina is gone?" Maddie's raspy voice pulls me from my thoughts. She winks.

I roll my eyes playfully.

"No. I'm enjoying the peace and quiet."

"Perfect time to pick up a new hobby. What about taking another stab at knitting." Clarice pats my arm. "I'll bring over my supplies." Her lighthearted laugh is comforting.

I chuckle. "Remember the last time you tried to teach me."

Maddie taps her chin. "You mean that hat you knitted that wouldn't even fit a newborn baby's head."

Clarice snorts and I scowl at her, amusement tugging at my lips.

"Maybe Larry could have worn it. Are you two best buds yet?" Maddie teases.

"Nope. You should have seen—"

I stop because I'm not sure if Sarina told Maddie what was happening. I promised her I'd keep it a secret. Maddie is her best friend, but I don't want to accidentally say something I shouldn't.

"He clawed my chest yesterday. I'd say we are off to a spectacular start."

They laugh.

"Well, I'd love for you guys to continue this Zach roasting session, but I've got to get back to work." My tone is lighthearted.

"I'm gonna join Miles for the game. It's getting good," Clarice says.

A loud roar from that side of the bar erupts. Clarice takes her drink from where Maddie left it on the bar. "Cheers folks! Go Islanders!"

I spend the next two hours waiting on tables. At one point Mark helps on the floor because we're so busy. It's good to see him smiling while chatting it up with the customers. The whole town loves him. I keep finding it harder to believe that this place could ever go under.

"I'm telling you this place does not have karaoke. It's a hole in the wall. They have nothing but—"

I whip around, tray in hand filled with table fives meal. The wind feels as if it's been knocked out of me.

It's my ex, Macy.

She hasn't changed one bit. Her blonde hair hangs in waves down her back. She still wears tight designer jeans and tops to get attention. Hell, I'd know that backside from anywhere, and yet, it does nothing for me now. Her purse probably cost more than the ring I bought for her. There's a golden designer label.

The group of women surrounding her stick out like sore thumbs. One of them has a bachelorette sash and the dress she is wearing does not fit the vibe of our smalltown pub at all.

Running into her would cause me to spiral enough with knowing the one thing she wanted me to do better is the one thing going under. *Why can't you get a job that pays more? Service jobs are for the people who didn't educate themselves well enough.* Her words still grind my fucking gears. I squeeze my eyes shut, feeling the tightness in my chest. It's fucking ridiculous she's even invoking these emotions from me. She doesn't matter. None of it does.

"Zachary?" My name off her lips sends one of those awful shivers up my spine.

I swing around and the tray of food ALMOST smacks into Connor, the other server on the floor with me. His brown eyes meet mine and I swear we both sigh in relief together.

"It is you," Macy says.

Getting a good look at her face as she walks in my direction, I notice that her fake tan has gotten darker. Her heels, I swear, are louder than the music and voices from the television.

"Still here, Zachary?" She gives one of those snide laughs and my jaw ticks. "I thought by now you'd have found a better—"

"Yes, Macy. I'm still here." My voice is flat. I do *not* want to deal with her and her mouth right now. "That shouldn't surprise you. You, on the other hand, shouldn't be here. This isn't your scene. You're better off across town at that new fancy place."

I have so much more I want to say but I bite my tongue because this is my place of work. Also, I don't talk down to women. That's not who I am.

She scoffs and rolls her wide blue eyes. "We ate there. Isabella is looking for a karaoke bar. I told her there wasn't one here."

"Well, I won't hold you up. I have work to get done."

I'm about to take a step when she says, "You can do better for yourself, Zachary."

I clench my jaw. "Doing just fine without you, Macy. Goodnight."

An hour later, it's finally time for my dinner break. I enter the office and once the door shuts, I let out a growl and tug at the ends of my hair. The not good enough feeling rears its ugly head, and I shove it back down. I'm tired of it.

My phone buzzes in my pocket. Taking it out, I lean against the desk and read the message.

> Unknown: So, are the strawberry eclair pops only yours? I mean they aren't leftovers, but you've sprawled your name across it.

The tug on my lips is instantaneous. My muscles relax. I'm confused by my body's reaction, but I text her back.

> How did you get my number?

> Unknown: Sarina gave it to me before I arrived just in case.

> I don't believe that for a second. You asked her, didn't you?

I go into the settings and change her name.

> Penny: You caught me, Zach. I just had to have your number. I couldn't go another second without talking to you.

God, why do my cheeks hurt from smiling so wide? I've lost my mind. Maybe I need to get laid. And *not* by Penny.

> Penny: So, are those off limits, or . . .

Walking around the desk, I settle into the seat. I lean back and exhale. The dots are bouncing on the screen. I should let her sweat it out for a bit longer. I'm imagining her right now pacing back and forth. Larry is probably watching her, and the axolotl, too.

> Penny: Zach, look, it's an emergency. I saw the box and now I can't stop thinking about it. I'm salivating, man!

> I don't know . . . I mean those are my favorite.

> Penny: Too late. You took too long.

Several seconds later a picture comes through of her biting the strawberry eclair with a grin on her face. I shake my head in amusement even though she can't see me.

> You're a brat. Worse than your sister.

> Penny: Sorry, can't twype bak ne more.

> *Penny: I'm too busy enjoyingg the last bar . . .*

I get to my feet, the chair sliding into the wall. I click the green phone button to call her. No way, there was more than one.

"Gotcha!" she shouts.

Her bubbling laugh makes me pull the phone from my ear. It's refreshing and much needed. I give her a few seconds to collect herself.

"I'm sorry, Zach. I had to. I may have raided the liquor cabinet. I had some rum with the mangos juice. It's chef's kiss."

I laugh. "It's fine. Enjoy. You should be celebrating your nomination."

"I should. Yes. Yes, I should! Alright. I'm cut off."

"Yup. Eat your ice cream and go lay down."

"Yes, sir. Have fun. Toodaloo!" she squeaks.

I'm about to say something when she hangs up. Well, I guess I'll have to go to the store to buy new ice cream.

The rest of the evening goes by fast. It's an easy clean up and we made a decent profit. I've almost forgotten about my encounter with Macy, thanks to Penny's call. It's still baffling that she can make that happen.

When I get home it's a little after four in the morning. The television in the den is on as I step inside. The lights are out, leaving a bright glow from the screen. I step into the threshold of the doorway. Penny is passed out cold. Larry is curled up in her arms. I don't move, only watch as she sleeps soundly. I tilt my head and can't help being pulled in by this woman. She's so fucking adorable cuddling with the cat.

I'm also fascinated by how the cat truly despises me but loves her as if she was his world. Animals are so weird.

I turn to go upstairs but something inside calls me back to her. Sarina's favorite forest green blanket lays on the back of the couch. Larry must sense what I'm about to do. His demon eyes open and he hisses.

"Screw you, cat," I whisper.

I'm able to get the blanket off, but he's still watching me like a hawk. I unfold it and set it over her. I shut off the TV and grab the open bottle of rum beside it on the coffee table. Vaguely, I make out the outline of her in the darkness.

In the kitchen I flip on the light and am shocked to see it clean. There aren't any dishes in the sink, no empty box of ice cream. In the dining area of the kitchen, there's a wooden liquor cabinet hidden in a small nook. I put away the rum and then go to check on my ice cream count. When I open the freezer side of the refrigerator I don't expect the sight before me. There's not one but two extra boxes. On one of them has a bright yellow sticky note with neat, flowing handwriting.

Sunshine, door-dashed you some extra. Just in case I get hungry again.

I almost smile but Macy's words creep into my head. I grip the door tight and close my eyes.

"You can't please a woman on the salary you get. They will be the ones taking care of you."

Ignoring the pain in my chest, I slam the door and rest my head against it. The cool stainless steel calms me as I take deep breaths. I listen to make sure I don't wake Penny. Her heart was in the right place and her note sent a wave of weird emotions running through me, but fuck, the past won't stop creeping in to all the places I thought I'd forgotten.

I get myself together, because I need to man up and head upstairs to bed. It's been a long night and while some of it—well, most of it—I'd like to forget, there's a part of it, mainly the phone call with Penny, that helps relax me enough to fall asleep.

Chapter 8

PENNY

My sister called as I was deciding where to put my box of sex toys. Finally after five days here I've started unpacking. The awards aren't until March 11th, so I have a little over three weeks before I have to head back.

I place the discrete, medium-sized black box beside me. It's something I had debated on bringing, but ultimately, I did. Self-care is important to me. Pleasure totally counts.

"I'm glad you and Zach are getting along."

Memories of the other night with Zach play in my mind. My drunk text, our phone call, the cuddles with Larry until I passed out. When I woke up in the morning I was covered by a blanket, and everything was cleaned up. No guy I have ever known has done that. Not even my ex. It was sweet. I thanked him the next morning and he said it was no big deal, didn't want me to catch a cold. He also was weird about me replenishing his ice cream.

"Yeah. He's sweet." I laugh and settle onto my bed.

"Sweet, huh?"

He's done nothing but make me feel at home. We've watched some shows together and eaten a few meals when he's not working. I mention my breakfast making disaster to Sarina and she laughs at me.

"When I get back, I'm teaching you how to cook."

Larry is curled up on the bed and I give him some chin scratches. His purr is like a loud motor.

"You've tried. Don't you remember the meatball incident? Or the steaming bread? The fire breathing cupcakes?"

My sister's laughter is light and fun. I miss it and her so much. We don't get to spend much time together. Our schedules are so busy. Her job sometimes requires her to work a lot of holiday hours. She works at local stores, but sometimes does out-of-state jobs. She loves her career probably more than most in her position. She always had a knack for organization, hence why her house is so neat and clean.

"So, are you excited about the award show? Have you picked out a dress?"

Mom's golden dress sticks in my mind, but I have no idea what happened to it after she passed. We spent some time in their house going through their things, but never found it. I would ask Sarina, but decide not to bring it up. I keep the memory of it alive with the video I always watch.

"I'm still trying to wrap my head around it honestly. I'm honored and excited but mostly nervous. You'd think after all this time I'd be used to the attention."

"You haven't been doom scrolling on social media, have you?"

"Zach told me to delete my apps."

"Oh, did he?"

Her voice sounds odd.

"I told him I wish I could ignore it all and then he was like 'well then delete them all'." I try to use my lower register to imitate his voice, and she barks out another laugh.

"It's a great impression of him. And have you been good?"

"Yeah. I've been keeping myself entertained with your streaming services. It's safer than cable. The last social media video I saw was from the documentary. Erick was babbling about how fake I am." My voice cracks.

She sighs. "Don't listen to it, Pen. Anything that comes out of that assholes mouth is not true."

"How do you feel about this documentary?" I ask, trying to deflect the focus off me.

Sarina is silent for a few seconds. "I mean, not great, but Dad was in the spotlight all the damn time so I've kind of grown numb to it affecting me personally. It's you who I'm most worried about. You're still in the thick of it. I can't believe he paid the producers so you'd win. I love him but what an asshole move. I want to protect you from all the corruption in the industry. It's why I . . ." She pauses. "It's why I got out and never looked back. I couldn't just take you with me. You were ten. You saw stars when you looked at Dad. I couldn't ruin that for you."

When Sarina left for college, I was sad. I thought she was coming back, but four years went by then another and suddenly we were both adults living separate lives.

"I know. It was my choice, and I have to live with the consequences of it." I shake my head.

"You followed your dream. I'm so proud of you for that. Mom and Dad too. You didn't know what was in store."

An alarm goes off on her end.

"Shit. Gotta get back to work. Keep me updated on what's happening with the awards. I hope I can be back in time. This might take an extra week."

My heart grows heavy. I want her there, but I understand scheduling conflicts. My sister works so hard. She refused Mom and Dad's money after college. She worked for the life she has now, but I still wish she had never left. She was my best friend growing up. One of my only friends since I was homeschooled.

"Hey, it's alright. I understand. You can just watch me on TV." I try to sound convincing.

"On, TV? Are you whacky?"

I laugh. "No, but I understand. Don't beat yourself up over it. Work is important too."

"Love you."

"You too," I say as a text notification goes off on my phone.

I adjust and Larry scowls.

Tanner: Sorry this is only a text, but I'm in a meeting. Erick was nominated for the same category as you. Don't freak out. You'll be fine.

I hold my breath. I'm being crushed under some kind of invisible weight. It's not only my chest, like it sometimes is, but my entire body. I hate allowing what happened with him to affect me. Memories from the road bring me back to a time filled with anxiety and worry.

"You're being too paranoid," he'd said.

"Paranoid? I'm not blind, Erick. I know what I saw."

I was curled in the tour bus on the road to the next city. Halfway across the country from where Erick was. Because of our schedules I had missed his debut album release, his first signing, and his appearance on The Late-Night Show.

"We all went out after the album signing. That's it. We were having a good time. Those women aren't you, Penelope."

I couldn't help the scoff. The pictures on social media showed the women sitting on his lap at some club. It was dark, but still a clear shot. One brunette had her arms around his neck. They were staring at each other with an intensity that I had never experienced with him.

"Would you have allowed that woman to sit on your lap if I was there with you celebrating? Huh? Answer me that." I tried to keep my voice low because it was the middle of the night for me, but early enough for Erick being a few hours behind.

He never answered my question that night. He danced around the subject and the sad thing was I let him. It was only the beginning.

"Hey, Penny?"

My phone slips from my hand at the sound of Zach's voice behind me. The box of self-pleasuring toys tilts. It falls and breaks open. A piece in the corner flies to the side. Larry is standing on all fours, his fur fluffed, tail puffy, as he growls like a dog.

Neither of us say a word, only look at the toys. My heart is freaking out as much as I am. What do I even say?

I clear my throat and try to make my voice sound normal. "What's the matter, have you never seen sex toys before?"

He laughs and tugs at the collar of his white T-shirt. "Oh, I've seen my fair share, but you have quite a collection . . ."

I get to my feet so fast it disturbs an already angry Larry. He jumps from the bed but is quickly distracted by a black discrete bag with a string. Larry inches towards it, picks it up with his mouth, and races for the doorway. Zach jumps as if there's a mouse running around and not a cat.

"Was that . . . did he . . ." The corner of Zach's lips turns up into a half grin. "Was that a sex toy?"

There's something bubbling in my chest. I'm not sure what's going to come out of my mouth. I almost expect a sob, but it turns into a bellowing laugh.

"Oh my God, get the damn cat!'" I yell.

"Me?"

"Ugh, never mind," I say, racing after the cat.

There are footsteps behind me as I go down the stairs. Larry makes his way through the entryway from the den into the dining room.

"Why did he steal it?" Zach asks, panting behind me.

"No—clue, but—that's the—best one."

"Maybe my question should be why do you have so many?"

"And maybe you should mind your own business."

Larry makes a beeline for the center island in the kitchen. He's up on top and skids across the whole thing, the bag hanging from his mouth.

"Larry! Drop the vibrator!" I yell sliding into the living room.

Zach is on my heels with each step but stops halfway. I pause and turn back. "Giving up already?"

"I might pretend to be all fit and shit but . . . that cat is fast."

I race up the steps but forget about the last one. My foot gets caught and I go down. Thankfully I hold my hands out in time, and I don't fall on my face.

"Penny? What was—oh shit."

He sits beside me and our eyes meet. I zoom in on his mouth and the rise and fall of his shoulders. His eyes crinkle and light with amusement and I'm lost in the view before me. Why does he have to be so handsome and nice?

Larry stands in front of us and meows. He drops the bag, walking away with his tail in the air.

"As embarrassing as that was, I needed the laugh."

"Everything alright?" Sincerity lines his voice.

"Nothing I can't handle."

He narrows his eyes. It's easy to tell he doesn't believe me, but he doesn't push it.

I get to my feet. Zach is still sitting there.

"Twenty?" he yells as I walk away.

I shake my head and groan. Why me? I'm going to permanently stain my cheeks pink with embarrassment if he keeps teasing me like this. At the same time, after the day I've had so far, it's given me something to laugh about.

"Fifty? One hundred?"

I bend and pick up the toy and give Zach one last glance before retreating into my room. I lean my head against the door. He's quiet, but there's a creak on the floor. He knocks.

"One hundred and fifty." His laughter is contagious, and I can't help myself.

"Go away, Zachary."

He chuckles. "Heading off to work. Later, love."

"Goodbye, sunshine," I say.

Chapter 9

ZACH

"I throw it all away, lock up the key for another day. Let it go and sing endlessly . . . ugh," Penelope sings as she frantically scribbles on the page in her notebook.

She's sitting on her bed with her door ajar, but I remain out of sight in the hallway. Her knees are bent, back against the headboard. She closes her eyes and hums a little. "Allow the day to take me away." She taps the pencil to her lips, jots down something, erases it, then does it again.

I can't stop thinking about yesterday's *cat*astrophe. Falling asleep last night was hard. I'm not going to lie, the idea of her being down the hallway with a box filled to the brim with sex toys gave my cock some ideas that I didn't give it permission to have. Like just thinking about it now. I'm confident it's not because I haven't had sex in a while, it's more than that. There's something about her that draws me in. Her passion, maybe. You can see it in her eyes; I'm watching it unfold right now. Like the way she lit up when she realized her nomination was a great accomplishment despite the world crashing down around her.

I don't want to disturb her, but a package arrived. She told me the other day she was expecting something.

"I throw it all away, lock up the key for another day. Let it go and sing endlessly. Allow the day to take me away." She speaks the words and flips the pencil, ready to erase, but then eases away.

"Hey, Penny?" I knock.

Her sleep deprived, shadowy eyes find mine. Her hair is pinned up but messy. Some strands fall loose over her face. Though her smile is there it's brief and stress lines crease her forehead.

"Yeah?"

"I'm sorry to bother you, but your package came."

She sets the notebook and pencil on the bed before getting to her feet. Something changes inside of her. It's as if the missing piece to her song has been written.

"Thanks, Zach."

She steps away but I hold out my hand and brush it against hers. She sucks in a sharp breath. Her eyes snap to mine. My hand lingers on hers. My fingers make a slow descent over her knuckles, down to the tips of her fingers. She shivers, her sights set on me.

"You alright?" I ask.

"Why do I feel like if I said yes, you wouldn't believe me?"

I give her what I hope is a genuine smile. It must trigger some kind of understanding because for a second she looks away. A soft grin slowly stretches onto her lips.

"I'm observant."

Her laughter isn't full but it's a start. I'm not sure when it became my mission to make her smile. Maybe it's me keeping a promise to Sarina or maybe it's something else.

She tilts her head, studying me. I understand her hesitation. I'm a stranger to her. I linger, allowing the tips of our fingers to touch for a few seconds longer before pulling away in case I've gone too far.

"I know you aren't a social media guy, but do you know anything about the award show coming up?"

"Not a clue. Award shows were never my thing."

"Are you familiar with Erick Platt?"

"The guy from the video?"

"Yeah."

She stares at the ground while rubbing her arm. Her skin grows red. Erick evokes fear inside her and it reminds me of what Macy does to me. I understand her and want her to know that. I reach out and place my hand gently over hers to stop the movements. She swallows hard and leans into my space. Lifting her chin, we're caught up in each other. I let go because I don't want to overwhelm her.

"He was nominated in the same category as me." She hugs herself. "He used me to get famous. When he got what he wanted and found women to get what he wasn't from me, he broke up with me. He's the reason I can't get serious with someone. Long distance relationships only lead to heartache."

"He missed out on something great. That's his loss. Don't let his nomination ruin this moment for you. You deserve it just as much, if not more, than him."

She gives a meek smile. "Thanks, Zach. I'm gonna go get my package."

I follow her down, leaning against the newel post of the stairs. Her eyes light as she rips the tape off the crease of the box. Amongst all the packing material she pulls out a black guitar case.

"There she is."

She places it on the ground and flips open the locks. The navy Martin guitar is in pristine condition. Once the strap is around her, she tunes it. Her fingers work magically. Her eyes are closed as she carefully listens to each note, fiddling with the tuning pegs. It's the first time I've seen her fully in her element. The passion returns and I'm enamored with her. The urge to get to know her better settles over me. I'd only set myself up for disappointment.

"She got a name?" I ask as her eyes open.

She startles as if she hadn't realized I followed her.

"Lita. She was my mom's."

"Oh. She played, too?"

This piques my curiosity. Everyone knows her dad. He was a Grammy award winning rock star, but I didn't realize her mom was part of it. She hesitates to speak.

"You don't have to tell me."

"Critics didn't take too well to her style. She had one album, and it flopped somewhere between my dad's hits. Her music was indie with a folksy vibe to it, I guess the world wasn't ready for it."

"What stopped her from trying again?"

Her eyes sparkle in the light leaking through the curtains.

"She settled for being a mom and the wife of a musician."

Her words pack a punch.

"I found someone else because you're settling and not trying to do better for yourself. You can be happy with your life and still be missing

out on greater things because you're comfortable. You're a smart guy, Zach, you'll figure it out one day."

Macy's words continue to haunt me. She left me for the doctor, because that's exactly what I did. Settled.

Penelope's fingers move over the guitar flawlessly and those thoughts vanish.

"What was the album called?"

"Take Flight. Her first single was "My Butterflies". Dad helped her write it, even got credit on the album, but it wasn't enough."

She continues to play. She closes her eyes, tilts her head and hums the melody haunting her. I'm drawn to how her cheeks turn a slight shade of pink, and a smile turns up her smooth and well-defined lips. The melodic, soft tune she's playing sounds like how she described her mom's music.

Her eyes open.

"Zach, are you okay?"

It takes everything in me to muster a smile. "Y-yeah." I clear my throat. "I'm good."

She furrows her brow suspiciously and never loses sight of me as she continues to play. I like how she's not pushing me to answer.

Her voice breaks through the sounds of the guitar. At first, she's humming, but then she starts to sing. I'm hooked on her presence, and I think she might be with mine, too.

My girls, be wise.
Tread lightly, my darlings
for this world can be cruel.
Your wings are soft and delicate,
but don't let it fool you.

Your strength comes from within.
Seek the harmony between two.
My beautiful butterflies follow the sun.
It will keep you in tune with time.
Tune out the darkness and spread your wings.
Show the world the light in the darkened springs.

"Was that the song? It's beautiful."

She blinks several times while nodding and turns to hide. I catch her wiping her tears.

"Yeah."

"The world missed out on a great one."

Her smile is faint. She continues to strum and her eyes close again. Her humming is so enchanting. I'd be happy sitting here and having more moments like this with her in the future.

The thought scares me.

"How is your song going?"

"We're about to find out," she says, then begins speaking the words. "I throw it all away. Lock up the key for another day. Let it go and sing endlessly. Allow the day to take me away. I hide from the pain to feel whole. I search my soul to find my voice again. It's strong and hidden behind a broken wall . . ."

She taps her lip with her index finger. "Hmm . . ." Her eyes dart back and forth as she falls deep in thought.

"What if," she says, as if almost to herself, "what if I took out one line? It's more of a chorus than a verse. Okay, start again." Her eyes flutter shut. "One, two, three . . ."

Lock up the key for another day.
Let it go and sing endlessly.
I hide from the pain to feel whole.
I searched for my soul to find my voice again.
It's strong and hidden behind a broken wall.

No matter how hard I try not to be pulled into this woman's orbit, I get sucked right back into it. It's only been a few days, but since her arrival I've been more aware of my life and the choices I've made. I've never taken the leap to prove myself—I've only coasted. Seeing her writing a song after everything is like a nudge for me to not allow the past to reflect on my future. If Penny can grow by taking small steps, I know I can grow and be better for it.

She opens her eyes and keeps them on me. There's a misty gaze clouding hers. "What?"

I shake my head. "Nothing. I'm just intrigued by the process. I don't think I could ever write a song."

She pulls the guitar off and places it gently into the case and locks it. Getting to her feet she wipes off her jeans and turns to me. "Want to know a secret?"

"Sure."

"My first two albums were written for me. A lot of my third too. It's one of the many things people hate me for. My dad could create these songs as if they were the easiest thing in the world. I struggle. A lot. I'm still learning. My voice is the most powerful instrument I have. The taglines of the articles and the hateful comments on social media over the years hurt and still do. I'm a fraud. Erick's not wrong.

A fraud because I won under false pretenses and because I'm not a song writer like he is." Her voice breaks a little.

She repeats Erick's words from the video. I don't know the guy and already I want to march up to his million-dollar mansion and make him understand what it's like to be told those words. Only, I'll be using more than words.

"You know what though? You didn't let it stop you. You didn't settle with others writing your music, you let it fuel you. That alone shows true courage."

She rests her warm, smooth hand on my upper arm. My muscle twitches at her touch. Her brows draw together as she leans in. There have been moments of closeness between us, but somehow this one takes the cake. I can't settle my beating heart.

"I hate that you had to go through it all. People have no idea what they're talking about. Your voice alone has broken records. Hell, you're even nominated for best artist. How many of those keyboard warriors can say that?"

Her bottom lip trembles. She turns her head, as the world between us blurs. I slide my index finger under her chin to make her face me. It's an intimate gesture but I don't regret it. She gasps. Her lips parting slightly and I zero in on them. My thoughts race to wanting to know what they taste like to; I shouldn't be thinking about that.

"I'm serious, Pen."

Her focus is all over, except for the one place I want it. On me.

"Look at me, love," I say, breaking her rules. Her face softens.

My heart jumps when she listens.

"I don't know what made you want to hide from the world, but no one should make you feel like you don't deserve every ounce of recognition you've gotten. I see the doubt in your eyes now and saw it when you got the phone call the other day. Tell me this, have you felt any better since deleting the apps? Be honest. You can say, 'Zach, you're an asshole and it didn't work'."

Her laughter is short and sweet. A smile is present but doesn't reach her eyes. It's progress.

"I don't know. It's helping a little to not see certain hot topics in the media. Like whatever Erick is posting about me. The only reason he's famous is because—"

"Wait. I remember now. Didn't that Erick guy only get famous when the video of the two of you went viral?"

Her eyes widened. "Y-you, you know. I thought you didn't do social media."

"It was everywhere, but I just didn't put two and two together when Sarina told me who you were."

The idea of someone using her to jump start their own career pisses me off. I don't know how she does it. I could never be in the spotlight and enjoy it. I like my quiet hometown life. I like privacy and comfort. I wish I could knock that guy down a peg and teach him a thing or two. I'm not one to fight, but if I ever had to protect someone I care about, I wouldn't hold back. Wow. I pause my thoughts for a moment. Thinking of Penny as one of those people comes as a shock.

"That fucker doesn't deserve to win the award. His music is like nails on a chalkboard. Every time one of his songs comes on the radio I change stations. He's trying so hard to sell himself to be like John Mayer. The truth is, not even music lessons could save that man."

Her laughter is sad, but I can't help but love how her eyes brighten.

"Not seeing the negative and focusing on the positive has helped me come up with those lyrics today. I can't tell you the last time I was confident in the words I had on the page. It wasn't easy, but it's almost therapeutic to write them."

"Then keep doing it," I say, lifting her chin slightly higher. My thumb caresses her jawline. "Write what's in your heart, Penny. Don't let the outside world get in your head. Don't let him in either."

She nods. "I don't know if I want this life anymore."

At her confession the first tear falls and grazes my thumb. She sniffles. I move my hand so I'm able to swipe away the tears easier. She leans into my touch, and I hold onto that feeling for a moment longer.

"What do you want?" I ask, pulling away.

"I don't know," she whispers, locking her gaze with mine. "I don't know." Her voice squeaks at the end. "A life where no one is scrutinizing my every move. A family. Spending more time with my sister. A place to call home. I don't want to settle, but I need a break."

"You've heard the saying home isn't always a place, right?"

She nods.

"To me it's the people you surround yourself with. That's home."

"Where is your home?" she asks, and I trace her lips with my eyes.

"Wingmans Pub. Not the place, but the people who make it Wingmans. Mark took me in when I needed it most. Madeline and Sarina. We are each other's support system. Hell, even Miles the regular who comes in to scream at the TV when the Islanders lose." I laugh and she follows suit.

I wasn't hesitant nor did I need to think about it. It's been home since the moment I stepped foot inside.

"I love that." She swallows hard. "I wish I could meet them . . . wait, Madeline. The name sounds familiar."

"She's friends with your sister."

"I feel so out of tune. Sarina is the only family I have left." She sniffles. "I'm sorry. I didn't mean to unload." She turns away again, but I tug her back to me.

"No. Don't apologize for being vulnerable. Alright? Your sister trusted me to make sure you are okay and safe. She saved me, too. She's family to me. I don't break promises to my family."

She nods frantically, the tears falling in rapid succession along with her movements. I feel bad that she's spiraling. I want to help her. Not only because of Sarina, but because I want to.

"I'm going to hug you, okay?"

"K," she whispers.

I don't waste a beat. She grips the fabric of my shirt, holding on. Maybe she does it because she's afraid if she lets go the comfort will vanish. How lonely is she out there in California? I've seen Sarina get off the phone with her and have this distant look in her eyes. Being miles away must take a toll on them. It's easy to notice it has done the same for Penny.

"Thank you," she says into my chest. My t-shirt is becoming damp with tears.

"Fifty-two toys?" I ask teasingly.

She backs away. A lightning bolt of complete adoration shoots through me at the bold and beautiful smile lighting her entire face. "Nope," she says. "You'll have to keep guessing."

Chapter 10

PENNY

The pink beauty takes a snap at her worm.

"Good girl, Petunia."

I finished cleaning her tank, cleaned out the litter box, the bathroom, and the kitchen. Then I mopped the floor along to *Wicked; The Musical* soundtrack, belting out "Defying Gravity" as if I were in the Broadway show.

My love for music varies. My parents gave me the best music education I could have asked for. On top of homeschooling, on Friday evenings when I was younger and Dad was home we would spend time in the living room listening to music of all different decades. The 90s and early 00s being my favorite, but I have a soft spot for the 80s.

It's Friday evening. I'm used to late nights on stage followed by after parties and being surrounded by people. Half the time I'd love to run for the hills, but ultimately stay to avoid the questions. When I leave with a group it's not as bad as leaving alone and being in the spotlight of the paparazzi.

Zach left a few hours ago for work. I keep fighting back this weird, lonely sensation. I recall the way he tipped my chin the other night. He commanded my attention. I have never experienced something so intimate before him. They've also never asked for permission.

I try to shake my thoughts. I can't go down that road with Zach. Number one, I only just met him. Number two, I don't live here in New York. It could never work.

"Petunia, I'm bored. Should we watch something on streaming?"

It's been peaceful but God, I want something to do. I'm not in the mood for songwriting tonight. I could google dress shops in New York City, but I have no desire.

Larry drops something from his mouth. He meows from the doorway, rubbing his body against the molding on the wall.

"I know, I know, Larry. I'm here on a Friday night talking to an axolotl. What has my life come to?"

I turn to Petunia. "No offense or anything, Petunia."

Petunia shimmies her pink external gills at me. I sigh and collapse onto the couch. Larry meows. He picks up whatever he has. It's something round. He struts over. I swear if this cat steals another vibrator, I'm about to toss his ass outside.

My phone rattles on the coffee table. I lean over as Larry jumps up beside me. The object is still in his mouth. The screen lights up with Zach's name. The sight alone causes a smile and strange warmth to course through me.

Zach: Sixty-nine.

I snort laugh. He is still attempting to guess how many sex toys I own. It's kind of weird but I love keeping him on the edge of his seat. I wasn't sure what to expect when I got here. I knew I'd be spending most of my time alone. It's part of my self-care. A nice orgasm can get your heart pumping and help clear the voices in your head.

Shouldn't you be working?

Zach: On break. Figured I'd give another guess.

Larry drops the object beside me. It reads *Wingmans Pub and Grille*. It's a round black coaster with golden words written in fancy font.

I think the cat misses you.

Zach: Yeah right.

I snap a picture.

Zach: That fucker went into my room.

I laugh.

Maybe that fucker actually does like you and he's mad at you because you leave him too much.

Zach: Okay, you've clearly been in the house too long. You're losing your mind, like the guy from the movie with the hotel . . .

I'm smiling so wide it almost hurts.

> The Shining?

> Zach: Yup. Shit. Breaks over. Are you sure it's not 69?

> Get back to work, slacker.

I sigh and pick up the coaster to inspect it. I'd love to see this pub he's always talking about. I could disguise myself, get a bite to eat, enjoy some hockey on TV, maybe some tunes. Is it worth the risk. Is *he* worth the risk. I laugh to myself. There I go again falling down the rabbit hole known as Zach. I like spending time with him. He makes me laugh and feel good. He listened to me and understood my feelings.

"Should I do it? Larry, Petunia? What do you guys think? I can order an Uber. No, I'd have to use a card. A cab?"

This shouldn't be about him. It's about me living my own life and taking charge. I blow out a breath. I need a night out without fame getting in the way.

The axolotl is climbing the fake rocks and swimming off them. She goes back around and does it two more times as if she's playing.

"I mean look, Larry, even the axolotl is finding a way to have fun tonight."

I'm here to hide, but at the same time I don't want to be confined to one space. It's a risk for sure. I spent almost a month in my L.A mansion by myself and it was the loneliest I have ever felt. If I thought touring alone was bad, being in a house with no one at all was even worse.

I get to my feet. "I'm going out."

The cat and axolotl ignore me and do their own thing, and I head upstairs to get ready. I rummage through my closet. I want to go for something out of the ordinary for myself while still being me. I pile things on my bed. Shirts, pants, sweaters, but everything feels wrong. I head over to Sarina's room instead. I flip on the light switch. She has the biggest one in the house. The high ceilings brighten up the space. I breathe in the lingering scent of vanilla. Her favorite. I admire the blue painted walls as clear as the sky on a cloud-free day. Her room is clean and neat.

Her closet is to the left of the door. My eyes dance over all the clothes. I spot a brown corduroy shirt jacket. It's so cute I can't help it. Cute? Who am I trying to impress? My cheeks heat and I try to push my thoughts away. I'm only going to have fun. Not because of Zach. Okay, maybe a little for Zach.

I tuck the jacket under my arm and browse more. A white shirt with blue stripes with a low dipped neckline. Perfection! Now pants. I shut the closet door and on the other side of the room beside a full-length mirror I go through her bottom drawer, which—*score*—are jeans. Some cute high rise light blue denim is on top. Once I'm set, I shut off her light, and head back to my room.

Thirty minutes later I'm ready, sporting some wavy locks, winged eyeliner with a light white shadow, and some nude gloss for my lips. I grab my black cap and black framed reading glasses from my suitcase and head down to wait for the cab I called five minutes ago.

The cab pulls up to a small red brick building on a side road off the main street. There are only two other stores before it. I pay the driver and slide out. My heart beats fast as I step onto the sidewalk. I tip my ballcap forward as I walk to the door. It's made of wood and is heavy and weathered. Inside darkness consumes me. There's dull lighting. I can use it to my advantage. To my right is the bar. There's a woman in a leather jacket, hot as hell. Her raven black bob sways as she walks. There's another man rushing around to get to each guest. He's much taller than her, skinny and lean. His blonde hair is messy, but the women watch him with a twinkle in their eyes.

There's a table of guys in hockey jerseys. Their voices carry as they speak about the Islanders finally winning a game. Their excitement is palpable as I pass by. Zach is nowhere to be found. I peer at a stage with a mic stand. It's towards the back of the pub. Small round tables sit close to the stage area. The tables are tall, and the guests all sit on bar stools.

Do I sit at a table and wait and see if Zach serves me? Or do I hide somewhere and go unnoticed? I did come to have a little bit of fun, so maybe some alcohol will help loosen me up a bit.

There's an empty space in the back corner of the bar. I slide onto the stool and take in the atmosphere as I wait. Laughter spills from behind the bar from the raven-haired beauty and the blonde guy. They tease each other. A customer jokes about the guy being a ladies' man and the woman makes a snarky comment. She reminds me so much of Sarina.

She is the first to take notice of me. There's something familiar about her.

"Hey, doll, what can I get you?" she asks.

I smile, but keep my cap tilted.

"I'm not much of a beer drinker. Do you have anything sweet?"

"I make a mean Mai Tai?"

"Mai Tai it is," I say with a smile.

"Coming right atcha! Be back..." She pauses and glances over her shoulder. I lift my gaze but not the bill of the hat. Our eyes meet. Her lip's part and her eyes soften. Maybe she recognizes me. I wonder if she's Madeline. She doesn't say anything and returns to making drinks.

She's back with mine in about two minutes tops and slides it over to me.

"All by yourself tonight?" she asks.

Her smile is warm and inviting.

"I was at home..." Home. That sounds kind of nice. "Um... I was talking to a cat and an axolotl as if they were my best friends. It was then I knew I needed to get out."

Her laughter fills the space around us. It's beautiful and friendly.

"Girl, I've been there. My cats are like my therapists. Although they never give good advice. Only smooches and love bites."

I laugh. "Nothing beats cat cuddles though."

"Nope. Sometimes they know when we need it the most."

"Yo! Add another round!" a customer from the other end yells.

"Sorry, duty calls. It was nice chatting with you. If you need another drink, let me know."

"Thanks," I say, lifting my glass to salute her.

She smiles and nods and heads over to the rowdy customer with hearts in his eyes.

I keep my eye out for Zach but haven't seen him yet. I'm sure he's busy. There are a decent number of guests sitting at the tables eating dinner. I assume he's somewhere in the mix.

For a good twenty-minutes this end of the bar is quiet. I'm enjoying the atmosphere. It might be a little loud between the music and televisions, but I like how everyone is too distracted to find a moment to check and see who the woman at the end of the bar is.

An older woman slides in beside me. She's got a little gray in her hair. It's pulled back into a ponytail. She places a keyring with a few knitted keychains on the surface of the bar, one of them being a four-leaf clover. She sneaks a peek over at me and I tilt my hat down a little but try to be nonchalant about it.

"Darling." She places her hand on the bar, in my line of sight.

I acknowledge her with a head tilt. Her eyes are a familiar golden brown. I've seen them before, but how? I can't put my finger on why this woman doesn't scare me. Like I'm not afraid she'll take my picture or run her mouth to the press.

"I'm sorry you're feeling lost. I have something that might help."

I narrow my eyes at her. Around her shoulder she has a brown satchel. She lifts the flap. Inside is knitting material, green yarn, pink yarn, and brown, sticking out as she moves things aside.

"Aha."

She pulls out a clover, like the one on her keychain and slides it on the surface of the bar towards me. Her smile is like the sun. It warms me like I'm being wrapped in a hug.

The yarn is soft, and I run my thumb over it. It's simple yet I feel comforted by the gesture. I lift my chin to get a better view of the woman and there's no indication in her cheerful gaze that she knows who I am.

"Thank you," I say, my voice a little raspy.

"Trust your heart," she whispers. "I love your locket too. A gift from someone special?" she asks.

I touch mine and peer over as she pulls a similar oval shaped one out from under her shirt.

"It's a picture of my family and I on . . ."

What do I tell her? I can't tell her the real thing, that it's me during my first concert.

"It was a really big moment for me. My parents passed and it's one of the only things I have left."

I'm surprised I'm revealing so much, but there's something so gentle about her.

She touches my hand and has a far off look in her eye. "Mine is of my son and I."

I'm about to speak again when the blonde male bartender comes over.

"Evening Clarice, what can I get for you?" He leans on the bar.

He peers over at me with a friendly smile. "You need another while I'm getting this young lady something?"

I hold up my nearly full drink but keep my head mostly down. It's my second. I finished the first rather quickly, which I probably shouldn't have, but I'm relaxed and it's a good feeling. "Still working on this one but thank you."

I hold the clover in my hand and close my eyes. Maybe it's a sign of good things to come.

Clarice snorts. "Young? Me? I think you're mistaking me with the beautiful lady beside me."

My chest tightens, as I'm being brought into their conversation, but I try to tell myself to breathe. They are trying to be nice. That's all.

She smiles. "Blue Moon, please, Pat?"

He winks, his blue eyes shimmering. "Anything for you. Be right up."

I smile at their interaction. It's like they've known each other for a while. I've noticed it with the female bartender too. She's called quite a few guests by their first name. I find it comforting that so many here know one another. Zach is right, it gives you that home feel.

"That's one of my favorite drinks here," Clarice says, nodding towards my glass.

My heart beats a little harder. She's sweet but I'm starting to second guess my decision to come here. I down a bit more of the drink before responding.

"It's really good. What else do you recommend?"

"If you like sweet, I'd recommend the Blue Hawaiian. Super sweet makes you feel like you're on a tropical island."

"If a drink can transport me to another place, I'm here for it."

We laugh.

"You won't be disappointed. If only it really could transport you. I'd love a good vacation somewhere warm. And if you're looking for a good meal, the Shepards pie is the best, then the nachos, or the double cheese bacon burger is to die for."

"Thank you. Those both sound delicious."

"Sure, of course. I've been coming here for years. I know all the good food and the secrets to getting the best stuff on the menu." She winks.

Pat comes back and slides the drink to her. "Taking this over to watch the game?" he asks.

"You bet your ass I am. We're gonna win tonight. I feel it in my bones."

Pat laughs. "Got your charm."

She holds up the key chain and touches the clover. "Sure do."

He tells her to enjoy and gives me a wave before going to help someone else.

"It was nice to meet you, sweetheart. Hope you enjoy your drink and your time here at Wingmans."

"Thank you. Enjoy your game."

She walks towards where a group of men are standing around a table. They are on this side of the pub all looking up at a big screen on the wall.

I'm about to look away but catch sight of Zach. He's dressed all in black, his T-shirt clinging to his body. He passes by a table, a red-haired woman with a princess crown on stops him. There are four other women at the table. One with short blonde hair reaches out to touch his arm and he politely smiles, but steps away. I can't read his lips, but his jaw line tightens. The one beside the blonde with black curly hair twirls her hair with her finger as she rests her elbow on the table.

I'm swept away by images of Erick with those women in the pictures. His excuses and lies. My heart starts racing and I feel the urge to get up and leave, which is ridiculous. I turn back to the bar as the woman bartender comes over. Maybe it was stupid to come. I keep telling myself it wasn't only to see Zach; it was to get out and enjoy the escape.

"Another, please?" I ask, downing the last of the one I have.

"Coming right up, doll," she says, wandering away.

I can't help myself; my attention falls back onto Zach as he's walking away from their table. He rolls his eyes and takes a deep breath as if he is maybe relieved to be away from them.

My drink is ready quickly. I'd go to talk to Zach but he's currently the only server left on the floor. I let him do his thing while I sip my drink and sing to myself.

Another forty-five or so minutes pass by. The music on the juke-box heals my soul. Fun pop music pours from it. It's easily heard over the television, but I'm swept away by my name being spoken by the news anchor.

In the corner of my eye, Zach stops beside where Clarice is sitting and watching the television.

"She's ungrateful for her nomination. What artist gets nominated and goes silent?" Ericks voice fills the pub, only for second, before the TV goes off.

Zach has a remote in his hand. He places it back inside a pocket on the wall and turns towards the bar and his golden stare finds me. My breathing falters at the sight of him. His frown flips and his lips lift, his eyes lighting up as if he'd been searching for me. I bite my lip and look away towards my little black clutch on the bar. I peer inside and act as if it has an endless bottom. A familiar touch has me sinking into him.

He leans forward, lips grazing my ear. "Spotted you from a mile away."

His voice alone makes me forget Erick. I'm flooded with emotion but hide it with a smile.

I snort. "You mean a few feet?"

I lift the hat and give him an innocent lopsided grin. The buzz keeps me warm or maybe it's the way he's watching me. His eyes roam over my choice of clothing. He stares intently at the exposed skin and cleavage right where the locket sits on my chest.

"You get feisty when you're drunk. What are you doing here?"

I wait for him to mention what was on the television, but so far he hasn't.

"Well, I was talking to Petunia and . . ."

He raises a brow, and I point to him, my finger doing some kind of weird whoosh thing. His shoulders shake with amusement.

"I was talking to Petunia and Larry and they both agreed I should go out. Well, Larry was the one who suggested it. The cat did bring over a coaster. Oh, hey." On the bar I find the same coaster. "That's the one he brought over. Anyway, I figured it was a sign I needed to get out and I wanted to see home for you."

His smile fades.

"I– I mean, wow. I should just shut my mouth. That was personal and you . . ."

He presses his index finger to my lips and in a low rumbling voice says, "Did you find what you were looking for?"

I'm warm from his simple touch. How does he do that? Make me feel things I shouldn't.

"Peace? Fun without the ambush? Yeah." I nod. "You're right about this place. There's something in the atmosphere. The second I stepped foot inside, I somehow knew I was safe."

"You should still be careful. And if you wanted to go out, I could have taken you."

I shrug. "You work a lot."

"I'm off on the 15th."

"The day after Valentines Day? You mean discount candy day?" I wiggle my brows.

A smile tugs his lips, lighting a soft glow on his scruffy, well-trimmed cheeks. His kindhearted grin is contagious. I can't help giggling, although it could be the amount of alcohol I consumed.

"The only real holiday in February."

"Agreed."

"Let me get some things together and then we'll go, okay?"

"Don't you have to stay?"

He shakes his head. "No. I usually stay after to help because I have nothing better to do."

"And now you have something?"

He averts his gaze then brings it back. "We have a discount candy day to plan."

I chuckle and shake my head. "Alright, I'll wait right here."

I stare at his backside as he walks off. I expect to sit here quietly while I wait, but instead a rough, yet feminine voice catches me off guard.

"Penelope. You're Sarina's sister, right?"

Chapter 11

ZACH

I was not expecting to see Penny sitting in the corner near the bar. I check back over my shoulder and find Maddie talking to her. I'm not worried. I'm sure she's the one that's been serving her tonight since Penny had one of Maddie's signature Mai Tai's.

"Goodnight, son," Clarice's familiar soft tone pulls me from watching Penny.

I turn in the opposite direction. Clarice has her heavy black jacket tucked over her left arm. Her smile is bright and caring. She opens her free arm for me, and I step into it. As always, I'm met with nothing but love from her.

"Oh, before I forget. In case I don't see you."

She pulls back and rummages through her brown satchel to retrieve her matching wallet. I don't mean to pry but inside are pictures. She swipes through them so fast, but I swear there is one of a baby beside one of her and I. My memory jolts me into the day I got into my grandma's photo albums and how fast she yanked me away from it.

"Aha! This. Happy Valentines Day."

In her hand is the gift card she gets me every year to my favorite donut shop.

"Clarice," I warn.

She gives it to me.

"Oh, hush. You're never too old to get a present from your—from me."

I narrow my eyes. What was she going to say? My mind races with possibilities that can't be. Clarice's cheeks flush. Penny's laughter carries across the room, breaking the moment. Clarice peers over my shoulder and I turn. I love Penny's smile.

"You know that young lady?"

Not good enough the voice in my head keeps telling me.

I try to speak but my voice comes out hoarse. I clear my throat and try again. "Yeah. She's Sarina's sister. She's staying at the house with me while Sarina is away on business."

I trust Clarice probably more than anyone and about as much as I trust Maddie and Sarina.

"Oh. So, it's only you and her in that big old house? Ohhhhh." A sly grin crosses her face in a teasing manner.

I chuckle. "It's not like that, Clarice."

She squeezes my arm. "I'm playing with you. Was hoping to get a smile out of you, son. It's been absent lately, but I saw a hint of one while you were speaking to her."

My face grows warm. Clarice teasing me doesn't bother me at all. There's a couple getting up and putting their jackets on, but their bodies are like silhouettes and all I see is Penny. She's so comfortable with Maddie and I love seeing her in this space. She fits.

"There it is again. Subtle, but it's there," she says.

I turn back to Clarice, feeling the smile she's speaking of.

"You're allowed you know. To be happy. To find real love."

She knows all about Macy and was never a fan.

"I know," I whisper.

" I'm sorry. Enough with the heavy. Go get your things and spend some time with that girl!"

I laugh. "Alright. Have a good night and get home safe. Thanks for the card."

"Thanks, Zachary. You, too."

In the office, Mark is at his desk. He glances up from the paperwork strewn about. His tie is loose and hanging off his neck. The top button of his shirt is undone and his hair is a ruffled mess. I've been wanting to talk to him all night. I spent part of my break researching ideas for the pub. He hasn't said much since the night he broke the news and it's totally understandable.

"Hey, do you need me to hang around tonight?" I ask.

"Nah. Your shift is over. You should head home."

I grab my jacket from the coat hanger in the corner and turn back to him.

"I hope it's alright to offer some ideas for the pub that I saw online in a forum."

Mark puts the pencil down and sits back in the chair. "Of course, Zach. You know I'm all ears and especially coming from you. You've worked your ass off since day one. I'm not sure how much I can do now to stop things, but I want to know your thoughts."

I play with the sleeves of my thick, black bomber jacket. My heart is picking up pace. Mark has never rejected one of my ideas for anything, but this feels different, because this time the pub depends on it. I can't lose this job. I refuse to go back to square one.

"Have you thought of maybe adding something different to the menu? Or a twist on an old favorite? Maddie could even create a drink; you know she's always experimenting. I'm not a fan of social media but you could always make a few videos or posts on the pages for a new item."

Mark scratches the scruff on his chin. "Ironically, I had a conversation with Danny earlier this evening."

Danny is one of our head cooks.

"At home he makes this homemade sauce for pulled pork and he was open to sharing. Our pulled pork sammy is a popular menu item, we could always spruce that up a bit."

Another idea goes off in my head like a light bulb. "What about pairing it with a drink. He and Maddie could work together."

Mark stands, a smile lifting his lips. "That's not a bad idea. Doesn't hurt to try. Thanks Zach."

"I mean I think it's more of a team effort, but I want to do whatever I can to help."

Mark sighs but still seems to be in better spirits. "Please, don't be afraid to come to me. My meeting was pushed back so I have some time to kind of get my thoughts together. It's not a lot but it's something."

We talk for a few more minutes before I say goodnight. The main floor is mostly clear now except for a few stragglers. Penny is no longer in her spot. Madeline is wiping the bar surface and lifts her eyes to meet mine. A soft smile flirts across her lips. I search the room for Penny as my protective side kicks in.

"Hey, she went to the bathroom," Madeline says as I walk over.

"Oh."

"You looked like you were about to have a panic attack. You okay?"

"Fine. I—"

Madeline's soft hand settles over mine. I take notice of something missing on her left ring finger. She shakes her head. She doesn't want to talk about herself.

"I was worried that's all. You know who she is?"

Madeline nods. "Yeah. You should have told me she was here. Sarina had mentioned it being a possibility, but she took off without saying anything else to me. I haven't heard from her since before she left."

"Sorry, Maddie."

"It's fine. Careful with her. Sarina is overprotective of her baby sister, that much I know."

"I'm taking care of her like she asked me to. Do you think anyone recognized her?"

"Nah. No one looked her way or anything."

Something grazes my arm. No, not something, Penny. The way her fingers dance along my skin sends a snake of electricity through me.

"Hey," she says, in almost a whisper from beside me.

She's watching me with thoughtful, hazy eyes. Her lip's part and she doesn't say what I expect.

"I think I broke the seal. I shouldn't have peed."

I snort. "Can you hold it for the ride home?"

Something passes over her features at the mention of the word home. I can't quite grasp what it was because it vanishes quickly.

"I promise not to pee on your seat," she says, breaking the moment. "Are you sure you don't need to stay behind to help?"

"He deserves a break. He hasn't taken a night off in weeks," Maddie says.

I shoot a glance over at Madeline. She raises a brow as if to scold me. She's not wrong. I haven't taken a day off in a while. In fact, the fifteenth is the first one I can remember.

"So, I'm right about Larry then," Penny says, removing her hand from my arm.

"What's that?"

"He's mad at you for leaving him. It's why he goes after you. If you spend more time at home maybe he'd be more loving."

"You've had a little too much to drink."

"Nah. I'm good. I could use a strawberry eclair though." She winks.

"Nope. I'm hiding those from now on. Maybe under a bag of peas or something healthy."

She shrugs. "I can just buy you more." She bops me on the nose.

My jaw tightens at the mention of her buying things for me again, but I bite my tongue. She doesn't need to know why it frustrates me. I don't stay upset for long because when I peer down at her wide, innocent hazel eyes, what upsets me fades.

Madeline is taking in our back and forth. She doesn't say a word, only a goodbye and for Penny to text her if she needs anything at all. I guide Penny towards the rear exit with my hand on her lower back.

"Did you have fun, miss runaway?"

"I did. The jukebox music was such a vibe. I had to stop myself several times from running up to the stage and singing. It's in my blood—I can't help it."

"I'm glad you enjoyed yourself. If you want to come again let me know, I'll drive you. No sense in having you take a cab."

I push open the heavy metal door to the left side of the stage. Across the rocky parking lot against the fence is my car. She skips over to it, a little wobbly on her feet.

"You know what Wingmans could use? Kar—a—oke. Or like an open mic, like how cool would that be?"

I use the fob to unlock the door. She opens it before I reach her. I hold onto the cool metal frame as she slides in. Mark has never taken advantage of the stage before. We have microphones. Maybe karaoke or open mic was his original intention when he opened the pub.

"Karaoke, huh?"

"People love that kind of stuff."

I hate thinking of Macy, but the night she and her friends came in, they were looking for karaoke.

"You might be onto something."

She grins and shakes her shoulders in some kind of happy dance. "And that's tipsy me. Just imagine what kind of stuff I can come up with sober."

"I don't doubt you one bit, love."

After shutting the door, I head around to the driver's side and get in. When I turn on the engine the radio blares to life and one of her songs plays through the speakers. I think hearing it might upset her, but she surprises me by singing.

Take me on the open road.
With the windows down
and the radio up loud and proud.
Summer days winding down,
I don't take this love for granted,
because I'm living in the now.

"I wrote this song"—she reaches forward and lowers the volume—"I wrote it when I was fourteen. It was terrible. So terrible." She chuckles lightly.

I put the car into gear and back out of the spot. Once I've straightened the wheel, I peek over to let her know I'm listening then set my sight back on the road.

She rests her head on the seat and sighs. "Years later I found it. I couldn't get the chorus out of my head. It had to mean something. It was at the point where I'd been criticized for not writing my own songs. I was determined to put it out there. I asked my dad how I could turn it into something better. He sat with me and helped me rewrite it. He refused to take credit for the work he put into it."

"It was a pretty big hit a while back."

"Yeah, because of him."

"He might have given you the tools to write it, but those words are yours and no one else."

As the song comes to an end, she's silent. She watches the buildings as we pass by. Within minutes we turn onto the block and another few seconds later pull into the driveway.

"I wrote more of the new song," she says.

"Oh, really? Do I get to hear it? Or do I have to wait for the next shower concert?"

The car light turns on as I open the door. Her cheeks are a deep shade of pink. She reaches over and punches my arm playfully. The banter between us has become something familiar. It's not quite like how her sister and I interact. It's different.

"If you get to listen to my shower concerts then I get to listen to yours."

"Yeah well, I don't perform for free you know," I say smugly.

She giggles and the sound makes me smile. When I turn to meet her gaze, there's something serious behind it. Her eyes are lit in amusement, but her furrowed brows tell a different story.

"I'm sorry. I couldn't stop listening. You have the kind of voice that sucks you in. It's really"—she inhales and releases a trembling exhale—"it's beautiful." She pauses for a beat or two. "I'm sleepy. Thanks for leaving work early to bring me back."

Without another word, she exits the car. I watch her enter the house and give myself a few moments before I do the same.

Chapter 12

PENNY

I spent the weekend enjoying the weather. For February it was mostly mild. It was freeing to walk in the neighborhood and not have to worry. It's a quiet area with families who mostly keep to themselves.

Walking must give me the strength I need to write more of my song. It's a slow work in progress but it's coming along. I'm becoming attached to the lyrics, wanting to keep them for myself, like a therapy journal. The words feel good and maybe I'll change my mind. Tanner keeps asking for updates, but I've been ignoring them.

It's mid-morning on Valentine's Day and another beautiful day outside. After a nice relaxing shower, I curl up on the chair Zach knocked over, trying to read Tabby Monroe's latest romance book. It's a small town, brother's best friend, close proximity, roommates . . . okay, that's a coincidence, I swear. I smack the pages of the book shut and stare off at the cherry wood front door. Sunlight beams in through the front windows, glimmering through the white curtains and leaving a streak across the area rug.

Starting a relationship with someone who doesn't live where I do brings back all the anxiety of being on the road while Erick was recording his album. The picture of the girls. The decline of phone calls as time went on. Leaving voicemails once a week and maybe hearing from him or not. Friends, I can do, but anything more, I don't have enough trust left in my heart.

Zach has been nothing but caring and helpful since I've arrived. He's given me the space to be me. He's not constantly asking about my career or the documentary. The only time we bring up my music is if we talk about my song, and he lets me bring it up first. I'm starting to see that he treats me like a real person and not a celebrity. His gestures are more from his heart than his wallet and I appreciate him. When he met my gaze from across the pub, something happened, like a switch went off and a light turned on.

A strange sensation of someone in the room with me catches me off guard. I slide the book between me and the arm of the chair and turn to find nothing. No one. Not even a cat.

"Larry?" I call.

When I reach for my book the floor creaks. I spin but again there's nothing. I settle back into the seat facing the door. Sarina didn't say her house was haunted or anything. After a moment or two, I pick up the book again. As I open the page the floor creaks. Quick footsteps skitter by, followed by a yelp, a *thunk*, then, "Oh, shit".

I'm afraid of what I'll find when I turn but do anyway. Over the back of the chair is a— holy shit—naked Zach with a navy-blue towel haphazardly draped halfway over him. Nothing is left to the imagination.

"Jesus, sunshine," I say, slapping a hand to my face.

I'm tired of the "Hollywood" image and the guys like Erick who, because they have all those things, grow a head too big for them to handle. They aren't all like that, but I can't ever see myself being attracted to that type because of what has happened in the past. Zach is perfect the way he is. I'm finding him more attractive by the day and I can't stop myself from feeling it. Although, what is sticking out from the towel might be a little above average from what I've experienced. It's not romance book huge but it's something.

"Are you staring at him?" he asks.

I shut my eyes and keep my hand in place. I'm burning up inside. My heart rate has spiked and if I was put on one of those EKG machines it would probably be off the charts.

"No. Can you please put that thing away, rule breaker."

"Hey, now. I'm not the one staring." His tone is playful.

I squint again through my fingers only to be met with said body part at eye level.

"Why are you tiptoeing naked through the house anyway?"

"Well, you see . . . towels in place, you may stare now."

I move my hand and make sure my eyes are on his face when I do. He has a devilish grin on his lips. A small dimple appears under his light scruff.

"I was taking a shower, hence the wet hair, the wet bod." He winks.

I roll my eyes.

"And I realized I ran out of soap and it's down here."

My attention slips to where he has tied his towel. I try not to let it linger there too long. His laughter lets me know I've been caught. My heart swells with an odd, overwhelming heat.

"You could have gotten dressed first. You need to stop being a rule breaker," I say, turning fully and getting on my knees in the chair.

"Who is the one who ate the box of eclairs when it had my name on it?" He lowers his face so it's level with mine, taking away my view of his lower half.

"Doesn't count, you specifically said leftovers. Those are fair game."

I bite my lower lip. He narrows his eyes. The closer he gets the less I want to look away.

"Are you gonna get dressed or stand there naked?"

He opens his mouth to say something, but I stab my index finger into his chest. "You know what, don't—"

The sound of "Wanna Be" by the Spice Girls comes blaring through the speakers of my phone. It's Sarina's ringtone. Growing up they were her favorite band.

Zach raises a brow at me.

"It's Sarina, and it's a video call. Shoo!"

I try to shove him while peering at my phone. I go too low and touch something hard. My hand freezes as the chorus of the song rings in the air.

"Uhh . . . Penny."

"Whoopsie, that's not your chest."

My face is burning hot. I pull away and accept the call. It takes a second for her image to appear on the screen. My heart stops the moment she does. Sarina is dolled up. It's more than she ever would be for work. It's odd seeing her with a full face of makeup so early in the morning. She's a few hours behind me. Her plump lips are bright red. She's got the perfect color foundation giving her a slight tan-kind of glow. The nude and natural eyeshadow is so her, yet not.

"Jesus, Pen, you are pale as a ghost. Are you ill?"

"What? No. I'm okay. I—"

I twist in the seat so I'm facing the front door again.

"You sure?"

"Uh-huh."

I lift the phone so I can see if there's anything or anyone behind me. A muffled curse followed by the shake of my chair makes me laugh. I throw my head back feeling a wave of absolute happiness, but I'm a little dizzy, with a mixture of the warm and fuzzies running through me. If only she knew what I saw. What would she think?

"I think you've totally lost your mind," Sarina says.

"I think I have too. I'm sorry. I was thinking of something that happened in my book."

Her dark eyes narrow, and I shrug.

"It's nice to see you laughing, Pen. It's been so long since you've seemed so like yourself."

I fiddle with my locket, but nothing stops my smile.

"How is the dress hunting going?" she asks.

"Tanner has been emailing me about designers and all of that jazz, but nothing feels right." I rub my thumb over the intricate engraved butterfly design on the front of the locket. Each tiny wing brings me peace.

"Go into my closet. On the second valet rod, check the white garment bag. On the shelf above it, is a box. I'd say more but I have to go. I'm, uh—I'm going out. Just go look. Okay?"

"Are you going on a date?" I ask, completely ignoring her request.

"I kind of sort of met someone." She scratches the back of her head. "Yeah. I don't know. It's not serious. We live too far away. It's nice to get out and date a little and forget I can't have Mad—"

Under her makeup her cheeks flush a bit pink and rosy. There's more she wants to say but stops herself.

"You deserve to go out and have fun."

"I'm not getting any younger," she says. She's turning thirty-five this year and I get that. She's been wanting to find a woman to start a life with but has been struggling to find someone willing to commit. "But I want to have fun too. She's fun."

"I'm happy for you. Go. Have a blast, and don't worry about my dress woes."

She chuckles. "Hey, I'm serious about the closet. Go. Look. It might help. Love you."

"Love you too," I say, and then she's gone.

"Oh, *thank fuck*," the voice behind me exclaims.

I jump up out of my seat at the same time Zach stands. He holds onto his lower back as if he was in pain from the position he was in. I laugh at him.

"You were back there the whole time?"

"What did you want me to do, jump up and say, SURPRISE!"

I laugh. "No, because then she totally would have had words for you, for me, oh god, she would think . . ." I gag.

"Hey, now! You'd be lucky to have this." He points at himself.

"You are so full of yourself, sunshine."

"You have no idea, love."

He turns and as he exits the room, sways his hips from side to side giving me a show. I hate to admit, but it's kind of nice to look at.

Chapter 13

PENNY

The wooden oak closet door is a barrier between me and whatever Sarina is hiding. The golden knob is warm under my touch. I twist and am met with an array of flannel button downs, suits, and a few dresses. Stepping forward I put my hand through the center. There's a black dress on one side and a red flannel top on the other. I part them. Behind it, the rod is almost empty sans a few dresses and one in a garment bag.

My fingers fiddle with the locket. The bumpy design comforts me as I press harder into it. I grab the white garment bag and step out of the closet. The material is old and a little yellow. I spin the hanger. A strangled gasp tumbles from my lips at the name written in black marker across the front.

Suzanna Clarke.

With trembling hands, I grab the zipper and slowly pull.

My breath catches in my throat as I reveal the gold sparkling dress with thick straps. It's the dress my mom wore for the Great American Music Awards in 1994. The one in the red-carpet video. How did Sarina get this? My lip quivers.

On the top shelf above it is a box.

I hook the dress onto the back of the door and peer up to find a shoebox. It's the only thing on the shelf. I get on my tiptoes but can't get it. Jumping doesn't help much. Shit. My eyes tear.

"Fuck," I yell, voice cracking.

I stretch my arm as the warmth of a body settles behind me. Zach reaches above us and grabs it before I can. The white dusty shoebox is placed directly in front of me. My lungs constrict. Zach's soapy aroma wafts around me in a comforting blanket. There's a coolness in the air as the heat of his body disappears.

"Stay," I say, in a strange high-pitched voice.

His hand grazes my lower back as he steers me out of the closet and over to Sarina's bed. I settle onto the sky-blue comforter, trying to calm down as Zach perches next to me. I gather my composure by absorbing everything or anything in my environment. Zach's scent, the blue comforter. I let go of the box with one hand and touch the butterfly wings on my locket. Zach's presence is like peace.

He's quiet and allows me the time I need to open it. It's like my body is in limbo. I lift the cover, and I expect to find shoes, but there's an envelope. Sarina's name and mine are written in Mom's fancy cursive. A soft whimper escapes me. Zach doesn't make a move to touch me. He allows me to cry.

I carefully open it and smile through my tears at the handwriting inside. The familiarity of it gives me a sense of home.

My dear girls,

I love you both so very much. I hope if you get this letter I'm reading it with you. If not, don't you worry, I see you. And Sarina, thank you for sending this message to your sister.

Pennyfly, my girl. I know you've made it big by now. I'm writing this as your first single is released. It took your dad many years for people to truly appreciate his talent. I don't want you to get discouraged if the world has a hard time accepting you too.

When Dad was nominated for a Great American Music Award, it wasn't from his first, second, or even third single. It was when he was a fully established artist with many under his belt. It was when he had grown into this amazing artist.

If you are reading this now, it means you need it for a BIG moment. I told Sarina that if something was to happen to me, she should give you this dress when you need it the most. So don't be mad if you're old and grey and she's finally giving it to you, but I do hope it's before then.

You had stars in your eyes over this dress. I spent countless hours with a friend who is a designer, who helped me create this beauty. They guided me in making it myself. It was my first of many, but you never forget your first. I just know you'll be the most beautiful woman at the ball. This is your time to shine, Princess.

Love,

Mom

By the time I'm done reading there are so many tears I can't see. I hold the paper tight in my hand. My shoulders are shaking with such intensity I'm starting to have trouble catching my breath. I turn towards Zach and meet his eyes. I nod frantically and before I can take my next deep inhale, I'm engulfed in his arms.

This is the second time in only two weeks I've been in this man's arms crying. It's weird having someone there to comfort me. It's been such a lonely road over the last few years. More so since my parents. The anger builds over how preventable their early death could have been. If the media would mind their own damn business, instead of running them off the road.

Zach stays silent and glides his hand over my back. I lift my head from his chest, and he wipes away the remnants of tears.

"Mom wants me to wear the dress she wore when my dad won the award. She made it. It's my favorite dress."

When I first met Zach, I never imagined him having a sweet gentle side to him. His sarcasm and how my sister made him seem, does not accurately describe the man I've gotten to know. I like how he makes me feel.

"Are you going to?"

I nod and whisper, "Yeah."

"I feel like there's more behind what else makes it special."

"It was the first time I had ever seen her on camera. I was maybe three or four. I don't remember much, only that I used to bug her to put it on over and over. She was a princess in my eyes. Her story is a fairytale. I still remember the way Dad embraced her on the red carpet. They were so in love then. He was her prince. Well, that's what younger me thought."

He smiles. "I love how you have that beautiful memory of her."

"I can't believe it's been here all this time."

He swipes his thumb under my lid where some more tears fall. "I believe you are exactly where you were meant to be when you got the call."

"M-me too."

I rest my forehead on his chest. Being here like this is calming.

"I'd to anything to have Mom see me in her dress. It shouldn't have come down to these paparazzi infiltrating their personal space. The accident could have been avoided."

"She knew it would be perfect for you, love. I'm angry for you and wish I could make it all go away."

We hold onto each other a little tighter. Words I'm not sure I should be saying, tumble from my lips. "I know we only just met but since I've been here you've treated me like a person and not the celebrity. You've made me feel safe, and while their deaths will always weigh heavy on my heart and you can't make it all go away, you do make it better."

I could spend the whole night here be comforted by him. It happened so quickly. The admiration I have for this man, but I like it. I try not to think about what could happen between us, the fear of starting something and losing it to distance is always lingering. Always. I don't think I could do it again.

"What are you doing tonight?" he asks.

I sniffle. "I was gonna read all night. It's usually how I spend Valentine's Day."

He stops his thumb from moving. "Come to work with me. Madeline keeps asking when you'll be back. There's a local band playing. They are good. I want you there . . .if you want to be."

My pulse picks up speed. I retreat from his grasp and stare into his soft eyes. He truly is different. Before I was famous it was just people who wanted to be friends with me because of my dad. After that it was because I was famous, and they wanted a piece of fame.

"Are you asking me on a date, Zachary?"

He grins. "It would be kind of rude to invite you on a date to my job while I'm working, but if that's how you roll." His wink sends my heart on a loop de loop. "I'm asking you to be my Valentine, but don't tell Sarina, she'd have my head."

I chuckle. The tears come to a stop and he pulls his hand away from my face. I miss the contact and fight the urge to grab his hand to put it back.

"Yeah, sunshine. I'll be your Valentine."

I am somehow a million times lighter and ready to bring some fun back into my life. There's no other way I'd rather spend my night. It's been a long time since I've looked forward to something. I hope there's more to come along with it.

Chapter 14

ZACH

We have half an hour before we have to leave. When she fell apart in my arms again there was intense pressure inside of me that grew heavier; not in a bad way as if she were a burden. I can only describe it as finding something you didn't know you were searching for.

A deep sigh comes from Sarina's room. I'm surprised she's in there again. When I returned from the store a while ago, the house was quiet, and her bedroom door was closed. I let her be and played some video games in my room. Valentines Day is one of the busiest nights of the year, so I wanted to relax beforehand.

The door is ajar. I peer around the frame, and I'm met with the curve of her backside in a glittery gold dress. It's not flashy gold, but more subtle. The dress compliments every part of her body. I'm so used to seeing her in flannel and sweats that it catches me off guard.

She holds the studded material at the bottom as she stares at her reflection in the floor-length mirror.

When she spins the bottom flares up only slightly and her laughter fills the room. It sure beats the crying. I do spy wet streaks on her cheeks, but she's not sad. She grabs hold of the locket and rubs her thumb over the engraved design. I want to ask her why it's so special. I've been hesitant in case it hurt too much to talk about.

I'm caught up in her smile and flushed cheeks.

I should leave the room. Instead, I'm entranced by her. She does another twirl, and our eyes meet. Her smile doesn't fade and something like relief washes over me. She glances at the floor, cheeks darkening.

"It suits you, Pen."

"You think? It's not too much?"

She lifts the dress and stares at the twinkling glow it gives off in the light. I cross the room to her, and I'm surprised to find there's a slight tremble in my hands as I reach towards her. She slips her hand into mine and it's a perfect fit, just like the dress.

I lift my arm and spin her. She takes my cues without missing a beat, as if we've done this a thousand times before. I pull her into me, pressing our bodies together with a jolt. I rest one hand at her waist and the other on her shoulder.

"Are you trying to seduce me, sunshine?" she asks, a tempting sexy grin on her face.

I'm caught between her feisty personality and her beauty. When I'd see her on TV it didn't do the real person justice. She's the exact opposite of everything I've come to know.

"Mmm, love, I don't seduce. When I see what I want I go right for it."

Penny inhales sharply, her lips parting as she watches me with a soft, adoring expression on her face. I lead her into another dance move and hum the first song that comes to my mind. The lyrics of "Somewhere Only We Know" come easy to me. It reflects a personal place of solace. Here with her, it feels right.

I don't want to look away as we continue to sway. I know she feels everything my body is saying. She's leaning into every touch and embrace.

She takes a few steps back. I lift my arm, and she spins once more. The bottom of the dress lifts slightly before she's back in my arms, my palm pressed against the small of her back.

For the first time since moving in, she's light and carefree. At the chorus, she sings with me. Our voices mesh in beautiful harmony.

With her back in my grasp, she rests her cheek against my chest. I wonder if she can sense how fast my heart is beating right now. I'd blame the dancing and singing, but it's all her. She makes me come alive. I wish there was a way I could live in this state every day.

"You are the first person, aside from Madeline, who has ever heard me sing like that. Sarina has heard a little, but I've never done that in front of someone I just met."

She stops dancing and lowers the hand she has on my shoulder, placing it right over my beating heart. Her tongue wets her lips as she watches me intently. There's something she's working out in her head. Her brows furrow and forehead creases.

"Zach," she whispers.

"Yeah, love?" I rasp.

Her hand remains on my chest, warming my entire body. I want to look at it, but I'm too captivated by her eyes over anything else.

She inhales a trembling breath, then releases. "Why would you hide such a beautiful talent?"

Her intense gaze, full of admiration, keeps me rooted into place.

"I . . . I guess I never had a reason to use it."

Somehow there's now barely any space between us.

"I can give you a ton of reasons why you should."

As I go to open my mouth my alarm goes off, letting me know it's time to haul ass and get to work. It breaks the moment between us, and she steps away as her gaze drops to the floor.

That beautiful connection between us is lost.

"I'll uh—it's time to leave."

"Oh, shit. I—I'm so sorry. Um, you can leave me here if you're gonna be—"

I take her hand, and she stops talking. Her skin is soft and warm under my touch.

"I'll wait for you," I say..

Her lips part and a soft sigh releases from them. I give her hand one last squeeze and exit the room to let her get dressed, shutting the door for privacy.

Something went down in that room tonight. It's been slowly unfolding since the moment she walked into this house. I don't see it going away any time soon.

Chapter 15

PENNY

Zach wasn't wrong when he said tonight was going to be busy. It's been nonstop since we stepped foot in the door. I've managed to snag the same spot I was in last time.

Maddie provided me with a new drink called *Whisk Me Away* and told me it goes best with their new and improved pulled pork sandwich or sammy, as stated in the menu. The drink is lemonade with whisky and my god, is it good. The tang and sweetness hit my tastebuds in the best way.

My head is still spinning from my moment with Zach in the bedroom earlier. Dancing to nothing but his beautiful voice was everything. Romance isn't dead. Zach sure knows how to take a moment of heartache and turn it around. I love that about him. I can't stop smiling every time I remember the way he held me.

The band is due to go on at ten, so in about two hours. I keep hearing chatter from the ladies at the bar about their favorite members. Apparently, all are taken. It doesn't stop them from talking about the hot delivery man Dominic, who is apparently their drummer.

The atmosphere is vibrant and music from the jukebox overpowers the television tonight. Beside me a kid—eight or nine at most—slides onto the stool. He glances over and his unruly blonde hair falls over his face.

"Hey, what's your poison?" he asks, nodding his head at me.

I blink, trying to figure out if I've stepped into some alternate dimension where kids are allowed at bars.

"Devin, use your manners, son."

An older man walks up behind him. His hair is much darker than the boy, but his eyes match from their shape to the sharp blue color. He smiles at me.

"You must be Penny." The man holds out his hand to shake mine.

I've got my cap low, the fake glasses on, and my hair tied back. I raided my sister's closet again. I went with a black blazer, a low-cut white V-neck tee, and some gray slacks along with converses. The hat and converses are a touch of my own self. So far, I've flown under the radar.

"I'm Mark. This is my place. You're Zach's friend, right?"

"Yeah, and uh"—I blow out a breath—"Sarina's sister."

"Right. Yes. And you'll be with us for a few weeks?"

I politely shake his hand. "Yes. It's nice to meet you. Can I just tell you; the pulled pork is to die for, and the new drink Maddie created? That one is gonna draw a crowd. So good."

Marks face brightens. "Thank you. My staff has been working hard to keep this place going strong. Tonight is one of our best nights in a while."

"I'm so happy to hear. And who is this fellow?" I ask, looking back at the boy.

Madeline leans over the bar and slides the boy a drink that looks suspiciously like a Shirley Temple. She messes with his hair, and he scowls at her. I take in the little man's attire. He's dressed up in a suit and tie. In his suit jacket pocket is a rose and I can't help but smile.

"This is my son, Devin. My wife is working, and I couldn't find a sitter on Valentine's Day."

"Hi, Devin. I'm Penny. Those are my favorite drinks. Do you think you can order me one?" I ask.

He turns to me while kicking his feet back and forth. The stool is too high for him. The seat shakes with each movement.

"What the lady wants, the lady gets." He turns to Madeline. "Maddie, may I have another please?"

Tonight, Madeline, although dressed head-to-toe in black clothing, brightened up her appearance with red lipstick and heart antennas. They bob with each movement.

"Of course. I'll add it to your tab," she says.

He slides over a pretend credit card, like the kind that come inside a brand new wallet

"Perfect. Thanks, doll." He winks at her.

Mark is shaking his head and pinching the bridge of his nose between two thick brows.

"What can I say? He watches a lot of movies . . ."

"Only the best movies, right, little man." Zach walks over and places a hand on Devin's shoulder.

The kid's face lights up like he's received the best Christmas gift ever.

"Zach!" He nearly wobbles off the stool.

Zach steadies him. "Careful there, buddy. What's up?"

"Nothing, just buying this beautiful lady a drink." Devin nods at me.

Zach lifts his gaze and meets my stare. My heart jumps a few beats. My lips dry, and my throat is suddenly parched. Where is that Shirley Temple when I need it?

"Oh, yes. She is quite a beauty, isn't she?" The question is directed at Devin, but his eyes stay on me.

"Hey, I saw her first," Devin says in the most serious tone.

Zach slowly backs away with his hands up. "Respect, dude."

I love their silly banter.

Another server walks up to Mark. He's young, maybe around my age. Exhaustion lines his features and his hair is a bit of a mess.

"Mark?"

Mark turns to the distraught voice.

"Destiny called out," he says.

"Shit. Um . . ." He looks at me. "I hate to ask, but do you mind hanging out with Dev a few minutes while I get things squared away?"

"Oh, yes of course. The man did buy me a drink," I say.

Mark chuckles, but his smile doesn't quite reach his eyes. Stress lines form at the corners as he nods and rushes off with the server.

"I should get back to work, too." Zach places a hand on Devin's shoulder again. "Take good care of the lady for me, will ya?"

Devin looks from him to me with a narrowed gaze.

"Of course."

Zach looks at me. It happens all over again. The faulty abnormal beat in my heart followed by the dryness in my throat.

"Your drinks are served," Madeline says.

I grab it and nearly chug it.

"Whoa there, beautiful. You must savor the taste," Devin says.

"Have fun, you two." Zach winks at me then turns to get back to work.

"So, do you go to school?" I ask Devin.

"I do. I am in grade three." He sits up straight. He faces me, but his attention is somewhere behind me or like he's looking through me. "I go to a special school called Horizon Academy. My teacher Mrs. Charlotte Holmes is the coolest. She used to be in Pre-K, but she thought us third graders were much cooler."

"Are you supposed to know your teachers real name?"

He shrugs.

"Third grade is awesome. I was homeschooled. My mom taught me and my sister."

His eyes widened. "Whoa. Was your mom a teacher?"

"It was one of the first jobs she ever wanted."

"My mom works. She's a nurse. She works a lot." He sighs.

"My dad worked a lot too."

He glances up, his blue gaze a little misty. "Really? It makes me sad sometimes."

"Mmhmm . . . it made me sad too, but do you know how special your mom is?"

"How?" he asks, leaning in.

I smile genuinely. "She's helping people in the best way. Comforting them when they have a scary test, like bloodwork. Making sure they are safe by figuring out what is wrong. Her job is one of the coolest ones out there. When I was little, I had to have my tonsils out. I was so scared, but there was one nurse there who held my hand.

She was there when I woke up. She made sure I was okay. I will never forget her."

Devin's face lights up. "My mom is a superhero."

"She sure is. And know she's doing it to give you the best life possible."

"We are going to Disneyland in two months, seven days, and twenty-six hours." He states it proudly.

"That's amazing. I went a few times when I was a kid. It's a magical place. Who do you want to see the most?"

"Stitch. He's the coolest alien on the block."

"He's my favorite too. In my house back in California, I have a collection of all things Stitch."

He beams. "So cool."

Devin stares off a little, his eyes drooping as he lets out a yawn.

"Getting sleepy?" I ask.

He nods slowly. "It's so loud though."

Mark is on the other side of the bar. He combs a hand through his hair and scans the room with a crinkled brow.

"Come on. Let's ask your dad if there is somewhere quieter, we can go."

I hop off the stool and hold my hand out for Devin. He follows my lead. We weave through the tables. Mark catches my eye from a few feet away and heads towards us.

"Hey, everything alright?" he asks.

"Devin says he's tired. Is there a place where he can rest?"

A loud roar of voices rips through the pub. Devin jumps beside me and tries to cover his ear with one hand.

"Yeah. My office is to the right of the stage. Up those stairs." He points behind him. "The only people going in there are employees.

I'm still trying to figure out how I'm going to manage tonight. I'm down two employees. Both with the flu. My wife should be here in half an hour to get him. I'm sorry to put this on you."

I hold up my hand. "No, don't apologize. I want to help. It's okay."

His tense stance loosens a little. "Thank you, truly. I appreciate it."

"Of course."

Mark bends to eye level with Devin and whispers to him before straightening and giving me a nod. I lead Devin through the crowd towards the stairs.

As I take the first step with Devin trailing behind, my eyes find a curious Zach's. He's standing between two tables with food trays in hand. He smiles. I'm swept up in the moment with him, so much I almost forget the small hand in mine.

"I'm so sleepy, Pen," Devin says.

"Alright. Let's get upstairs."

"Zach looks like my dad to my mom," Devin says.

"Huh?" I ask, as we stop at the top step.

"Dad always looks at mom. Zach looks at you too. Like that."

"Oh— oh."

"Does he love you?"

I choke on my own spit and cough a few times to clear my throat. "N-no, no. Zach and I are just friends."

"Sure. That's what they all say," he says, and I chuckle under my breath.

Once inside, I shut the door to drown out some of the noise. The bass from the music and the murmur of voices decreases but not one hundred percent. I sit in what I assume is Mark's chair behind the desk. Devin curls up on my lap. I take in the small space, the lockers, and awards and licenses on the wall.

"I still hear it," he says.

"Do you like books?" I ask.

He nods. "I like books about pirates."

"What about audiobooks? Are you alright with wearing headphones?"

He nods. "I have some for when things get too much and too loud, but dad forgot them."

I smile. "Ah. These are perfect for that. Let's search through my audio app so we can find a pirate book to fall asleep to."

Tonight, I've brought one of my bigger purses. It's not deep but is big enough to hold my small set of headphones.

"I can listen to books in my ears? Like a movie?"

I nod. "Uh-huh. And it's so cool, because the narrators who do the books make it feel like a movie. They are actors like you see on TV but use their voice only."

"That's the coolest."

We scroll through the app until he finds one that jumps out at him. His eyelids are droopy. I don't have any doubts he will be out quickly. I press play and close my eyes along with him. The weight of him in my arms becomes a little heavier and his breathing slows. I find myself nodding off a bit and enjoying the company of this little guy. I can almost imagine a life like this: being a mom, holding a child, reading and listening to bedtime stories together. I smile at the idea.

Having a family is something I do want, but it's also not a thing I think about often. What would life be like if I wasn't famous? If I could be like this always. Not worrying about leaving my house because someone could snap a picture of me picking my nose, turning it into a scandal. I could live life under the radar and enjoy the peace and quiet. It's nothing I've ever experienced. I've been in the spotlight since I was born.

The last two weeks with Zach have given me this whole new perspective on life. To have someone who likes me for the real me and not for personal gain. I allow the thoughts to sit there and relax into a light slumber.

Chapter 16

ZACH

I'm supposed to take a thirty-minute break. It hasn't happened, because tonight has been one disaster after another. I stand at the bar and pop a few fries into my mouth. It's not a lot but it's something. I can't believe how many guests we have. I've gotten so many compliments on our new menu items, and I'm filled with a little hope that we can turn things around. Penny's idea about karaoke and open mic have been on my mind. I'll have to bring it up to Mark when we're less chaotic.

I feel bad about inviting Penny here and not being able to spend a little time with her. I thought I'd have my break to sit and chat, but I'm basically eating on the go.

"Hey, Zach. Have you seen Mark?" a familiar soft yet exhausted voice asks behind me.

"Hey, Cynthia. How are you?"

Cynthia is Mark's wife. Her shoulders are slumped, and her usual bright smile is lost within her tired features. They are both clearly worn out.

"We had two servers call out with the flu. It's been rough. I'll go and get Devin. He was tired and my . . ." I pause. My what? What is Penny to me? My roommate's sister? She's much more than that. A friend? For some unknown reason that doesn't feel like quite enough. It's the best for now. "My friend Penny is with him upstairs. Poor kid looked exhausted. I can go get Devin for you, while you search for Mark."

"Thank you. I'll hang out here. I'm sure he'll appear eventually."

I give her a nod and then head towards the stairs. It's been about an hour since they went up there. The band tinkers with their drums as I get to the last step. They should be going on in a few minutes. As with everything else going haywire tonight, the band's van broke down, so they were delayed by a half an hour getting here to set up.

The door to the office is shut. I knock softly and press my ear against it. When I don't hear anything, I twist the knob. Penny and Devin are passed out in the desk chair.

As the door clicks shut behind me, I zero in on the sight before me. Devin is on her lap, his head is resting in the crook of her shoulder as his legs dangle over one side of the chair. Are those headphones?.

Penny has her arm wrapped protectively around him. Her phone is loosely held in her hand.

The sight makes my heart stutter. I loved watching her and Devin together at the bar. Her entire face lit up with amusement as he babbled to her. Even from afar you could see, despite the short time Penny had known Devin, the way she cared for him. She engaged in conversation, asked him questions, and played along with his pretend play.

An image flashes through my head and it nearly jolts me backwards. It's one of Penny in the den of the house holding a young boy who could be mine. I cover them with a blanket and watch them sleep soundly.

I close my eyes. My breath hitches for a second before I'm slammed back into reality by the door smacking into me.

"Oh, there you are. Cynthia was wondering what happened."

Mark pauses beside me. I peek over at him, and he grins. He sighs and pats my shoulder.

"I know that look."

"There's no look," I say.

He chuckles. "Deny it as much as you want, but I get it."

Penny stirs. Her eyes fluttering open slowly. She meets my gaze and blushes.

"I'm so sorry. I don't know why I fell asleep."

Mark laughs. "It's alright. Thank you so much, Penny, for taking care of him. I don't usually bring him, especially on a busy night like this, but I had no choice."

"I didn't mind at all. He's a spectacular kid."

Mark crosses the room. Penny carefully takes the headphones off Devin's ears and he stirs but instead of waking, cuddles deeper into Penny's arms.

"Bye, bye, Pen," Devin whispers. His eyes are still closed as he's lifted into Mark's arms.

"Bye, Devin. Thank you for the drink."

Devin's sleepy eyes remain closed, but he gives her a thumbs up. Upon Mark's exit he tilts his head and winks at me before heading out the door. It takes me a few seconds before I turn back to Penny. She gives me a sleepy smile as she puts away her headphones and phone into her bag.

"Do you want me to take you back to the house?" I ask as she stands.

"No. You guys are swamped. I know I have no experience but if you guys need an extra hand, I'm a quick study. I could be waiting tables in minutes or whatever else you guys need help with. I could be a bouncer too and watch all those women here for the band. Some of the ladies at the bar earlier were feral for these guys. My god! Thirsty, thirsty women."

I scoff playfully. "And you're not thirsty with your dirty books."

She gasps as she crosses the room. "I don't read dirty books." She pokes my chest. "I read sexy, smutty books and I'm damn proud of it."

I stare at her finger for a few seconds before lifting my gaze. I lose the ability to breathe. Her heated green eyes are on me.

"I'm serious," she says, being the first to break the silence. "I want to help."

"Aren't you afraid someone will recognize you."

She shrugs. "I am but you can clearly see Mark is stressed. I want to help, and I want" —she pauses—"to feel human and not like an animal on display or a puppet for the world to control. If Mark can't allow it, I won't but I'd love to help."

There's genuine desire in her voice. Her eyes sparkle at her confession. She's seen both the good and bad sides of fame. There's a longing in her eyes for something deeper, something more. The urge to find a purpose rather than living as if driven by some motor. I understand it.

"Can we ask?" Her pleading voice does me in.

"Come on. Let's see what we can do."

I've had my eye on Penny almost all night. I keep checking in to make sure she's alright. I'm in awe at how easily being a server comes to her. Mark didn't hesitate to let her join the crew. One of our servers, Rachel, helped her navigate the floor. On a busy night, we usually have five servers; on slower ones it can range from two or three. Tonight, with two out, including Penny and I, it makes four. Everyone was so welcoming and helpful. Through the chaos we do find time to connect. Our eyes met several times from across the pub.

There's something different about Penny with the hat, glasses, and Sarina's clothes. I don't think anyone has recognized her. The lighting in the pub is dim so between that and her outfit guests seem to be oblivious to her. I love both versions of her, but as I watch I start to take notice at how much more at home the Clarke Kent side of her is.

The band has been in full swing for almost an hour, so their set is almost over. A lot of people are focused more on them. They aren't paying much attention to us other than for food.

I'm at the bar, taking a quick breather.

"Thank you so much, Wingman's, for an amazing night," the lead singer says into the mic. He's got his guitar wrapped around his neck as he grabs hold of the microphone.

If I had to guess he's probably around my age with much darker hair and a rocker vibe I don't possess with piercings and tattoos.

"We're going to play two more songs. You've all been incredible. But let's end this on a high note. Everyone get out of your seats for this one. It's a cover I think you'll all know. Picture this. You're on this stage with a karaoke machine. The crowd is hyped and waiting for you to nail this song."

They start playing opening chords to "Don't Stop Believing". A lot of guests stand, cheering.

"Best karaoke song ever!"

I shiver at the way Penny's familiar, loud feminine voice vibrates in my ear. My heart kicks up a notch like the drum beat of the song. She bites the corner of her lip and grins.

"You're so wrong. 'Sweet Caroline' takes the cake on that one."

"If there was karaoke here, I'd prove it to you that I'm right," she yells back and bumps into me with her hip.

"Did someone say karaoke?" Mark comes up and stands on her other side.

"Have you ever had a karaoke night here? Or an open mic? If a band can draw a crowd like this, I have no doubts karaoke would do amazing," she asks.

Mark smiles. "We did for a bit when we first opened, but no one came and if they did it was the same few people."

Penny taps her lower lip with her finger. I can't help my wandering eyes, but they keep going right to her mouth. She wets her lips with her tongue and for a second, I'm not in this room anymore and in my head, I'm kissing her with everything I've got. And it's good. So fucking good I can almost taste her.

A hand touches my arm, and I jolt out of the desirable daydream.

"Right, Zach? I said it when I came here last about karaoke?"

It takes me a moment to get my bearings. "What?"

"I was just saying how I told you there should be karaoke here or an open mic."

"You sure did. I think you even yelled Kar-A-oke."

She chuckles. "I think it could really bring in a whole different crowd and could be a ton of fun."

"Hmm . . ." Mark hums loud enough to hear over the volume of the music.

"It's a good idea, right?" Penny asks, excited like a kid on Christmas.

"Zach, what if you ran a karaoke night? I'll have to look and see what day might work best, but if you two want to create something together. It can't hurt to try new things. I am willing to try anything to save my home here."

Mark's eyes sparkle with some kind of joy for the first time since breaking the news to us. He glances around the room, soaking in the energy in here and I do the same. A satisfied smile tilts his lip upwards. It's nice to see him with determination on his face unlike the night he told us the news.

"Sure, anything to help," I say.

Penny stares over at me and narrows her brows.

I lean in. "I'll explain in the car."

Mark seems happy with the suggestion, so I'll roll with it. If it helps give us more nights like these, I'm all in.

* * *

Penny leans her head back on the seat of my car. She and I are both exhausted once the night is over. When it was only Mark, Madeline, Penny, and I, she let her guard down. Her glasses and hat came off.

No one treated her any differently than they did each other. The fact that she felt safe amongst my friends speaks volumes. She's nothing like I expected.

"You alright over there?"

"I'm . . . really good actually."

"What were you going to tell me earlier? Is everything okay with Wingman's?" Penny asks in a sweet quiet voice.

I start up the car and turn on the heat. A heavy quiet falls upon us. I grip the wheel and think about how I want to approach this. My chest tightens. Penny is not Macy. She's not going to tell me that keeping this job will never be enough for any woman. It's hard to shift gears out of that mindset. When I see Penny beside me the doubts creep in and I keep telling myself she doesn't belong in this beat up old hunk of junk. I wait for the moment when she comments on what I drive because Macy did all the time. It tied into her telling me, if I had a better job, I could afford a "real car" or a "real house".

It's becoming hard to breathe, my chest tightening like an iron fist is wrapped around it. *She's not Macy. She's not Macy.* I try to push back the thought of her buying groceries and shut my eyes to make it go away.

"Zach? I'm sorry, did I overstep or something?" Her tone is softer, concern etched in it.

She reaches for me but hesitates for a second before placing her hand on my arm. I let go of the breath I was holding. She has been open and honest with me about her past. It's my turn.

I swallow hard and face her. She doesn't look away. My heart warms. She's a safe space.

"Right before you got here Mark told us the pub isn't doing well. We've had good years and bad ones but ultimately have been alright. I guess it got so bad that he's not sure what is going to happen. We've all been trying to help in any way we can. The new drink and sandwich were one of our attempts to get more people in."

She squeezes my arm and a soft understanding smile dances across her lips.

"What can I do to help? I'll get on social media and shout it out to the world—"

"I can't ask you to put your own mental health at risk for me."

She leans in and our eyes lock in an intense stare that I can't look away from.

"You're not. I could help by making a social media video on Wingman's page if there is one. I could hype up open mic or karaoke. I mean it could blow my cover but if it helps you, Mark and all the others who could be in jeopardy of losing their job. I'll donate—"

I rest my hand over hers and her breath hitches.

"Zach, if this place is your home, I want to help you fight for it."

I'm starting to feel that overwhelming sensation of not being good enough because I could never afford to make things happen the way she could.

"You're mad."

I take her face in my hands. Her lips part as our eyes dance all over each other.

"I'm not mad at you. I'm overwhelmed," I admit.

She puts her hand right over my rapidly beating heart. I love when she does this. Her eyelids flutter as she stares at the spot.

"I got a little too eager there. You tell me how I can help. Sometimes I can be a little pushy."

I chuckle. "You, pushy? Never"

She smiles and I catch hints of pink on her cheeks.

"We have some time to talk about it. I appreciate you wanting to help. I'm sorry. Sometimes a voice from the past, my ex almost fiancée, likes to creep in and make me feel like I'm not good enough. She never thought my job was enough. My job, my life, nothing was. Like me and my feelings didn't matter."

"But you are good enough, Zach. You matter to so many people."

She doesn't look away from me when she says it. That's how I know it's genuine.

"I don't believe that voice inside of you, not one bit. I also totally understand your past sneaking in and making you feel like less. I've got it in there all the time. We should both promise ourselves we won't listen to it. Help each other."

I smile the best I can.

"And yes. We should go home," she says. "I'm exhausted. I thought performing was tiring but being a server is hard work. You're all doing amazing."

What I love is how she didn't push me or question the fiancée thing. I didn't want to elaborate, not yet, and she got it.

As I start to pull out of the parking spot, she reaches for the knob on the radio. My car is a bit older, a 2009, so although it has a screen, the radio is controlled below it. There's something oddly comforting about this scenario. I imagine us cruising down the road for a late drive, Penny fiddling with the radio. If it were summer, I'd have the windows down allowing the warm breeze to circulate the air.

She stops when she hears her name on the radio. It's not bad. It's the song by the Beatles, "Penny Lane". She hums and sings along.

"Were you named after the song?"

She shakes her head, continuing with her own rendition. I admire how she gets lost in the music and the way it affects her tone. At a red light, I'm finally able to fully watch her. She's smiling and in her own world.

"Nope. I'm just me," she finally says. "Not named after anyone, but I can tell you who my favorite Penny's are. There's Penny from *Big Bang Theory*. Hey, I got to be a waitress like her today. It's kind of backwards though. I'm already famous and Penny strived to be."

The car behind me honks. I check the intersection before going. As I continue driving, she rattles off more names.

"Then there's Penny Lane from *Almost Famous*. It was my mom's favorite movie. I met Kate Hudson once. She's the greatest. And then there's Hanson. I discovered them when I googled songs with my name. They have a song called "Penny and Me" and it's one of my all-time favorites. It reminds me of summer and driving down the coast."

When the Beatles song fades, she lowers the volume on the radio. Without warning she belts out a song I've never heard before. I assume it's the one she mentioned. She enunciates every word clearly. She gets louder when she sings the word NYC and throws her hands up during the chorus.

She's right about the lyrics. They're fun and carefree. A Long Island summer is something I always enjoy. The beaches, the concerts, and events. I could do it all with her. My heart jolts in my chest as if it were being brought back to life. It's crazy. I'm so caught up in it, I don't even realize I'm pulling into the driveway, until the spotlight goes on.

"Hey, Zach?"

I put the car in park and face her.

"Yeah, Pen?"

"I—"

She tilts her head. Her eyelids flutter, and she bites her lip. Her nervous twitches make me smile. I love those little quirks about her.

"Thank you for tonight. For the first time"—her voice breaks a little—"For the first time ever, I felt normal."

I wish I could fix the way she's been treated by the public. She doesn't deserve any of it and has worked as hard as anyone else, and it shows. She's not some princess who wants the world to bow down at her every move. I might get upset when she buys me things, but I have to realize that she's doing it without thinking. It's not to make me feel bad, but because she's a truly genuine person with feelings. The need to protect this woman's heart is so strong. What she has gone through fills me with rage.

The spotlight on the garage goes out. Neither of us move. There's a soft yellow glow from the light above the front door. Her chest rises and falls rapidly as I reach out to cup her face without a second thought.

"Don't allow the outside world to take away your sense of normal. You deserve it as much as anybody. You were thrown into being in the public eye. You deserve to find peace. No matter what it is."

She's trembling from head to toe. There is so much happening inside of me. The image from earlier settles back into my head. The one of her holding my––no, our child. It hits me like a ton of bricks out of nowhere. God, I could imagine myself with this woman, but what do I have to give her? There's nothing I can offer her other than, I don't know, great sex? That sounds fucked up, but it's kind of true.

Her lips call to me. They are a perfect pale pink with a delicate cupid's bow. I want them to be swollen from my kiss. There are so many things I want with her, and I barely know her. What if I did it once? Kissed her. There's something there between us. It's been there since the moment I locked eyes with her across the room, crouched on the floor fearing my life from a cat.

"Fuck it!" I say out loud.

"What?" she asks. "Zach, what's––"

"Your sister is going to kill me. You might too, but Pen, love, I can't hold back."

I move forward and crash my mouth against hers. She gasps at the contact. She's so soft. Her moans are like music to my fucking ears. Everything about her sends these sparks of something I've never been privy to before. She opens her mouth first, inviting me in for more. I hum at the connection, and she leans into my touch.

I bring my other hand to her left cheek. It only makes her kiss me harder, faster, and feverish with desire. Our tongues tangle and I want more, but I also don't want to overstep or go too far.

"Zach," she sighs when there's only a sliver of space between us.

"Your lips feel so fucking good against mine, Pen," I say.

"I wanna know"—she pants—"what else ca–can they do."

"Oh, love, you have no idea how badly I want to show you right now."

She rests her forehead against mine as we try to catch our breath. I'm finding it incredibly hard to formulate the next sentence. There's so much I can do with her right now, but I'm choosing not to. I need to get my head on straight.

"Maybe not tonight, though. I don't know what's happening but whatever it is I need to be cautious. I'm afraid to start something when we live so far apart. Does that make any sense? I don't regret the kiss. Not for a second."

I nod. "It makes a lot of sense. I like you, Penny, and I don't want to do anything that would hurt you. I'm still trying to work through my own insecurities. So, take your time and let me know. Okay? I enjoyed our kiss. "

We fall silent until her chuckle fills the space around us.

"Don't make it awkward now, sunshine," she teases.

Her ability to tease me in this situation only solidifies my feelings even more.

"With you, things are always awkward."

She hits my chest. I rest my hand over hers.

"I mean, how many people can say their cat stole their vibrator and you had to chase them around the house in front of a man you just met?" She shrugs, her eyes sparkling.

"Sixty-two," I whisper in a growly tone. "Wait, did I already guess that number?" I tease when I catch a smile on her face.

"Nope. You'll just have to keep guessing." She lowers her gaze and her cheeks flush.

I push into her with my nose and her smile widens.

"I want to be selfish and ask for one more," she whispers, and I barely have time to nod before she tilts her head so our lips meet again.

There's no urgency behind the way her lips claim mine. She takes her time. My mouth opens to hers and our tongues meet. It's a slow, steady embrace, but the impact is a fucking jolt to my system.

"We should stop," she says.

"Hey, I'm not the person who initiated that one."

Her eyes dance with amusement. "I'm not sorry."

"Neither am I."

She pulls away and opens the door but stops and turns to me with a smile.

"Night, sunshine."

"Night, love," I reply

I watch her go inside, leaving me speechless once again. I don't know how she did it, but Penelope Clarke has somehow found her way deep into my heart.

Chapter 17

PENNY

L ast night I went to bed with a smile on my face. It was hard for me to fall asleep. I kept thinking about the moment his lips were on mine.

I like Zach. He's been so welcoming, and I love how he sees me for me. I found him attractive from the moment I laid eyes on him. It never occurred to me how good it might be to kiss him.

Until now.

It was ten out of ten, no notes needed. The man got me so hot and bothered, I'm forced to use my newest dual end vibrator to get relief. It's great but still doesn't give me what I need.

I need him. Those lips. That low voice.

No, I need to stop.

I was worried he would be upset that we didn't go any further, but he understood, and it wasn't awkward. With each passing day I'm finding it easier to not hide or hold back how I feel. I've been burned and trust doesn't come easily. My sister is a good judge of character and so far, Zach has lived up to all of it.

And yet, I'm still not convinced we can make anything of what we are.

My relationship with Erick wasn't perfect. Things were okay and headed in the right direction. When Erick's first single "Fighting Temptation" dropped, the groupies started crawling out of the woodwork. It was then that he decided he didn't want to be in love. He wanted sex and fame and he got it all.

I don't know if Zach will do the same, but it's why I have to protect my heart.

My stomach growls and I start to get out of bed. I get an agitated look from Larry as the mattress shifts from my movement.

"Stop looking at me like that, cat," I say.

My phone goes off and Larry hisses.

"Oh, stop, Larry. It's Sarina," I say, showing him the screen as if he can read. "Hey, Sarina." I roll onto my back and stare at the ceiling.

"I'm checking in. Are you going to wear it?"

I forgot to call her last night in the heat of everything.

"Yeah. How did you keep it a secret for so long?"

"Mom gave it to me for safe keeping. She wanted to surprise you."

Out of habit I reach for the locket. With my phone beside me on speaker, I open the clasp and lift the chain so I can peer inside. It's a family picture from my first performance. We were on the stage. They were so proud of me. I sniffle but no tears fall.

"You alright?" she asks.

"Do you ever feel like maybe you took the wrong path in life? When somehow a moment you're having makes you feel like you were meant to be there instead?"

Last night flashes in my mind. Sipping Shirely Temples with Devin, chatting with Maddie at the bar. Mark trusting me with his son, and Devin feeling safe enough with me to fall asleep in my arms. Then when I wrapped the apron string around my waist and took orders from the customers. They didn't know who I was and saw me the same way Zach did. The pub became my safe haven.

"Um," Sarina's voice pulls me from my thoughts, "I don't know if it's the same thing, but remember Bradly Fisher?"

"Yeah, of course." I close the locket but keep it in my grasp. "Your college boyfriend."

"Growing up as a millennial, it was different. Coming out wasn't viewed quite like it is today. My friends knew I was bisexual, but then things changed. I remember when I realized I was no longer attracted to men sexually. I also couldn't lie to him. He would have given me the world. He asked me to marry him, you know."

"He did?" I ask, sitting up as the shock of her words hit me.

"Mmhmm. He was on his knee, and I kept thinking over and over, I love him. I still do with all my heart, but I wasn't in love. Internally I was beating myself up over not being attracted to him sexually. He looked at me and said, 'I had a feeling, but I thought maybe if I proposed, you'd change your mind.' He stood and wrapped me in his arms. He told me how much he loved me and how letting me go wasn't going to be easy."

She sniffles and I hate that I've upset her.

"I'm so—"

"No." She chuckles. "You didn't do anything wrong. These are happy tears. We talked all night long. He held me in my dorm room bed. While we sat there together, I realized how much of my life I'd missed out on. I wanted a change. I needed it. I'm happier because of it. He and I still talk. Did you know he had twins three months ago?"

A lump forms in my throat. I would have known this story if I wasn't famous. If we were closer. I didn't even know Madeline existed. I only knew Zach as "the roommate".

"Aw, well congrats to him."

"I went to his wife's baby shower. I'm so happy for him, ya know? But yeah, the road I was about to go down suddenly changed for me. So why the question?"

I inhale and release a shaky sigh. "I met Mark, and Madeline."

Her breath hitches at the name, but I continue.

"Last night for Valentine's Day, Zach invited me to come and hang out to get out of the house. I was a bit of a wreck after the dress. Not in a bad way but I needed the distraction."

I tell her about the rest of the night, and she listens to every word, responding here and there.

"It felt . . . I don't know how to describe it. And Zach—since I've gotten here, he treats me like a person not a celebrity. Everyone I've ever met sees me as Christopher's daughter or Penelope the fraud. To him, I'm none of that. I'm Penny. I'm me." My voice breaks on the last word.

I pause for a moment and we're both quiet.

"Also, I miss you. We haven't had more than one, maybe two holidays together since everything. I'm tired. I'm so fucking exhausted of it all."

"Oh, sweetie, I wish I was there to hug you. I think whatever you decide, make sure it's what truly makes you happy. I'm sorry I'm not there. If I could have, I would have been when you arrived. I miss you so damn much."

"I think I'm going to stay an extra week. All I know right now is nothing has felt right until I got here."

"Take the time you need. For years, I wondered why you kept at it. I supported you because I thought it was what you wanted, but it hasn't been the same since they passed."

"No, it hasn't," I whisper.

Her alarm goes off. "Shit. I've gotta go. Please, don't wait until you're ready to burst to talk to me about things like this. I love you."

"Thank you for listening. I love you, too."

The door to the room flies open. Larry hisses and jumps from the bed. Zach appears with his arms wide open.

"Are you ready for some chocolate," he yells, and then dive bombs beside me on the bed. "I figure maybe we could have a limit--"

From my position on my back, I turn my head to meet his gaze. A huge smile crosses his features.

"The limit does not exist."

His finger slides down my lip and dips under my chin. My heart can't handle his boldness.

"Let's play a game. You pick out candy you think I'll like based on only knowing me the last few weeks. I'll pick out the candy I think you'll like. When we get home, we will give each other the bags and see how many we can get right."

"Bet."

"Maybe fifteen dollars for each store?"

"That's a lot of candy," I say.

He grins and rolls onto his side. "Isn't that the point?"

I shove his chest, and he swaps to his back again. Our laughter fills the room and it warms my whole body.

"And what about dinner? Candy? Or I can order something fancy for us after. There's a new place that keeps sending postcards in the mail. I'll door dash."

His lips turn down, brows furrowing. The change in him is startling. His jaw ticks and it's the same kind of reaction I got when we spoke about the groceries and the ice cream bars.

"Zach?" I ask, my excitement softening. I touch his arm, and he starts to jerk away but stops.

"Pen," he sighs.

"Did I say something wrong?"

He rolls onto his back and runs a frustrated hand through his hair.

"No. It's a me thing. I always chip in around here. I don't live under this roof for free. I appreciate you wanting to buy food for us, and you've done more than enough of your fair share of making sure the house is stocked, which is totally fine but . . ."

His throat bobs and eyes go distant while he thinks. Last night he said something about his ex and how she made him feel.

"Say no more, Zach. We'll play dinner by ear."

While his smile doesn't fully return, it makes its appearance. I don't want to upset him anymore, so I get up off the bed and change the heaviness in the room.

"Okay. I bet you I'm better at this candy competition than you."

He sits up with a competitive gleam in his eyes.

"Oh," he chortles. "You're on!"

I race towards the door, grabbing my bag from the floor beside the small bedside table.

"Last one to the car is a rotten egg," I say, over my shoulder as I run ahead of him.

Chapter 18

ZACH

The candy lands on the table with a thud. It's loud enough to make Larry jump from his cat bed in the dining room. He gives us one of his kitty scowls before lifting his ass in the air and walking out with an annoyed swagger.

"Someone is grumpy today," Penny says.

"When is he not?"

"That's only around you." She grins and sticks out her tongue. "Okay, let's see, what did you get for me?"

We spent over two hours going from store to store. It was much more enjoyable than going alone.

"Oh, here. There's this too."

I had my bags concealed by an additional reusable green shopping bag. I lift it onto the table and slide it across.

"More candy?" she asks, peering up over the bag.

"Just open it."

She narrows her eyes at me. I find myself completely enamored by her as she digs through. Her eyes light and her giggles fill the kitchen as she lifts the fluffy brown bear holding a purple heart. The song "Wild Thing" originally by The Troggs plays from it. At one of the stores, I caught her at the register waiting in line. In a display beside her sat several Valentine bears. She kept picking up this exact one. She hesitantly put it back. After she left the store to wait in the car, I grabbed it with my stash and hid it.

She holds the bear tight to her chest. "But why?"

Her eyes are misty. She hugs it like it's her lifeline. As cheesy as it sounds it warms my heart.

"I might have seen you."

She gasps and points at me. "You weren't supposed to be looking. You cheated."

I chuckle. "I didn't see what you got, only you and the bear."

She presses the button again. "You don't know what you've gotten yourself into. I'm playing this all night long."

"It's worth it to see the smile on your face."

She brings her eyes to mine and something hits me like a bolt of lightning. I'm struck frozen by her. Her wide smile softens into something more beautiful and real. I want to capture the moment.

"You should see what I got you." I attempt to deflect. Maybe she won't notice.

She places the bear on her lap then peers over at the array of treats.

"Oh! Rings? A bracelet . . . a necklace too. It's funny, I had men think the way to my heart is gold jewelry and fancy diamond rings, but you cracked the code."

I try and push back the feelings of not fitting into her world because right now I know I do.

"You've only known me for two-weeks and you know me better than any of them ever did."

A calm washes over me at her words.

Penny continues to browse through, keeping the jewelry separate. Her brows pinch together in concentration. I want to explore what is happening between us. I want something real. Penny is real. She's easy to be with and with each passing day I want to spend more time with her. I hate that she's leaving in a few weeks. I'm still bothered that I can't give her more.

Grinning, I take her all in as a shiver runs over her frame She stares up at me, embarrassment creeping up her cheeks.

"I did good, didn't I?" I wiggle my brows.

She points at me. "Don't get a big head now."

"You didn't get me peanut butter ones." She pauses. "Good. Because those are gross. You got me all the sweet stuff. It's perfect."

She tears open the necklace, the plastic crinkling. She tosses it aside and slides it over her neck then brings the candy to her mouth. She does the same with the bracelet and hums in approval as she chews.

She stops almost mid-bite. "Why did you choose the jewelry?"

"For that reason alone," I say, staring at her lips.

She shakes her head and smiles. "Get your mind out of the gutter. Did you know that edible jewelry goes back to ancient times? They made it from fruits, nuts, grains, but these specifically were dated back to the 1950's or so."

"Way to kill the buzz with your facts," I tease.

She growls with amusement and goes back to sifting through her pile. Instead of playing with the locket, she's fidgeting with the candy necklace.

"Did you see what I got you? Did I do good?"

There's a little bit of everything.

"When we had lunch together you always ate peanut butter and jelly, so I did get you the peanut butter cups," she says.

"You hit the nail on the head. Those are my favorite. I also love this—sour patch kids?"

"You're so sour sometimes, but you can be sweet too."

I shake my head as I sift through what I have on the table.

"Conversation hearts?" I grab the box and lift open the flap. "You know what's funny? They taste so chalky almost like that stomach medicine, but whenever I get them, I can't stop eating them."

"Same. And I got them for you because of the phrases."

"Honey?"

She lifts the bear and hides behind it, then presses the button and starts dancing.

"Thought we said no nicknames, love?"

"Well, sunshine, sometimes they are necessary."

"Yeah, and sometimes this is necessary."

I stand and reach over the table for her wrist with the bracelet and gently grab hold. She yelps and drops the bear into her pile. I lift her wrist and lean so I can place the candy bracelet to my lips. She inhales a harsh breath, and I can't help smiling.

"That's mine," she says, definitively.

I don't lift my head, only my eyes. Her lips part. After our kiss, I've done nothing but want her. Before I sang in the shower this morning, I made use of my hand and got myself off to the way her lips felt on mine.

"Roommate tax. It's in the rule book."

I lower my voice and enjoy the way her eyes light with hunger. She shivers as I bite on one of the pieces. She doesn't look away. Instead, she observes every movement. My lips touch her skin and the taste of her mixed with the sweetness of the treat causes me to moan. I'm rock hard. I have been since she started eating with a fire in her gaze. It's as if she wanted me to do this.

She closes her eyes and sighs. I also kiss her wrist while biting the candy. I finally let go and we stare at each other. She sits back in her seat.

"You know this taste better." There's some hesitation in her voice, but there's a seductive layer behind it. She lifts the necklace to her mouth and hums as she eats it.

She stands with determination and stalks towards me. She radiates this sexy confidence and it's an absolute turn on. I want her to be mine and I don't mean that in a possessive way. It's the feeling of falling and wanting her to be part of my life in every aspect of it. The new sensation causes my heart to react.

I adjust to face her, asking for permission with my eyes. Her nod is barely visible. I reach out and take hold of her waist. Her body trembles under my touch as I bring her closer. She moves forward to straddle my lap. I guide her to sit, and she rubs against my erection. Her head falls back from the friction dancing between us. I grab the necklace. She bats it away and I laugh.

"Don't touch. Use your mouth." Her voice grows deep and velvety.

My jaw goes slack at her boldness. I blink with wide eyes and chuckle.

I whisper against her skin. "You like the way my mouth feels on you?"

She nods. "I know we stopped last night, but I can't stop thinking about how your lips felt. I want more."

I don't know what changed between last night, but I don't have it in me to deny her request.

"I'll do whatever you need to feel good. Don't hesitate to tell me what you want."

She says nothing but watches me with lust flickering in her gaze. I lean forward and her chin lifts slightly. She moves her neck to the side, giving me full access. The second my lips meet her skin she moans and shifts on top of me. The motion sends a prickling sensation up my spine.

I open my mouth around the candy and bite, taking my time to explore her.

"Zach," she moans, as I greedily eat three pieces.

I chew and swallow, my eyes on her the whole time.

"Can I kiss you, Penny?"

"My lips are yours tonight."

I groan as we adjust so our faces are level with each other. She rests her forehead against mine.

"Where can I put my hands?" I ask, anxious for a touch.

She takes mine and slides them onto her waist under the hem of her tee. I dig my fingers in and gently massage the area. She throws back her head. Our lips crash together. She's rough in her approach but also adds in tender moments with slow swipes of her tongue.

"You were thinking about me last night, weren't you?" I say, pulling away.

Her cheeks easily flush. "Were you spying on me, sunshine?"

"There are some pretty thin walls in this house." I lean in for another taste and she pulls away.

"Yeah. I did. So what?" She's trying her hardest not to smile and uses it as another moment to kiss me.

I open my mouth and passionately give her a kiss that indeed knocks the breath out of her. Her cheeks flush and she looks away, but I take her chin and make her look at me. There's nothing to be embarrassed about here. I did the same exact thing.

"Eighty," I whisper to try and calm her.

She laughs. "I was thinking about you."

Her words shock me. The tone in her voice is sweet yet sultry. I can't help the grin sliding across my face.

"What did you fantasize about?"

Tonight has taken a turn. My mind flickers to Sarina's warning, but I dismiss it. I need to have her. Even if it's only while she's here. There's nothing else in the world that I want more right now.

Instead of talking, she grabs one of my hands resting on her waist and brings it up to her chest so I can cup her breasts. I knew they'd fit perfectly in my grasp.

"I was thinking about how it would feel for you to do more than kiss me."

Penelope Clark will be—no—she is my undoing. I keep trying to remember what life was like before she barged into this house, and it pales in comparison to what it is now.

"Look, I know we probably shouldn't do this, given how long you're going to be here, and because your sister will probably chop off my balls, but after our kiss, I'm not so sure I can stop."

"Who says we can't enjoy each other while I'm here? My sister doesn't have a say in who I fall—who I let in."

I'm stunned. Was she about to say fall? If we are being honest here falling for her would be the easiest thing in the world. I go to take my hand away from her breast aiming it for her cheek, but she holds it there. As much as I want this for myself, I have to set some kind of boundaries. Not only for me, but for her as well. She needs to know I'm not here to steal what isn't mine and I'm not out to sleep with the celebrity. I'm here holding her because it's the only place I want to be.

"Pen. I know you're hurting from what's happening out there and I need you to be sure you want more from me."

She sighs and leans her head against mine. "I'm asking for it. I'm not saying let's have sex tonight or I want to marry you right this second or be in a relationship. I'm saying let's explore each other. I want to make you feel good, Zach. I want to show you how much I appreciate what is happening between us. I don't want to think about the next few weeks, I only want to be here in the present with you. I've never lived in the now and you make it so easy to do."

She retreats only slightly so our eyes meet and whispers, "I want this. I want you."

I almost stop myself, because I know I'll want more, but instead, with her words hanging in the air, I claim her mouth with mine.

Chapter 19

PENNY

My guard slips. His kisses drown out the noise in my head. All is quiet aside from what is happening between us. His moans and my own mix. The subtle sound of fabric rubbing together. I've relaxed into him. I don't think, only feel. I'm wanted, cherished, and taken care of in his arms.

I know I said I wanted to slow down and take a step back, but today was something I'll never forget. Holding back is too hard.

He places my hand on his shoulder. His eyes meet mine as he goes in for another bite. I love how his lips are a gentle caress against my skin. He's tender yet packs this punch behind it. I'm wet and rock against him a little more. He stops me by gripping my hips.

A devilish grin tugs at his lips. "Two thousand."

"That is an unrealistic number."

"Which one did you use last night?" I love when he lowers his voice for me.

His golden gaze roams over my body. It's as if he's imagining everything that I've done to myself with those toys.

"Is that something you're interested in seeing?" I ask.

He nods. "Will you show me?" His deep growl penetrates through me as if I've been zapped by lightning. "I want to watch what you did to yourself while you thought of me."

"On one condition." I move ever so slightly, making him moan. The sound of it alone has me craving him. "After I show you, I want you to do the same."

He leans forward, and in a hush tone against the shell of my ear says, "That turns you on?"

"Only the thought of you," I admit, my cheeks heating.

He's awakened something inside of me. The desire to watch him while he does the same to me has me moving again. He holds me tighter.

"If you keep going like that we aren't getting far," he chuckles. His laughter fades as he touches my cheek. "Tell me you're sure, one last time."

I swallow hard and get up off his lap. I reach for his hand and am met with another devious gleam in his eyes. He stands and in one fell swoop I'm tossed up over his shoulder. I can't contain my giggles. With a bit of stumbling, he heads for the stairs. He makes sure each step is taken with caution but is done quickly.

He opens the door and curses.

"Shit. The demon cat is staring at me."

He spins us around so I'm facing the bed, and sure enough Larry is loafing, but his head has lifted. He's glowering at us as if we've interrupted something important.

"You know, maybe if you stop calling him demon cat he'll love you."

"I'll stop when he stops."

"You are such a baby, let me down." I giggle, hitting his back.

He does as I ask, but the second my feet hit the floor he tugs me back into him. I gasp upon the contact and his hard cock against my backside. I close my eyes and allow him to take another piece of the necklace. He lingers there, kissing my neck and my shoulder.

"What are you doing, sunshine?" I ask, voice hoarse.

"Just getting another taste, love."

"Zach," I cry out.

My center pulses and there's a buildup deep inside. He cups my breast. I close my eyes and allow the ecstasy of his touch to take over my whole body. I won't complain. It feels too good. Between his fingers he rolls my nipple through my shirt. They are hard and ready for him.

I moan. "That feels so good."

He doesn't stop. The friction makes me so wet. I turn my head enough to get a taste of his sweet lips from the candy he just devoured. Sparks of pleasure cause my body to tremble.

His soft laughter against my ear makes me smile. I step out of his grip and whirl around to meet his hungry eyes. He takes a deep breath in.

"You have magic hands."

He closes the gap between us. I walk until the back of my knees hit the bed. Larry hisses in displeasure. He meows before leaping off the bed with a thud and running out of the room.

Zach lowers me onto the bed with ease. It's gentle and he holds the back of my head until it hits the soft mattress. He leans forward and kisses me. The voices in my head have vanished. There's no one telling me who I should be or what I should do. No one telling me I'm a fake. He makes me feel real.

"What do you like? I could do this first . . ."

He lowers himself, lifting the hem of my shirt. Then he slowly peels the waistband of my black yoga pants. His lips graze right below my belly button. I thrust upward at the sensation. He continues to push the fabric lower.

"Stop," I whisper.

His eyes meet mine, concern flashing in them.

"I've never really enjoyed it."

The idea of someone tasting me is embarrassing for some reason. I like mostly everything else. He lifts quickly and adjusts to hover over me. He lowers his lips to mine.

"Okay. It's okay. I won't. Are you alright?"

"Thank you," I say, shakily.

"I want to learn what gives you pleasure."

My request for not doing that has been laughed at by Erick. He told me all women like it. Zach on the other hand was more concerned and open to my comfort. I like that.

"The box is under the bed," I say.

He kisses me hard but takes his time with each stroke of his tongue. I enjoy his slow steady movements. I like that he wants it to feel good for me. After a few more long, drawn out kisses, he gets up to get the box. I sit up and grab the toy from last night. It's a simple pink vibrator but the speeds on it are what sold me.

"Hold up," he says.

Without hesitation, he tugs at my pants. I grant him permission by raising up, so they easily come off.

"You missed something," I say, taking note of my—oh dear lord—my high waisted granny panties. I clearly didn't think this through when I got dressed this morning.

"Why are you blushing?"

I throw the toy at him, and he grabs it with a grin.

"I like these."

I roll my eyes, and his laughter crowds the space but in a good way. He touches my shirt. "This too?" he questions, and I nod.

He takes all of me in as my long-sleeved purple tee is up and over my head. Revealing a black-laced bra that does not match the underwear. His eyes roam over my curves. I have some insecure thoughts as he does. I have tiny breasts and a pear-shaped bottom. Fear vanishes as he continues to run his gaze over me. He nods as if I'm the only person who matters. I feel more and more beautiful by the moment.

"You're perfect," he says, when our eyes meet again.

His fingertips dance over the waistline of my underwear. I've almost forgotten how to breathe.

"I forgot to shave," I say.

"Doesn't matter, I'm obsessed with all of this." He runs a finger down the center of my chest, over the front clasp of the bra, and to my belly button.

"Hey, if I'm naked you need to be, too."

Without hesitation, he takes off his shirt, then stands to release his belt and jeans. His cock stands at attention through red and blue plaid boxers.

"Holy hell."

He laughs and I cup my hand over my mouth. I said it out loud. Shit.

The buzz from the toy brings us back to focusing on it. I've never done this before in front of someone. I try and pull out the confidence I know I have with my sexual desires. He watches intently as I lower the toy and situate it where it needs to go. The second it's in place I'm already feeling the buzz.

"Can I touch you while you do that?"

"Yourself," I say, almost out of breath. "Touch yourself."

He frees himself from the boxers. I'm in awe at the way the veins in his hands become prominent with each stroke. He stands there while I lay on the bed and I'm so turned on right now. His muscles tighten with each movement.

"I like this, watching you," I say.

"Me too," he croaks.

The intimacy between us with his eyes on me and mine on him is everything. The build-up is so easy. I lift my hips off the bed as my entire lower half tightens. I prepare for the release. We find each other in the heated moment and only then does my body fully feel everything. The release jolts me and I fall back as the release causes tremors of pleasure inside me.

"Help me this time?" I ask.

I love how he doesn't look away while kneeling beside me on the bed.

"Can I touch you?"

"Yeah. I want you to," I say.

I'm nearly bursting at the seams to feel him again. He hasn't taken his attention away from me. Our lips part as he takes in all of me. I shiver. He trails his fingers down the front of my body, stopping to play with my hardened nipple. I groan and he grins. With his other hand he strokes himself. His hand covers mine holding the vibrator and I moan.

"Zach," I pant, my voice breaking.

"Yeah, Pen?"

"I love the way you're looking at me. You make me feel like a real person. No one has ever—"

"You are a person, Penny. You are a beautiful, kind, and sexy woman. Has no one ever told you this?"

I shake my head. I'm being honest; not even my ex did.

"Well, I'm telling you right now. I love watching you, too. Your confidence is sexy."

There are so many firsts happening right here. Only in the span of a few short weeks. Never have I experienced dirty talk or speaking of feelings during intimate moments like this. I like it. A lot. It's such a turn on for me.

"Can I?" he asks.

I move my hand, and he takes over. The motion of the toy helps build my orgasm. I call out his name.

"Are you close, love?" he asks.

"Mmhmm..." I place my hand over his and the vibrator to push it harder into my clit. "Like this. Fast and hard."

His grin is everything and I want to eat it up. I love how he's using the toy to pleasure me and it's turning him on.

"Kiss me, please."

He does as he's asked. It's only for a second or two and the moment he pulls away and our eyes meet, I teeter over the edge and let go of my orgasm. It's so intense I cry out in pleasure but only for a second as my scream is muffled by his lips pressed to mine.

I tremble as he pulls back, and my mouth falls open. He looks down. A mischievous grin lights up his face. His laugh is deep and sexy.

My cheeks flush as I feel what I've done. "Okay, that's a first."

"Do you want more?"

I nod and he continues to make circular motions with it, while getting himself off. He lays down beside me on his back and I take over my vibrator.

"God damn it, Pen. I'm so close," he says.

Our eyes meet and somehow, I end up on the edge all over again with him and I watch as it happens. I've never been more turned on in my entire life. Time doesn't exist in this moment with him. We lay there in awe at what happened between us staring up at the ceiling. With trembling hands, I shut the toy.

"Wow," he says. "That was . . ."

"Yeah. It was."

Our laughter surrounds us. I want nothing more than to record it for when we no longer have these moments. When I'm three thousand miles away.

Gah! Penelope, stop! Live in the now.

I get up and pad across the room to my desk to grab some tissues for him to clean up.

"Well, I'm going to need a shower after that. Would you care to join me for a shower concert?" he asks.

"Will you sing with me?" I ask.

"Only with you."

I follow behind him to the bathroom. He throws out the tissues then reaches for me and pulls me into him. I'm not scared about what happened between us. There was something so intimate about enjoying each other's company while getting off. Three more weeks doesn't feel like enough time to be with him. My heart is heavy. This is all new and I need to try to take it one day at a time, instead of planning the future. It's much easier said than done.

We stay locked in the embrace for a few moments.

"Come on. We have a concert to perform."

I bite my lower lip and grin. "Should we do an encore?"

"How about two?"

"You're on!"

Chapter 20

ZACH

I sense her beside me. Last night was unlike anything I've ever experienced before. We didn't need to have sex to feel the connection. I promised Sarina I would keep my hands off, but with each passing day, and after what happened between us, there's no going back. I'll have to let go when she leaves. I won't fit in her world nor am I the man good enough to be at her side in the public eye. As much as it pains me, I'd never want to be the one to hold her back. She has to get out there and show the world who she is—that she's not the person they suspect her to be.

The mattress creaks under her movements. She backs up into me, curling herself into a ball. Without opening my eyes, I wrap my arms around her. Nothing has ever felt more right in the world than having her in my arms.

I run the pad of my thumb across the soft skin of her arm. She hums. Memories of what happened replay in my head. The way I made her come so easily and how she opened to me, allowing me into her heart a little more. She's ruined me for other women. How will I find this ever again? Her laughter is a sound I've gotten so used to. The house will be so empty without it when she leaves.

Once we finished in the shower last night, we chipped in for takeout and had more candy for dessert. Then we sat on her bed and talked for hours. It was nothing heavy. I learned so much about who she is. I gave her every bit of the real me, minus my childhood. We stuck to safe topics. From our guilty pleasure movie to our favorite music.

"Do you have to work tonight?"

"Yeah. Why? Do you want to tag along?"

She hums. "You want to know something weird?"

"What's that?" I ask, continuing to run my fingers up and down her arm. She shivers, goosebumps forming with each pass.

She grabs my hand and runs her fingers over my knuckles.

"You were right . . ."

"About?"

Whatever she is trying to get out seems hard for her. Quiet buzzes through the room while I wait for her response.

"Penny?" Her name comes out soft against her ear and she shivers.

"Wingman's is like home. You could feel this, I dunno, this energy in there. Everyone on the staff was so kind and didn't ask questions. Even the guests I was serving. If anyone noticed, they said nothing. It's like . . ." She sighs, then turns to face me.

I shift slightly to make room for her. I open my eyes to find her shimmering green ones on me.

"I was happy to serve those guests. I loved chatting with some of them. There was one woman who was quietly knitting in her Islanders jersey, she left before I started helping, but I remember her from the first night I was there. She had this warm inviting presence about her. Clarice, was her name I think."

"Clarice Johnson."

She smiles. "I think so. Do you know her?"

I open my mouth and at first nothing comes out. Talking about me and my past is so hard. It's why I've focused so much on finding out more about her past.

"She—she was friends with my grandma."

Penny almost smiles but stops. She lifts her hand and places it gently on my cheek. Her head tilts to the side like she's trying to get a better read on me.

"Oh, they aren't friends anymore?"

I look away for a second. Invisible pain catching me. It's the one that comes when I think about my childhood. When I return my stare to Penny, it's gone.

"My grandma passed away years ago."

"Oh. You alright?" she says, instead of telling me she's sorry for my loss. I hate when people say that. There's always pity, or sorrow hidden behind it.

"Yeah, we weren't close."

"Clarice had a locket like mine." She holds onto hers. "She noticed mine and I shared my story. She said it held a picture of her and her son."

Son? I try not to look too confused. I never knew Clarice had a son.

"I told her the story behind mine without giving myself away too much. Are you close with Clarice?"

I'm still caught up in what she said. My stomach knots. Clarice and I are close enough that I feel like she would have mentioned something big like having a child.

"Wow. I'm sorry for prying. That was rude."

"It's okay. I am close with her," I say, reaching out to touch her hand on my cheek. "I don't remember my parents. They were never around. My grandma was given custody of me. I'm grateful she took me in and that I didn't end up in the system. She made sure I was fed, clothed, and had a roof over my head, but was also closed off. It was when Clarice came over, she changed and paid more attention. It wasn't right away though. I was almost ten before Clarice came around. When my grandma passed, Clarice would send me care packages."

Penny smiles. "She's a sweet woman. I'm glad you had her in your life."

"Me too," I say, my voice breaking a little.

Without any hesitation she leans in and kisses me. I tilt my head, parting my lips but I let her decide where she wants to take the kiss. She hums and when her tongue meets my lips I open fully to her.

In sync we suck in a breath. My whole body is aware of her presence. My erection is straining to break free against my sweatpants, but it's her decision on how far we take this.

She drapes her leg over my body and tries to pull me closer as if our proximity isn't enough. I moan at her hot center pressed to me. We align together and she rocks against my hardening erection.

"What do you want, love?" I give a short thrust and devour her whimpers as she returns the motion back to me.

She answers me with a deeper kiss. Our tongues tangle in frantic movements. She's in control. I want her to take the lead. I'd rather her share her boundaries with me than to have her hurting when we part ways.

She pulls back with a gasp.

"What is it?" I ask, thinking she's second guessing this.

"Oh my God, that's it. Zach, you're a genius."

She untangles herself from me and rolls towards the edge of the bed. She's so determined to get up, she completely misses putting her feet down first and goes tumbling to the floor with a *thunk*.

"Shit, Pen are you okay?"

I hang my head off the bed. Even on the floor she's so fucking breathtaking. Her hair is around her in a wild mess. The top half of her boob is spilling from her light blue tank top. The hem of her shirt is raised, while the folded waistband of her light-colored striped pajama pants lay low on her hips.

"Shit," she chuckles.

"Did you find what you were looking for down there?" I ask.

She glances at me and the image of her lying on her back makes me so hard. I may need another shower to get myself off. I can't help how she makes me feel. It's sappy and horny all at the same time. Two feelings that have never been combined before.

"Oh, were you looking for your toys? Is that what got you all excited?"

She rolls her eyes playfully. "Next time I want your hands on me not my toy. Oh!" She cups her mouth. "Did I say that out loud?"

I'm so screwed with this woman around. I love the soft blush on her cheeks. Along with her laughter, it's the one thing I'd be happy to wake up to every day.

"Oh, is that so?" I wiggle my brow.

"Yes, but I can't think about that right now. I need to find my guitar."

I quirk a brow. "How will we use it?"

"You, my friend, have a dirty mind." She sits up, using her elbows to prop her.

I lower my head to get closer while still laying on the bed.

"What happened to the young man afraid of a pussy cat? He was so innocent."

I can't help the loud rumbling laughter that escapes me. "Young? Did you forget I'm seven years older?"

She narrows her eyes at me. The right side of her lip turns up in a grin. "Old man."

I stumble off the bed. She squeals and attempts to sit up. I tug her back into me. She rests her head on chest, giggles unwavering.

"What do you need your guitar for?" I ask her, once we've both calmed down.

She tilts her chin back and I peek at her.

"I was inspired," she whispers.

"Am I your muse?"

"Don't get a big head over this. Okay?"

I laugh and let her go. She stands and peers at me.

"It's already growing."

I glance at my lap.

"Not *that* head."

With an amused sigh she rounds the bed to get her guitar. It's propped up against her desk.

I get onto the bed, and she does the same then unzips the case.

"Can you grab the notebook from the drawer?" she asks.

I retrieve it for her and notice a tube of lipstick beside it. It's not ordinary lipstick, it has a button. I grab it with the notebook and pull them out together holding them up.

"What?" she asks, face flushed.

She has the guitar in her lap. Her fingers ready to strum.

I shake my head. "This I'm saving for later."

"Whatever," she smirks and grabs the notebook while I hold onto the toy.

She plays the chords to the song she's been working on. Before she burst into my life her songs were all over the radio. While I heard her music it wasn't something I ever paid much attention to. Did I think she had a nice voice? Yeah. Talented? Most definitely, but I never took the time to truly appreciate the beautiful woman sitting beside me.

Even as she transforms into musician mode, the person I've gotten to know the last few weeks shines through. The media paints these awful pictures of celebrities at times but with her none of that is true.

Her voice carries through the room. I settle onto the bed and place my back against the headboard. A sense of longing reaches inside of me taking hold. This could be my—no—our life together. A life where she doesn't have to worry if someone is going to put her face in a tabloid. One where she wouldn't have to look over her shoulder. As I think the words, her lyrics coincide with my thoughts.

Freedom is close enough to feel.
Unlocked yet forbidden to yield.
The golden tides that greet me are on edge
but pull me back from the sharpness of the sea.

She pauses to write the words. I expect her to go back to playing, but she turns to me as if my opinions matter.

As if *I* do.

I find myself getting swallowed up by the rough waters of my own metaphorical sea, drowning in the voices telling me that my lifestyle isn't enough to support someone else. It's not good enough for a woman to contemplate a future with me.

I'm lost in the depths of Penny's green gaze, trying to latch on to the idea that to her what I do for a living and my status in the world doesn't matter. I'm good enough for her.

The bad rolls in, too. If I wasn't good enough for my parents to stick around, why would I be for her? What makes me think this gorgeous celebrity in front of me would think twice?

Could what we have be real? Can she be a part of my future now? She has her life to live, her music to create and her fans to please. In the grand scheme I'm only a small blip on her map.

Her touch sends shockwaves through me. I didn't notice she shifted to face me.

"How's this?"

I only have enough power to nod. She swallows hard and let's go of me to tuck a few strands of her loose hair behind her ear. Her beautiful, raspy voice isn't what pulls me in, it's the lyrics she wrote.

A ray of sunshine peeks through the clouds.
The warmth guiding me to the sandy shores.
A hand to hold, to save.
One to cherish me unlike any other.
A safety net is thrown,

as he stands on shore in the vast unknown.
The golden tides push me forward instead of back.
Who out there can help me be... me.
It's only him I see

She stops her hand, caught in mid strum. Her eyes dance and shimmer with what I believe is hope. Maybe if I show her I can be the place she's been searching for, we can solidify a future. I try my hardest to push the insecurities of my past to the back of my mind.

Her lip's part. There's doubt in her eyes. I go to her, get on my knees and cup her cheek. I love those tiny gasps every time I touch her. I tighten my grip on the lipstick toy and urgently press a kiss to her open mouth. The intake of her breath does me in and I devour her.

Before I have time to think, she's pulling back and removing the guitar from around her. She wraps her arms around my neck and continues the kiss as if it were never broken. We dive back in as her phone rings. It's lying face up on the bed as Sarina's name flashes across the screen.

"Sorry," she whispers.

I lean in for one last kiss before grabbing my clothing and shutting the door behind me. I rest my back against it for a moment. What a night. I'm not sure how to describe it. It felt so right, and I don't regret a single moment of it. I wish she wasn't leaving soon.

Chapter 21

PENNY

I can't wipe the smile off my face. The past few days have been perfect. It's exactly what I needed. I keep replaying the way it felt to have Zach touch me. Foreplay was rare in my previous relationship, and I don't think I missed out, because I know for a fact it wouldn't have come close to feeling as good as it did with Zach.

I stare out the window at the houses passing us by as Zach and I drive through the neighborhood towards Wingman's.

It's Saturday and I'm trying not to let the idea of leaving get to me. Having those intimate moments with Zach has given me another reason to stay, but how can I? I could move to New York, but it doesn't mean I'll be here all the time. There's still recording an album, going on tour, and all the other responsibilities that come with being a singer. My own insecurities play a huge role. Erick's lies and betrayal somehow still feel fresh.

Music plays through the speakers and he's humming along and drumming on the wheel. The lingering scent of the cherry air freshener hits my senses. I take a deep breath and feel how good this moment is. What if this was my life with him? Nights of cuddling with intimacy. Drives to work together. Pulled pork sammies, hot wings, and specialty drinks. Being close to Sarina again.

We pull up to a stop sign and Zach checks the rearview before looking over to me. I love the way the corner of his lip quirks up and his eyes gleam.

"I like seeing a smile on your face."

My face heats. "You're the one who put it there."

He reaches over and rubs a thumb over my cheek. A car horn sounds behind us, and he lets go and focuses back on the road. I close my eyes and breathe deep, then stare out the window again.

My phone vibrates. Tanner's name lights up the screen again. She has been calling all morning. This one is only a text.

> Tanner: Penny, I need you to call me back. I can't push back any more interviews. You have a few set up the week before the awards. You need to be back in town by March 4th to do them. You really need to get on social media and make a statement, too.

I release a shaky breath. That cuts my time here by almost a full week. I was going to go back the Friday before the awards, but now there's this. My leg starts to shake, but calms as Zach's warm caress steadies it. With one hand on the wheel and one on me it helps, but not enough.

"What's going on?"

I close my eyes. "It's Tanner, she's trying to get me to post on socials about the nomination. I also have to be back the week before the awards for interviews. I don't know. I feel like maybe I should post and then I can delete the app again."

My leg has a mind of its own and I try so hard to make it not move, but the pressure he's got on me helps. He rubs his thumb in circles. My jeans are in the way, but his touch feels good.

"You should do what you feel is right."

"What if I sent her a statement to put out on my socials? I won't have to show my face and it's still coming from me."

"I think that's perfect."

I won't have to worry about redownloading the app and seeing the comments. It wouldn't tempt me to check in on Erick's posts either, which I'm sure he's made a ton of. He's a social media king. I send her a quick text stating just that and throw my phone in my bag on the floor.

Zach squeezes my leg. "So, karaoke and open mic night."

I'm grateful for the topic change.

"Yes! Two weeks from now, right?"

I'm excited but also sad because that Monday I'll be leaving. I try to hide feeling any sadness over it. I have to shake this feeling. We said we were living in the now. I need to focus on that.

"Yeah. I was thinking open mic can be first, we make it a double header for this first time. From six to nine there will be an open mic. We could do karaoke from ten to two or midnight."

"I think that works. I can create some graphics. I didn't delete those apps," I say.

"And what about one of those google forms to fill out and maybe some sheets in the pub itself. We can get an idea of how many are coming," he suggests.

I nod. "Yes! Exactly. We could also use QR codes for the fliers placed in the pub?"

His face lights up with hope. Although I'll be leaving, my goal is by then I'll know Wingman's and its staff are okay.

"Maybe for our next one we could have theme nights. Like 80's rock," he says.

"And we can do 90's, boyband themes, too and . . ."

I stare down at my lap, stopping my words because a lump forms in my throat. Zach isn't looking at me. He's staring out the windshield. Both of us said *we* as if we were creating plans. My heart hurts.

I touch his arm and try my hardest to smile and not let it get the best of me. "I think it's perfect."

We pull into the parking lot and he shifts the car into park. He leans over the center console. I follow his lead and rest my forehead against his. The opening chords of a familiar yet old tune starts playing on the radio. I grab my locket and smile. My heart is feeling full yet sad.

"This was my parents' wedding song," I say, unable to stop myself from remembering their wedding video.

It was the first song they ever sang together after they met so it was only fitting it was their song. I adored the way my dad looked her square in the eye while they danced and you could see him mouth, "Just look at me, Suzy baby. You and I are the only ones in the room. Sing only to me."

Zach sings a little of the chorus.

"You know this song?" I ask.

"Who doesn't? It's a classic."

I smile. "One day I'd love to sing it in duet with someone, maybe on stage as a cover. Dedicate it to them. I don't know. That's silly, isn't it?"

"Not at all and I think it's the perfect love song. Who doesn't want to find someone to take on the world with them. Am I right?" he asks.

This man melts my heart. He knows what to say to make me feel cherished. My heart wants this life.

The moment is broken as the song finishes and another starts.

"I think I might kiss you, Penelope Clarke."

I bite my lower lip. "What's stopping you?"

His breath hitches as he brushes his warm, beautiful lips to mine. My heart pounds hard as if it wants to reach his.

"Absolutely nothing," he says, and closes the kiss.

I melt into him and allow my tongue to slide easily into his mouth.

What if I stayed?

* * *

"Hey, Penny. I'm so glad you're here again. Love your outfits. You and Sarina have similar taste," Madeline says, leaning on the bar.

I lift the brim of my usual black hat to greet her. "Thank you. The clothes are from her closet, and I love it here."

She chuckles. "I wish I had a sister to steal clothing from."

Tonight, I've got on a tan corduroy jacket, with a white turtleneck, and light blue jeans. When we were kids the age gap made it hard to do, but it didn't stop little me from raiding her closet. As an adult she loves plaids and corduroy. I love how the style is so not me, but it works.

Zach and I arrived about thirty minutes ago and it's been a busy but steady night.

"I'm glad it's less chaotic tonight."

"You're telling me. I'm still tired from it. You did amazing, babe. I had a few customers ask me when the new girl was returning."

Her comment catches me off guard. A warmth spreads over me. I'm wanted somewhere for something other than my money and fame.

I smile. "They couldn't have meant me."

"They sure did. They specified the one with the cap"—she bops the bill of my hat— "and the glasses. These are cute by the way," she says, tapping the frame.

"Thanks. They are for disguise. I wear them on occasion when sunglasses aren't exactly necessary."

For someone who gives off tough girl vibes, her smiles sure are sweet.

"Well, not to be weird, but you look hot."

I flush. "Thanks. Not weird at all."

She fidgets with the red rag tossed over her shoulder. "How's Sarina? Have you heard from her?"

I don't miss the longing in her voice. I wonder what it's for, but don't ask, because it's not my place.

"She's alright. Working hard. I'm hoping she'll be able to come to the awards."

"That's right. Congrats."

"Thank you."

"You two are close, right? I sometimes feel like Sarina has this whole other life I'm unaware of and I should be. She is my sister, and I didn't even know about her friends here."

Madeline sucks in a deep breath. Pain flickers behind her hard eyes.

"Yeah. She's a good friend. She's been there for me. My marriage has been on the rocks, and I think at this point officially over and your sister truly has a heart of gold."

Guilt plagues me at the mention of Sarina. Our phone conversation earlier helped ease some of it, but I still feel like a horrible sister for not being around as much as I should. We lost both of our parents and not even two weeks later I was back on the road touring. Life doesn't stop for a musician. We barely had time to grieve. I hated leaving her when we were in such fragile states. I wish I knew more about her relationship with Maddie. I barely knew this side of her life existed and I'm angry at myself for it.

"Relationships aren't easy."

"You're telling me," she says amusedly. "So, I don't get in trouble—do you want a drink?"

I shake my head. "I want to be sober tonight."

"Shirley Temple?" She winks.

I chuckle. "Yes, please."

She places her hand on the bar, and I look up at her and into her dark eyes. There's a heaviness there. "I'm on it." She smiles and without another word goes to make my drink.

"Hey, sorry, we've been super busy tonight." Zach comes up beside me.

"It's okay. I hope it's a good thing."

"It's very good," he chuckles. "But also, we're down a server who quit. It's one thing after another I guess."

An idea hits me. It's probably not feasible, but I want to do more for this place while I'm here. I love the people and the atmosphere and if I can get away with no one figuring out who I am just yet, maybe it could work for now.

"Do you think Mark will hire me? I mean I'm only here for a short time, but I don't know. I know it's ridiculous and there's a process, but I loved it. It felt like I was doing something good for once."

He regards me and my question with soft, nonjudgmental shimmering eyes.

"What?" I ask, huffing a laugh and giving him half a smile.

"I'll see what I can do, okay?"

Chapter 22

PENNY

W hat a rush. The relief on Mark's face when Zach and I asked if he would hire me was palpable. I'm filling in for the person who quit without notice. The idea of not being on his staff permanently actually twists at my gut. It only makes leaving more real. The closer I get to my departure the sicker I feel.

I don't want to sound ungrateful for the life I've had. My dad was already an established musician when I was born. I never had to worry about losing everything. I had stability—well, minus being uprooted constantly. I had a life that most people don't get to lead. Even so, the strong desire to pick a new life route is weighing heavy on me. I love my fans and singing for them is the best part of my life, but there comes a point where the burn out becomes too much. The consequences for having people knowing your business could take a turn like it did for my parents.

I finish filling some drinks when I catch sight of Clarice.

"Hey, sweetheart."

Clarice has a bright smile on her face as I approach. She devoured one of her favorite meals, the shepherd's pie. Danny, the chef on duty tonight, is a master at making it and promised me before I leave—I hate those words —he'll teach me the secret to a good pie. I told him I was a terrible cook. He laughed and said he'd change that with this simple recipe.

"Hey, Clarice. Are you finished?"

She nods and continues making what appears to be a scarf. It's a mixture of purples. She's gotten a fair amount done since she's been here.

"Sure am."

I pat the side pocket of my jeans and smile because her clover is there with me. As I reach for the plate she wraps a delicate grip around my wrist. She lifts her chin and there's something sad in her usually bright eyes.

"You make him so incredibly happy."

With her free hand she tinkers with her locket. It's all I can focus on as I remember what she said about it, who is inside. My mouth opens but I don't say what I'm thinking. I can't. Zach would know, right?

"I've worried about him for so long. I wish he would have come to me when he was living out of his car."

"What do you—"

"Oh dear, I've said too much. Before your lovely sister gave him a place, he refused to accept our help. Stubborn boy always. My boy." Her voice breaks.

His car? What is she talking about? She shakes her head and attempts to smile through her sorrow filled face. The place, aside from glasses clinking and utensils scraping against plates, goes silent. I'm about to open my mouth when the familiar opening chords to "Nothings Gonna Stop Us Now" play again.

Clarice's hand drops from my wrist as Zach's voice comes over the speakers. In shock, Clarice and I turn our attention to the stage. My heart leaps in my chest. He's holding the microphone as if it's his lifeline and if he lets go, he'll crumble. The part that gets me the most is the way his eyes are focused on me as if there's no one else in the room.

Without thinking I start moving. This could blow my cover. It could ruin this sacred spot for me. If someone with ill intent wanted to film this moment they could, then my reprieve would be over. The closer I grow the less fearful I become. It's Zach. He's the reason. I'm comforted by the admiration radiating off him. I don't say love, because it's far too soon for that.

I don't know how things sparked so fast between us, but I can't help the hope of a new path when I'm with him. The glimmer of something incredibly special shines through with every heartbeat.

His eyes follow me the whole way as I take the steps and walk towards him. He's singing the female vocal and nailing it. When I'm only inches away, he reaches his hand out for me. I take it. His lips brush my ear. "You said you wanted to duet this song with someone. Do I count as someone?"

Is he serious? Does he count? Of course he does. Only for his ears, I lean in and whisper, "You're more than just someone to me."

It's not a lie. I no doubt have a watery smile. He squeezes my hand and doesn't lose sight of me as he sings. Is this how Mom felt when she and Dad sang to each other at their wedding? The pull towards Zach right now is indescribable. He said he doesn't sing for anyone, but here he is singing for *me*. Fear in his eyes is present, but somehow without words I keep his attention focused on me.

He lifts my hat only slightly, like he needs to see more of me. His golden eyes collide with mine and his entire body loosens. His voice opens to the volume and strength I've heard in the shower. Singing with him is so natural, almost how it is to be in his presence. Between the flutter in my chest and the butterflies running the show in my stomach I never want this moment to end with him.

A fear I'd forgotten until this second tries to push through. The last time I sang with someone on stage, he used it to better himself. It's not who Zach is, and this moment will forever go down as one I won't ever forget.

His grip tightens on my hand as if he needs more reassurance. I rid the intrusive thoughts and focus on what is happening between us. I'm so caught up in him, us, and this moment that I'm startled when the applause starts. Not even when it ends does he look at the guests. Our breathing is heavy as we stare into each other's eyes. Can you make love through singing? God, that's the dumbest question, but I'm so charged that I couldn't think of another way to describe it.

I get up on my tiptoes and lean in. He clutches me and rests his hand on my back. In his ear I whisper, "You fucking rocked it. You're amazing."

"No. You are. Only for you. Couldn't have done that without you."

His vulnerability is beautiful. He's sharing a part of himself he's never had the courage to do before.

I press my hand to his cheek. "You did that all on your own, sunshine."

"Kiss already!" Maddie yells. A few voices in the crowd whoop, holler, and echo his words.

Zach's cheeks turn a deeper shade of pink. I'm about to tell him he doesn't have to but then his lips are on mine and there's no stopping my body's reaction and how I melt into him. He tilts his head, so he fits under the bill of my hat without having to move it. I listen to our guests still hyped from what is happening between us. It feels like nothing will break our kiss. We're locked tight. It's a perfect kiss that leaves promise for later.

We both end it at the same time.

"I have an idea," he whispers. "What if we mention the event?"

I grab onto his arms. "Yes. You can tell them to come out and to keep an eye out for the signup sheet."

Zach grins. "You get me."

I shrug. "It's one of my superpowers."

He chuckles and then turns towards our guests and addresses them. Some have already gone back to what they were doing before our performance, but even in the dim room I see some perk up and keep their attention on us.

We head off the stage and I start to walk towards Clarice's table and stop short. She's not there. I approach and take note of the hundred-dollar bill, which more than covers her night. I glance around to see if maybe I'm mistaken and she went to the bathroom, but she's nowhere to be found.

The rest of the night is steady. I'm worried about Clarice. What she told me about Zach sits heavy on my shoulders. Plus, the locket. I don't know what to think.

In the car the heaviness of sleep takes over. Zach starts the engine and the radio comes to life. I rest my head on the back of the seat as a popular tune by Taylor Swift drifts over the speakers. The lyrics to "Enchanted" come naturally for me to sing. I respect that woman for who she is and what she has done for the industry.

Zach hums along and puts the car into gear. He rests his hand over mine, which I have on my leg. I'm basking in it and close my eyes. I love the way he squeezes my hand. I peek over at him. For a second, he does a quick sweep of me. The corner of his lip lifts in a smile that lights his eyes.

"Can I ask you something?"

He looks both ways before stepping on the gas. "Sure."

"What happened before you moved in with Sarina?"

He flips on the blinker as we get to another stop sign. Another quick peek over at me before his eyes land back on the road.

"Clarice slipped up, huh?"

He turns the wheel with one hand, keeping his other clasped with mine.

"I wasn't going to rat her out, but yeah."

He sighs and tries to pull away. I stop him. "I don't want to talk about it. It's in the past."

"But, Zach, I--"

Headlights flash in our direction from an oncoming car. I glance over to find his cheeks colored pink. We're close to the house, only one more turn.

"It's not important."

When he pulls into the driveway, he lets go of me to put the car in park. My heart hurts because I've been open with him and he's closing again. He goes for the door handle like he can't get out quick enough. I grab his wrist. He stares at it. My thumb moves in long gentle strokes over his skin. I watch the way his shoulders rise and fall.

"It's important to me," I whisper. "You're important to me. I know we just met and that sounds absurd but I——"

He moves me towards him. His lips crash into mine and our breaths mingle as our tongues tangle. I run my fingers through his wavy locks.

"Zach," I pant, pulling away and resting my forehead against his. "Why are you afraid to talk to me? Do you think I'll judge you because I'm famous or something?"

He cups my cheek.

"Because if you think that of me maybe we shouldn't——"

"I lived out of my car," he whispers and closes his eyes. "I lived out of my car because I was too embarrassed to ask to crash on someone's couch. I'm an adult and I should have been able to handle it on my own."

"On your own? You do know that it's okay to ask for help, right?" I hate how he shakes his head and looks off to the side.

"Zach, don't be afraid. True friends don't leave you hanging."

Our eyes meet and I hate how sad his look. He sighs. "I know, but it was hard for me to admit what was happening. My apartment had mold, and I couldn't stay. It wasn't the first time I'd been knocked down a peg. Mark caught me one morning in the Wingman's lot. Later that day Sarina said she had an extra room, and I moved in that night."

"I don't know what our future holds, but if you are ever in a bind like that again, reach out. You never have to be embarrassed about something like that around me."

I hate the downcast look on his face.

"I'm glad you moved in," I say.

He half smiles and my heart sores.

"Is that so?"

"Yeah. Look don't be so stubborn next time. 'K?"

He laughs. "I'll think about it."

I roll my eyes. "I guess it's better than nothing. Now, can you please finish the kiss we started before I lose my ever-loving mind?"

I don't have to ask twice. He kisses me with everything he's got. Zach has shown me so much grace and respect over the last few weeks, I want to respect his boundaries, too. I hope I didn't push by asking, but despite me having to leave in a few weeks, I want to know this man. I have to know him.

Chapter 23

ZACH

I t's been a week since Penny and I started whatever this is between us. Even though there is a nagging voice in my head, this new normal is fucking amazing. She worked all weekend at the pub, and I've closely kept an eye on the news and socials. I'm grateful none of the guests in the pub on Friday night took a photo or video of our performance. If they did, I haven't come across anything about it yet.

Each night we'd take care of each other and then fall asleep after talking. We eventually need to have a serious conversation about where this is headed. It's growing into something more. With her return to L.A. and her career, I have to prepare myself for the inevitable downfall of it all.

Penny took the last two nights off. Wednesdays and Thursdays are slow. She spent it reading and writing her song.

It's an early night for me, but not too early. I've got my jacket, and I'm heading down from the office. Clarice is standing by the door, wrapped up in her gray peacoat with a knitted scarf around her neck. She's more than likely waiting for her cab or uber.

"Hey there, my boy," she says, as I approach.

"I'm surprised you're still here. Isn't it past your bedtime?" I tease.

Her soft tired smile gives me that warm home feeling again. She fidgets with a silver locket peeking out of the bottom of the scarf. I remember what Penny had mentioned about her saying it was her son. It's been on my mind, but I don't know how to broach the subject. I don't want to upset her.

"Well, my uber never showed up."

"Come on, I'll take you home."

She's about to protest, but I give her a stern raise of my brow and she chuckles. It's not the first time I've given her a ride home from here. She lives a little further away from the pub than I do, but I don't mind. She's done so much for me, it's the least I can do.

We haven't even driven out of the parking lot before she says, "So, you and Penny, huh? She's a lovely young lady. I'd love to get to know her more."

I smile. "She's pretty awesome. Isn't she?"

We pass under the streetlights and it illuminates the inside of the car a bit. Clarice is grinning from ear to ear.

"Sure is. We've had some nice conversations."

"What about coming over for lunch one day before she goes . . ." I pause. "Home." My voice has a weird tone on the word *home.*

Beside me Clarice's eyes narrow. Her intense stare makes me think she knows my feelings for Penny run deeper than I ever could have imagined.

"Lunch sounds wonderful. I'm free Saturday."

"We don't have work until later in the evening, so Saturday sounds good."

I try hard to disguise the hurt of her leaving. Before we even started whatever this is between us, she mentioned her dislike of long-distance relationships and how Erick ruined it for her. It's something that has stuck with me. On top of my own insecurities, I don't know why I gave into my feelings for her, but it felt right when I did.

Clarice places a hand over mine on the wheel. I glance over as a car honks behind me.

"Light's green, son."

The rest of our car ride the conversation is a little lighter. We talk about hockey and how she's convinced her team will make it through and we solidify lunch plans. She and Penny have taken a liking to each other and the thought makes me feel good.

When I get home my phone goes off. I turn off the car and the lights before pulling it from my jean pocket. It's Sarina.

"That asshole. He posted some shit on my sister. I'm fuming."

"Woah, woah. Hold up a sec. I literally just pulled into the driveway from work."

All the lights in the house are off. It's nearly three in the morning. I stayed after to make sure things were good.

I put her on speaker, then open the app.

"Why are you up so late?"

"I was having a hard time sleeping. I sent a text earlier to Maddie and never heard back. So instead of sleeping, I was doom scrolling on social media and came up on the assholes video."

I groan. "What did Erick post now?"

"Hold on. I'll play it for you."

A few seconds later my phone pings. I take a deep breath because the more I see this asshole on screen the more I want to knock his lights out. As always, he's got his blonde hair looking neat and tidy. I swear the guy wears makeup for all his posts. His teeth are so white you wouldn't think they were even real.

"I don't know about all of you," he starts to say, "but I know that I'm so grateful for my nomination for artist of the year. It's been a long time coming and I'm blessed to have so many amazing people on my team for this."

I narrow my eyes at the screen. He's on the deck of what I assume is his house. There's a hot tub and palm trees. His yard looks like a fancy oasis with a brown stained fence, twinkling lights, and off the deck his grass and the bushes along the fence are perfectly manicured.

"Unlike some nominees, who can't even show their face in a post regarding the award, I at least will address you all the right way. Cough, Penelope Clarke, cough. It just goes to show how much of a coward and fraud she truly is. Of course, you'll all get a nice glimpse of that in the documentary, which is coming soon." He winks and I can't take it anymore and swipe out of the app.

Sarina sniffles on the other end. "Do you think they are going to release it early? To make her look bad? Oh god, Zach."

I run a hand through my already tangled hair and rest my head on the steering wheel. Sarina lets out a frustrated growl.

"Fuck. I just want to protect her from all of it."

"Sarina, do you trust me?"

"Yeah," she whispers. "There's something there between you and her, isn't there? I don't have to see to know."

I sigh. "I'm not going to lie to you Sarina, your sister means a hell of a lot to me and it's not going to be easy to let her go when she leaves to live her life."

Sarina is quiet for at least a minute. I try to be patient and wait her out, knowing she's trying to process everything.

"You don't have to let go," she says, voice breaking a little.

I do. Her world is in L.A. and I'm not part of that circle. I'll never be enough for it. I don't argue with her, because I don't want to upset her further.

"Thank you for taking care of her."

I would have even if she didn't ask me to.

"I'm sorry you're both going through this. It's not fair to either of you."

"Thanks, Zach. I should go. It's getting late. I know she can handle all of this, it's just my big sister claws coming out."

"Understandable. I know she can, too. She's just got to see it for herself."

We say our goodbyes and hang up. I rest my head on the back of the seat and stare at the dark house. When I enter it's quiet. I hang my jacket and leave my shoes at the door before walking upstairs. Her reading light is perched on the headboard and she's out cold. I smile at the sight I find. The cat is fast asleep on her stomach and there's a book on her chest. As I step towards the bed Larry lifts his head, glares at me, then hops off her. She groans and turns but remains asleep. I catch her book before it falls and place it on the nightstand and then undress.

In only my boxers and the undershirt I had under my tee, I climb into bed beside her. I reach over, shut off the reading light. As I pull the blankets over us, she half wakes and mumbles, "Zach?"

"It's me. I'm here," I whisper.

"Mmm." She scoots herself closer, fitting herself so our bodies mesh together. Her back to my front. I wrap an arm around her and hold on.

"Night, love," I whisper.

She sighs. "Night, sunshine."

"Hey Zach."

Her soft voice catches me off guard. Early morning sunlight peeks through the curtains. I've been up for a little while but have been enjoying having her in my arms.

"Yeah, love?" I ask, breathily.

She sits up and rests her back against the headboard. I do the same. Her forehead scrunches. She blows out a breath and for a few seconds she remains quiet, like she's trying to decide how to say her next words.

"I don't want to lead you on, because I care deeply about you. I've got two weeks left here and I'm not sure if what we're doing can go anywhere. Long distances are not something I'm sure I can handle. Maybe sometime in the future, but not now. Thing is, and it might be selfish, but I want the extra week with you. Would it be wrong if I asked you to be my date for the award show? It's selfish of me to"—she groans—"I'm fucking this up."

"No, you're not, love."

"Maybe it could be like—"

"One last hurrah?"

She peers over at me, her soft eyes shimmering.

Two weeks. Is that really all we have left? Not good enough. I close my eyes because it's not her fault I'm hearing those fucked up voices in my head.

"Zach . . ."

Her shoulders fall and her lips are turned down. I find her watery gaze and I don't know why, but I want to do this for her.

"Okay," I whisper, giving a half smile. "I'd be honored to be your date, Penny. I care about you, too. A lot. Maybe the distance can help us both."

I touch her cheek and run the pad of my thumb over her warm smooth skin. She melts into my touch.

"We don't have to stop being friends when I leave, right?"

I wish this could be our every day. She's made it clear that when her time is up here it's up for us at least romantically. I hate the idea, but I'd do anything to have her until then.

"Never," I say, giving her a soft quick kiss.

"So, I spoke to Clarice," I say, changing the subject, because it hurts.

She leans back and the slightest of smiles tugs at the corner of her lip. "Oh, yeah?"

"I invited her to have lunch here with us on Saturday."

Her entire face lights up. "I want to cook."

I wiggle my brows, "Oh, do you now?"

"I promise I won't burn anything or make a huge disaster of a mess. What's her favorite lunch food?"

"Make PB&J?"

Her melodic laugh surrounds me. I take it all in. There's a brightness to her now.

"No, you dork." She shoves my chest and I chuckle.

"She's a huge fan of tacos."

"Tacos. That's easy. Ground beef and mix—we can do a make your own taco. I'll spread it out on the table in containers and we can pick what else we want in our taco. We should go food shopping," she says.

"Food shopping?" he quirks a brow.

"Yeah, that's what I said, food shopping."

"You mean grocery shopping?"

She narrows her brow. "No, food shopping."

"But you're not just getting food."

"Yeah, but that's the intention: to go for food."

I lean forward and press my lips to hers. She hums and the vibration goes right through my whole body. Her hands find my face. She rubs her thumbs over my scruffy cheeks.

"What was that for?"

I shrug. "You're incredibly sexy when you go on a tangent."

"That was not a tangent," she says, crossing her arms.

I laugh. "Come on, let's get dressed and go FOOD shopping."

She pushes my chest and grins. "Yes. Lets."

Chapter 24

PENNY

Zach is walking ahead of me. We're in the aisle of the store filled with taco mixes and shells. He's leaning over the handle of the shopping cart; his ass is sticking out. I'm not gonna lie, the view is nice. I laugh to myself. He turns and I can't help the way my face warms.

I can't believe I invited him to the awards show. Zach knows this me, not the one who puts on an image for the cameras. What if he . . . it shouldn't matter what he thinks, because he and I can't be anything more than friends after this. Can we be that after all we've done? Maybe.

"Like what you see, love?"

"Just admiring the taco shells, that's all."

"Right, uh huh."

He turns and goes back to scrolling his app for the store. Go figure, the man is a couponer. It's definitely a turn on.

I scan the shelves, checking out all the different brands. While I do, my mind wanders. He makes me happy. This whole place does. The countdown is on.

Zach walks over and bumps into me. Our eyes, as always, connect in a way that causes the butterflies in my stomach to flutter uncontrollably. I shiver at his touch.

"You're thinking too hard. These are the best shells." He reaches up to the highest shelf.

I would have needed to get on my toes to reach or maybe even stand on the bottom shelf.

"Okay, you win. They totally are."

"How about this mix?" He tosses the shells into the cart and grabs the same brand of mix.

"Nope."

I pull out my phone. "I promise I was good. The only thing I googled was taco seasoning recipes. So, we need the spice aisle."

"Are you sure you want to tackle that on your first try?"

"Pshh, it's tacos. How badly can I fuck those up?"

He snorts. "With you anything is possible."

There's a twinkle of jest in his eyes.

"Ye of little faith," I say.

He tucks his index finger under my chin and lifts it, so my eyes meet his. "You're sassy today." His tone turns low and growly.

"Yeah, and? What are you gonna do about it?"

He uses his other hand to tip up the bill of my hat ever so slightly to look me in the eye. I'm wearing my disguise glasses. He lowers them only enough for him.

"You'll have to wait until we get home."

I inhale sharply and he grins. The word home coming from his lips when he's talking about us makes me want to stay even more. My pulse beat a little harder and my heart flip flops in my chest. That turned on tingling sensation pools low in my belly.

He's about to lean in for a kiss when his phone goes off. He sighs and pulls back to take it from his pocket.

"It's Mark, hold on a sec."

He steps away and once again leans on the cart. He gives me a little wiggle. I roll my eyes as he glances over his shoulder with a smirk.

"Hey, what's up?"

Zach looks around the shelves while listening.

"Really? That many have signed up for open mic? And for karaoke? I can feel it too, it's going to be great!" He pauses again. "Saturday? What time? Clarice is coming for lunch. Yeah. I love the little guy. Okay, yeah, I'll bring him when we go in for our shift. Perfect. Later gator."

He turns and I quirk a brow. "That's how you talk to your boss?"

"It's Mark." He shrugs. "First, amazing news. We have—drum roll, please."

I make a weird noise with my tongue, and he chuckles.

"We got fifteen people signed up for open mic and twenty-five for karaoke! Can you believe that? Just from the social media post and signs around the pub."

My mouth falls open and I jump, still holding onto the car. "That's such good news."

"Sure is! And I hope you know how to babysit a child."

I snort. "Are we watching Devin?"

"Yeah. Saturday. Mark is dropping Devin off around one. He has some errands to run before work. We can bring him with us to the pub where Cynthia will pick him up."

"Does this mean we can buy kid friendly snacks?"

His eyes widen. "It sure does."

Shopping with Zach is fun. Now that we have everything, we're on our way to the register, taco and kid snack ready. The best part is I'm here doing this without a camera in my face. I don't mind fans coming up and wanting an autograph or picture, that has never bothered me. Some days I want to shop in peace. I watch everyone else who can easily move through aisles and not be bombarded, and I've never been able to do that. My whole life has been in the spotlight. I've never known this kind of life. It was something I imagined on nights when things got too hard. It never grew into anything fathomable until the last few months and now being here solidified it even more.

I bump into a hard body. Zach grunts. I lift a hand to touch his shoulder. He's stiff like a boulder.

"Zach, what is—"

And that's when my eyes land on the one thing I've been avoiding for weeks.

My heart sinks into my stomach. Not only one magazine, but a couple of different ones have a picture of Dad and I from the night I won Talent in America. We're standing on the stage with confetti of all different colors raining down. His arm is around my shoulder, and I'm glancing up at him with an adoring look shimmering in my eyes. He had performed that night so was already on stage when they made the announcement.

It's not the picture getting to me, although it's a memory that has been ingrained in my head since the image started to circle social media; it's the headline.

Star Power: The Downfall of a Rockstar's Daughter, Leaked.

My chest starts to tighten, and the world is in tunnel vision. I barely register Zach's arm around me.

"Come on. I'll come back and buy this another—"

"No. It's okay. We'll buy this stuff and, and, and we'll go home."

I start to rummage through my purse on my arm, but Zach rests his hand over mine.

"Love, I got it. Okay?"

I nod my head and something like relief washes across Zach's face. I go through the motions of taking the items out of the cart and placing it on the belt. My movements are robotic. It feels like it takes forever, and I'm grateful once we are headed to the door.

The cold February chill hits me and flurries of snow fall on the tip of my nose. When we get to the car Zach has me wait inside while he puts the bags in the trunk of his car along with placing the cart back to where it belongs.

He slides in and the door closes. I knew he was there, but I jump. His hand laces into mine. I feel him but don't. It's like an out-of-body experience. There's pain but numbness all at once. If that even makes sense.

"Can we go home now?"

"Okay. Yeah."

I let go of his hand and I don't miss the way his entire body tenses. I turn and rest my head against the seat and spend the whole ride staring out the window.

Chapter 25

ZACH

I stare out the kitchen window. Snow started to fall when we were on our way home. By the time we pulled into the driveway, the ground was covered in a light dusting. The crinkle of a paper bag behind me pulls my attention from the storm brewing outside.

Penny stands at the center island, her hand on the blue package of cookies. It's as if someone hit the pause button on her life. She looks off into the distance. Not out the window. Not at me. She's lost.

I know she can handle herself and she chose the career which ultimately put her in the spotlight. It doesn't ever stop the urge to want to shield her from the chaos surrounding her name. Even if it's a few minutes of reprieve. Her safety is the most important thing to me.

I gather my thoughts and go to her.

"Penny?"

Nothing. Not even a flinch.

"Hey, Pen," I say.

I'm not sure if touching her right now is appropriate, so I hold back. I may need to if she doesn't respond. She's far away from here, so I give it another few seconds.

"Penelope," I say, this time firmer, but gentle.

She blinks. Her head turns slowly and her eyes lift. Between her brows are wrinkles that are not normally there. I reach for the cookies but my hand accidentally brushes with hers. We both make a noise at the contact. It's a soft inhale. It shouldn't shock me, but everything does when I'm around her. We lock gazes again.

"Hey, love," I say, trying to get a reaction, but nothing. Shit. This is bad. She's not fighting me. Not even a hint of a smile.

I sigh. "Pen."

Her hand slides off the cookies and immediately grabs hold of the silver locket. She rubs it with her thumb and index finger as if it's a magical cure.

"Why don't you go take it easy. I'll take care of this last bag. Okay?"

She nods, lips parted but doesn't say a word. I hold up my hand, so she feels my presence. She stares at it for a moment and then back at me.

"Yeah. Okay."

Without another word she turns and disappears through the entryway. It takes me a minute to gather myself and send Sarina a text.

> *It was released early. It was on the tabloids.*

The dots appear before I even have a chance to close out the app.

> *Sarina: Shit. Thanks for texting.*

If you'll let me, I got her.

Sarina: Yeah. Let me know if you need me. Have her call me.

Of course.

I finish putting away the last bag and then go to find Penny. She's in the den, facing Petunia's tank. I quietly observe her. I wish I could lift the burden causing her defeated posture. Her head hangs low, shoulders hunched forward. The rise and fall of them come in long, drawn-out movements.

I turn to leave when I'm met by Larry standing at my feet. He's not all fluffed as he usually is. He tilts his chin, so his slit green cat eyes find mine. I prepare myself for a fight of epic proportions. Instead, the moody bastard purrs and weasels his way between my legs.

"Whoa," I say, not meaning to, but his gesture catches me off guard.

"Did you know axolotls can regenerate their limbs? Chop a hand off? Oh, here's another. It takes about four to eight weeks, but can you imagine? Her laughter is short lived and small. "I wonder if it could work on broken hearts." She sniffles. "Oh, and something else cool, they are solitary animals. They rarely like to be in groups or pairs. They are smart creatures."

She hiccups. Her hand flies to her mouth to muffle her cries. I'm watching the woman who has come into my life and unexpectedly invaded my heart in ways I never imagined fall apart.

I cross the room and gently take her arm. She whirls around with a gasp. I hate the sight I'm greeted with. Her beautiful face is streaked with new and old tears. The creases on her forehead increase every time she attempts to hide the hurt.

She tries to back out of my grasp, but I pull her back to me. She lowers her gaze but pauses when I press my hand against her cheek. She reaches for it. Our fingers interlock and she leans into my touch, closing her eyes and pushing until the pressure is enough to feel good.

"You're stronger than this, Penny."

"Y-you can't possibly know that."

I shake my head. "I beg to differ. I know that you're contemplating giving up your career, but you're afraid to because you fear you'll disappoint your father."

The moment I say father, she tinkers with the locket again.

"You blame yourself for what is happening on social media. When you are feeling anxious or sad you say it all out loud to animals. You know they can sense when we are distressed."

"Brr meow." Larry chooses that moment to weave in and out of my legs again and between hers as well. He pushes his head against me and then does the same to her.

"I know you have a big heart and that you are searching for a place to call home. You are also starting to contemplate a normal life. Like this one. One where you have family dinners with your sister more than once a year or every other year. You are emotionally exhausted from being pulled in every direction with short breaks and from everyone needing to know all the skeletons in your closet . . . am I close?"

She inhales and exhales. "I know you, too. You're afraid of what could happen if you put yourself out there. You may have found a home but there's still something more you're searching for. There is something in your life you want to prove but can't quite find the strength to do it. Your heart is always in the right place even if it doesn't seem like it. You love with all your soul and are protective over the ones you love," she says.

A lump forms in my throat. I lick my lips and swallow hard to push it down.

"I guess we both know each other better than we thought," I whisper, leaning in and resting my forehead against hers. "I'm sorry. You make me—"

I'm cut off by her soft salty lips pressing against mine. Her eyes are closed so tight they line with wrinkles. I slide my hand to the back of her head, getting my fingers tangled in her silky hair. A whimper from her prompts me to open my mouth. I guide her in with the flick of my tongue and when we meet stroke for stroke I get enveloped in the sheer intensity of the moment.

"Zach," she moans into my mouth and that only makes me kiss her harder.

I follow her lead, giving her full control. Her head tilts and I go with it, leaning into her. My hand moves from her hair and catches her around the waist to sit against her lower back.

"Mmmm," she hums.

My cock is straining against the zipper of my jeans. She moves her hips, and fire shoots up my spine.

"Is that for me?" she whispers. "Do you want me, Zach?"

The rasp in her voice does me in.

"Always," I say quietly.

She stops kissing me and raises her hand to place it on my scruffy cheeks. She watches me closely as if she wants to make sure I'm not lying.

"Seventy-two," I say, unable to hide my smile.

Through her tears, her face finally lights with something.

"You're still doing this?"

She shakes her head, giggling. It's easy to show her what she does to me. The bulge in my jeans doesn't lie. I love seeing her smile. I'm both worked up and turned on. I'm a strange mess of emotions over it.

"I want more, Zach." A blush creeps up her neck and covers her cheeks. She bites her lower lip.

"You're running off emotions."

I lift her chin. I love the small gasps she makes every single time I do. It was easy to fall under her spell. More than anything I'd love to take her upstairs and fuck her. The things I'd do to this woman are endless. I want it all with her.

"Hey, don't look away from me, I'm not done talking." I say it softly and smile to let her know I'm teasing.

"You'll have me, don't you fucking worry about that. I'm not letting you go without knowing what it's like to sink inside of you. I want to get lost in how damn good it's going feel, but that's not what you need tonight."

"What do I need?" she asks, her voice meek.

"Support. An ear? A movie night? Take Larry for a walk?"

Her laughter is present but sad.

"Or we can lay in bed, and I'll hold you. I don't fucking care. You're hurting."

Her eyes sparkle. "Thank you. I don't know what I did to des—"

I kiss her hard for only a few seconds before I rest my head against hers. "Don't you dare, woman. Keep that—no scratch it, throw those thoughts out the window."

"I need ice cream bars of the strawberry kind," she says.

I purse my lips and give her a playful scowl. Through a tearful smile, her cheeks turn rosy.

"Fine, but only this once."

"You can't hide them from me."

"Wanna bet?" I chuckle.

She laughs with me for a few more seconds then relaxes. Her eyes focus on mine.

"My heart wants to believe my dad didn't pay those producers, but my brain is telling my heart to stop being so stupid. He had the power to do so. He always said he'd do anything for his daughters. Even if he did it out of love, it will feel all wrong to have won the show."

"Either way, you deserved that win. I'm not saying that because I have this huge crush on you." I pause and hope for a smile, but it falls a little short. "Look, I'm being serious now. Okay? You're incredibly talented. Your voice has helped thousands of people. Maybe they had a bad day, and your song came on the radio, and it brought them joy, or you made a fan's day by helping them to believe in their own voice and power. Penelope, I can't say I understand what it's like to have the world watching and criticizing your every move. There will always be haters, gossipers, keyboard warriors, corrupt media outlets to tear you down, but remember you have done so much good by being who you are. You've given hope to people who need it. Don't let them put out your fire. Everyone had to start somewhere, but you are the one who made it grow into something more."

Tears stream down her face. I wipe them away as fast as I can but can't keep up.

"Come here," I say, and she throws her arms around me and holds on extra tight.

Chapter 26

PENNY

"**I** can't believe he . . . I can, but still." Sarina sighs.

I've got her on speaker as I attempt to make tacos. Today is going to be a busy one. I've been grateful for the distractions.

I go from angry to upset to numb and it's a never-ending cycle. It feels wrong to be mad at someone who is no longer here, but it hurts. It's almost like a betrayal. He paid those producers and it's now officially out there. I love my dad but I'm not sure I like him very much right now and out of anything in the world it's what is most painful.

On top of it, Erick's words keep ringing in my head. *Fraud.* I truly am now.

"I know." My voice breaks despite me trying to be strong.

Last night I worked, which helped. With each passing evening, I love it more. I try not to think of what will happen when I leave.

The people I've met, the friendships I've made. My heart fears the worst. I was easily forgotten by my L.A. friends; what's to say it won't happen again.

"Today is supposed to be a good day. I don't even want to think about it. Shit. Ouch."

My phone is set on the counter beside me on speaker. The grease jumped up and got my hand as I stirred around the meat.

"What are you trying to do over there?"

"Make lunch."

Her laughter is the best thing I've heard all week.

"You?" she teases.

"Yeah, and you're distracting her, Sarina."

Zach's voice startles me. Some of the meat I've been mixing around flies up and out of the pan. I hang my head.

"Zachary." I sigh.

"Zach Efron, be nice!" Sarina teases.

"I'm starting to think I should take that as a compliment. He's a good-looking dude."

He comes up behind me and slips his arms around my stomach while resting his chin on my shoulder. I look back at him or at least try, but the angle is hard. His fingers dance along my stomach over my clothing. I sigh and then realize who I'm on the phone with. He must notice the switch from relaxed to tense because he lets go and stands beside me.

Sarina chuckles. "Why are you allowing her to cook in my kitchen?"

"She insisted. Clarice is coming for lunch and we're babysitting Mark's kid."

She chokes. "Babysitting? Both of you?"

"No, I'm going to let Zach watch the kid."

"Oh, yeah, yeah, you're right, both of you are better."

"I'm offended, Sarina," he says playfully.

"He's a cool kid. He bought me a Shirley temple with his fancy credit card."

"He's such a cutie," Sarina says. "So, you've been going to the pub a lot?" Curiosity is prominent in her tone.

I look up to find Zach keeping a watchful eye on me.

"Mark kind of hired me. I wanted to work. It felt so good to do something normal. I had real conversations with people that had nothing to do with music or gossip. It was nice. Madeline is sweet."

Sarina gasps on the other line. "Oh. Wow. You know what, I love that for you. That place is a home away from home. They all accept me and my loud singing to the jukebox."

"Hopefully when you return you won't need to sing to the jukebox, because we're starting open mic and karaoke. Next Saturday is the first one and so many people have signed up."

She squeals. "Are you serious? Don't play with me. You know I'm a karaoke queen."

I laugh. "Promise. No joke. Maddie mentioned she thought you'd enjoy it."

Sarina sucks in a breath.

"Oh. Yay!" Her voice sounds off. Almost sad. "How is Maddie?"

I have this inkling Zach knows a lot more about Madeline and Sarina's friendship than I do, so I look to him for some kind of guidance.

"She's hanging in there," Zach replies for me.

"Good," her voice squeaks.

There's an awkward silence on both ends until another splash of grease pops up. "Shit."

"Okay, I'm gonna let you go before you burn down my kitchen. Are you sure you're doing alright with all the rumors coming to light?"

"Yeah. I'll be okay."

"Love you. Oh, and Pen, keep your head up. Okay? We can't change the past, but we can choose the way we react to it. You are where you are because of your own strength."

I sniffle, but there are no tears. "Love you, Sarina."

The doorbell rings the moment I'm off the phone and I curse again. "You need to hold her off for like twenty more minutes at least," I say, turning to Zach who is already making his way out of the room.

"Zach!" I hiss.

"Maybe I should take over?"

"Nope. Stall her!"

I turn back and the grease pops. Oh man.

A half an hour later I stare at the display I made on the dining room table. I have it all laid out in the center in plastic trays. There's lettuce, cheese, shells, sour cream, black beans, tomatoes, the works.

"Okay, lunch is ready!"

They stroll in smiling and chatting. In the short amount of time I've known Clarice, I've never seen the two side by side before. My heart does several flips as I take in her eyes. In this light there is something different about them. Like they are clearer. When their gazes both meet mine, I am struck square in the chest. My mouth parts but no words come out.

"You alright, love?" Zach asks when he reaches me.

His hand grazes mine.

"Y-yeah. O-kay."

"Wow," Clarice states, clapping her hands together. "This looks amazing, and it smells great."

I push Zach's arm, so he scoots over. Clarice comes forward, inspecting everything.

"You did this, young lady?"

I nod. "I sure did."

"It's fabulous. I can't wait to dig in. Tacos are my favorite. You know when . . ." She trails off and shakes her head. "When I'd come to visit him, his grandma always had tacos cooking."

"Yeah." His tone is a bit clipped.

"Well, I know this will taste amazing," she says.

Clarice sits across from us on the side with the windows and Zach and I sit together on the other.

"Warning before you bite in, I am not held responsible for any deaths by tacos," he says.

I shove Zach playfully. "Maybe I slipped something into yours."

He sticks his tongue out at me, and I do the same to him. On the other side Clarice's watery smile catches me off guard.

She laughs. "You two remind me of me and my first love." Her laughter fades as the memory takes hold of her. She gives a hesitant smile.

"Clarice, we're—"

"Friends?" She lifts her brow and wiggles it. "Sure, we'll go with that. My Chester, he was a good man—or boy, I guess. We were fifteen but things happened and his parents made him move. It was this whole big thing. I found out years later through a friend he had passed." She waves her hand. "Look at me being sappy. Let's dig in, shall we?"

"On three we all try so if its poisoned . . ."

"Zachary, behave yourself, young man," Clarice states, pointing her finger.

Her brows crinkle and I take note of how similar in shape they are to Zach's. A perfect arch that's hard to come by.

I wait for them to take a bite first and when they do appreciative noises fill the air. Zach puts his down, finishes chewing, and then grabs his throat making a gagging noise.

"Oh my God. You are such an asshole." I laugh, smacking him.

He pushes his arm into me, and I lean into his touch. "It's actually pretty amazing," he says.

"He's right, Penny. These are delicious. Homemade seasoning?"

"Yes, ma'am."

"Wow, Zach, you've landed quite a lady. Talented, beautiful, a good cook."

"Who knew?" I say, in a squeaky voice. "Confession, I've never cooked tacos before."

She chuckles. "I'm impressed. These are delicious. I'll have to have more."

Our conversations remain light. We go for seconds and even thirds.

"Well, I'm full. What are your plans for the afternoon?"

"Mark's son, Devin, is coming over. We're going to watch him for a bit—make a cardboard box into a pirate ship and play pirates. The treasure is going to be the snacks."

She smiles. "That sounds so lovely. Zach used to love pirates you know. He'd always be outside with his eye patch using anything and everything as a pirate ship."

"So, you've been secretly loving this idea, huh?" I say. It's my turn to nudge him but there's something in his stare that catches me off guard.

"One holiday," she says, not realizing, "I bought him a pirate costume and he never wanted to take it off."

"That was from you? How did you know that?"

She stops talking, her smile fades. Her mouth opens like she wants to say something, but it's caught. Tears well in her eyes.

"That was before you . . . before . . . I knew you."

Zach keeps his eyes on her. She touches her locket, and he focuses on it. Her son. Maybe my inkling was right. Just because she wasn't around at that age doesn't mean his grandma couldn't have talked to Clarice about her grandson. Although, from what he's told me, she wasn't a caring woman, so why would she?

"I should probably go," she says, her voice breaking.

She goes to stand, and Zach calls out, "No! Wait!"

Clarice stops moving and sits. His brow furrows. He assesses her as if he's looking at Clarice for the first time in his life. Tears fall from her eyes and the answer is laid right out there for us to see without either of them having to say it.

"You're my mom. Aren't you?"

She sniffles and attempts to wipe her tears. "I—look, Zach, I—"

The doorbell rings but no one moves.

Chapter 27

ZACH

C larice is my mom.

"I'll go get that," Penny says.

As she stands, she rests a hand on my shoulder in a comforting squeeze. I cover hers, returning the gesture. I hate when she walks away, hate it so much.

Clarice's shoulders shake. All the memories come together from the moment I met her to now. She places her elbows on the table and buries her face in her hands. Her cries are soft and muffled. I'm holding back my own emotions. I don't cry often. The last time was when I was sleeping in my car. I was frustrated and angry, but this is different. The urge to hit my hand on the table is strong, but I stop myself.

"Why?" I finally ask after a few moments.

She sniffles and wipes her eyes. "I was fifteen when I got pregnant." Her tearful eyes meet mine. "His parents shamed me when we told them. A month later they moved. I never heard from him again. He was the boy who passed away. Your grandma was pissed. I tried the whole teen mom thing. My grades slipped; school was a nightmare. We almost went the home school route, but I was so depressed because I lost friends and was in a bad headspace. We agreed my education was most important and maybe if I distanced myself, I could come back and be ready to be a parent. So, she sent me to an all-girls boarding school. She became your legal guardian. I finished high school, went to college, got my degree, and tried to grow into a person who could take care of a child. There were so many times I could have told you. Once I returned, it became harder. I found myself in failed relationship after failed relationship. I was in a marriage that didn't last. I never felt worthy to be your parent, and I"—she sighs—"I know I'm making excuses, and it's not fair to you."

I'm trying to comprehend and wrap my head around this story. She lifts her hand to the locket around her neck. It's a gesture I'm used to since Penny does it often. Then I remember what Penny said.

"What's in that locket?"

She closes her eyes and takes a few deep breaths.

She unclasps it. Holding it tight in her palm she reaches out and gives it to me. At first, I sit there, still stunned and not wanting to, but something inside of me makes me do it. Our hands touch and it's like I'm zapped to life. Inside is a picture of the two of us. It must have been right after birth. She was so young. A knot forms in my throat. She had curly hair; it was light brown and sat on her shoulder.

I've never seen a baby picture of myself. Grandma rarely ever took pics. The only ones that hung on her walls were school pictures, but only up till third grade. I lift my gaze and meet hers.

"I'm s-s-s-orry. I should go. I'll give you time to process. I understand if you never want to speak to me again."

I let her go, not sure what else to do. There's some conversation in the living room between her, Devin and Penny, but I can't bring myself to move. I look at the locket and allow the tears to take over.

❧ ❧ ❧

Penny came into the dining room a little while after Clarice left. She placed a hand on my shoulder and told me to go upstairs and relax. She offered to take care of Devin. He came in as I was getting up, in search of the tacos she had promised. I gave the little guy a hug and told him I'd be down later to hang out.

It's been over two hours since then. Now, I'm back in the kitchen to get a drink of water. Their laughter from the den allowed me to smile for the first time since everything happened. I stop midway through the kitchen and look over at the dining room area. The tacos are cleaned up, the dishes in the sink as well.

I place a hand on the counter as a wave of dizziness takes over. All the events of the afternoon play through my mind. Squeals of happiness continue, but I'm lost in my head. A future possibility floats through my head. A child's laughter mixed with Penny's, but it's not Devin. It's our kid. I imagine Clarice spoiling them like she did for me. I close my eyes and squeeze the edge of the island. It's so strong it almost feels real. It's like the wind has been knocked right out of me.

I grab a glass to fill. I spin and lean against the counter, placing the water behind me. My phone buzzes. I don't want to answer but I look anyway. It's Madeline.

"Hey." I try to make my voice sound as if I'm alright.

"I heard you were babysitting a cutie. I was calling to check in on Penny."

"We're fine." My tone is a bit harsher than I mean for it to be.

"Zach . . ."

This woman has a sixth sense when it comes to feelings.

"C-Clarice is my mom."

Glass breaks on her end of the line. "Ouch. Shit. Fuck. Damn it. She what?"

I laugh although it's not full. "You alright?"

"Mark is gonna take that one out of my check." There's some shuffling on the other end. "Okay, now what happened?"

I'm not so sure where to begin. I start with lunch and how the conversation came about. She listens to all of it. When I finish, she's quiet for a moment.

"Wow. I mean, there have been times when I've seen a resemblance of some sort between you two, but I thought it was a coincidence. You know how some people have similar features even if they aren't related. You're not holding up well, are you? Whose—oh, is Penny with Devin?"

"Yeah. They're in the den now."

Their laughter grows louder. Despite everything I find it in me to laugh too. I love the sound of theirs. It's helping me cope with whatever turmoil this revelation has brought. I'm stuck in this back and forth of why Clarice didn't tell me. She had all this time to come forward. I can sort of understand when I was a kid, but what about when I was eighteen? Did I not have a right to know? Or when my grandma passed, she could have said something. I flex my free hand, trying to calm the raging bull inside.

"Ahoy matey!" Penny says, pulling me from the chaos.

"Clear the poop deck!" Devin yells and then falls into a fit of giggles with Penny.

"Poop deck." Devin repeats the word, his voice hitching as he says it.

On the other line Madeline chuckles.

"You heard that?"

"Yes. Sounds like they're having a blast. You should join them. I know for a fact it's what you want."

"Penny's leaving soon." It's out of my mouth before I can stop it.

"So then tell her how you feel."

I sigh. "Why didn't you?" I pause, realizing I've hit a sore spot with her. "Shit, Maddie, I'm sorry. That was an asshole move on my part. My head is so fucked right now. I know you're stuck between a rock and a hard place with that."

Her situation is different.

"Zach, it's fine, no offense taken, okay? Maybe what I'm saying is don't let Penny be the one who got away if it's what you want."

My head is spinning with so many things. Clarice is my mom. All this time I was wondering why I felt this connection with her. I don't want to talk to her, but at the same time when I think about not having her in my life that hurts so much more.

Then there's Penny. She's leaving. She doesn't do long distance relationships. I can't give her what she needs.

"I'm not going to be the one to hold her back. We will be thousands of miles apart. She's going to record a new album and go on tour. There is no room in her life for me. We're going to be friends. That's all."

"I don't think that's what is stopping you."

She's like a mama bear and when she knows one of us is hurting, she's there in a heartbeat, no questions asked.

"I don't own my own house. I rent a room. I don't make a lot of money. I'm not good enough to give her the life she deserves."

"Zach, that's not true and you know it. She's not like your ex or any of those other women. She likes you for who you are. What you do for a living, at least in her eyes, does not define the man you are."

I run a hand through my hair. I need to pull myself together.

"Go be with her. If your time is limited, spend it together because when you least expect it, she'll be gone. As for Clarice, I think you should talk to her. Not right away. Give yourself time to understand the situation and when you're ready maybe find out more. That woman loves you. I've seen it in her eyes. I should probably take my own advice with all of this. Maybe one day. One day I might regret not saying something, because life is unpredictable. It can take any of us away in a heartbeat."

I inhale. "Thank you, Maddie. I have a lot to think about, but first I should help clean the poop deck, it sounds messy."

"There isn't really poop on the deck. It refers to the stern or highest deck on a ship."

"Pshh, I knew that," I tease.

Her laughter makes me smile. "Sure, you did, Zachary. Now go get your pirate on. I'll see you all later."

"Bye, Maddie."

I stare off towards where their voices are coming from. Something soft touches my leg. I yelp and scurry from my spot. I spin and find Larry watching me. He rubs himself against me again.

"You drunk, Larry? Maybe ill?"

He weaves between my legs, and purrs, then heads towards the entryway of the kitchen. When he gets there, he stops, turns to me, meows and runs off.

"Well, shiver me timbers."

Penny's voice keeps me grounded. Thinking back to what Madeline said, she's right. I've got a limited amount of time with Penny, so I might as well stop getting caught up in my own thoughts and spend what time I do have left.

They've built a pirate ship out of a cardboard box. There's a black pirate flag attached that looks to be painted and designed by Devin. The skull and crossbones are a bit lopsided, but you can easily see the pride and joy put into the work.

Their backs are to me. Penny is kneeling inside the makeshift ship while Devin stands behind her. They are both wearing the costumes Penny purchased online. Thankfully they were next day delivery. She couldn't wait to try hers on. Hers has a long red skirt with a fake black corset top. It's held together by loose strings. Devin's has black pants that are cut on the bottom with a black and white striped top. On the couch beside the ship is my costume. It's laid out nicely as if they were both waiting for me to join them. Emotion clogs my throat. What I wouldn't give for this to be our future.

They move the cardboard box as if they are stuck in the wild waters of the ocean.

"Zach is a Scallywag. We should make him walk the plank when he returns."

"I agree, matey. We can feed him to Petunia," she says.

He chuckles. "Petunia isn't a shark."

"No, but she's a fierce axolotl."

His giggles don't stop. As the two pretend a huge wave is coming, they lean too far to the right and the entire ship along with them goes over.

"Guess I can't walk the plank now," I say.

Devin gets to his feet first. "Zach!"

When he whirls around, the smile on his face nearly knocks me over. He races towards me and wraps his arms around me.

"Hey, there buddy." I ruffle his hair.

I try to keep my voice even. It's not working too well. I lift my gaze and immediately lock eyes with Penny from her position on the floor. The force of what I feel for her hits me harder than Devin's smile. She gets up and comes towards us. Devin doesn't pull away until she's nearby.

"I'm gonna go fix the ship, then you can join us."

He happily runs back to where they left the box tilted on its side. She doesn't hold back. Her fingers slip between mine as she takes my hand, holding on tight. Her eyes light up. "You're just in time to be axolotl food."

"Oh, is that so?" There's a bit more strength back in my voice.

"Yup. Petunia is rather hungry."

I run my thumb over the smooth skin of her hand. She inhales a trembling breath. She tilts her head, staring deep into my eyes. I nod and she squeezes my hand a little harder.

"I don't think that's gonna happen."

"Oh?" She smirks. "And why is that?"

"Because you're gonna walk the plank first." I unlink our hands and lift her up and over my shoulder to carry her. She squeals and tries to squirm out of my grip.

"Hurry, matey, prepare the plank," I tell Devin.

In this moment, despite my heavy heart, I feel whole being surrounded by the echoing laughter and the comforting hold of the woman I've fallen for.

Chapter 28

PENNY

Three days left in New York and a week in L.A. with Zach. That's ten days. I've been lying here in bed staring at the door while listening to Zach lightly snore. My phone went off about an hour ago and I should never have checked the message.

> Erick: Now that the truth is out there, only a real artist can win the award. See you in L.A., Penelope.

The tension in my body causes an ache in my bones. I gasp at Zach's warm hand finding his way up the back of my shirt. I breathe in and allow the feeling to relax me.

"You're so tense, love."

"Erick texted me."

There's no point in hiding it from him.

"What? Give me the phone, I'll—"

I roll over and come face to face with his scrunched brows. I touch his face to smooth out the wrinkles and shake my head.

"I want to forget about it."

A heaviness hangs over him. It's been there all week.

"Are you okay?" I ask.

He's been quiet about his situation with Clarice. I was afraid to bring it up and when he didn't, I figured he needed time to process. I caught him in his room when we got home after work on Saturday. He had Clarice's locket. He held it in his hands and was staring at it, dazed. I didn't linger. Not long after he crawled into my bed where we held each other.

Mark put me on schedule this week so we could prepare for tomorrow's events at Wingman's. We both welcomed the distraction. Last night we came back, got into bed, joked around, and fell asleep holding one another.

"No, but I will be," he finally speaks.

It's easy to see how affected he is by Clarice's confession. While he's been beside me this whole time throughout the night, I know he didn't get much sleep. Sometimes I'd feel him watching me. Other times he'd shift or rub my back. I couldn't tell if he was doing it to comfort me or himself.

"What was in her lock—no, that's rude of me to ask. I'm sorry."

He adjusts to sit up. I do the same and we sit crisscross on the bed, facing each other. His hand tinkers with something in the pocket of his sweats. Slowly, he lifts out the locket and holds it out for me.

"Are you sure?"

"Yeah."

Our eyes meet. His are soft and if I'm not mistaken, there are so many unsaid words dancing in his golden gaze. There's trust, admiration, love— no, there can't be. I hate looking away but it's too intense. I click open the locket and find a woman and her baby. A young teen Clarice with Zach. I smile at the sight.

"This is . . . it's beautiful," I say.

His eyes fill and tears spill over. I touch his flushed cheek and wipe along the bottom of his eye. He turns away from my touch, but I pull him back.

"It's alright, Zach. No judgement from me."

He closes his eyes and nods. His hand covers mine and we sit in silence for a minute. He's given me my space, now it's my turn to give him his.

"My grandma was the one who sent her away the first time. She was only a teen when she had me."

He explains to me what he knows from the conversation he and Clarice had during lunch. I don't say a word, only listen.

"Knowing that my dad was forced away because of his family boggles my mind. I still don't know what to feel about it. I can't believe the first love she spoke about was him. He's not here now. If he was alive, would I even have the guts to find him? It's a lot. I need time to process."

"And that's okay." I place the locket back into his hand and close his fingers over it and hold on. "After all these years, you have some kind of answer. You're allowed to be angry, sad, relieved. Feeling anything is okay. You don't have to be the strong one all the damn time. It's okay to be vulnerable." I touch his lips with my index finger and a slow grin grows under it.

"It's hard for me to show it. All week I've watched her usual table waiting for her to be there. When she wasn't . . ." His voice breaks.

I touch his leg and squeeze.

"Sorry," he whispers.

"For what?"

He sniffles. "This."

"Don't ever be sorry for feeling."

I move my hand to his face and lean in to kiss him. It's a closed mouth kiss but it says so much. His arms move around me, and we stay in the embrace with our lips pressed together, his warmth surrounding me. I breathe him in.

"You don't have to hide your pain behind your sarcasm."

"Yeah, but you like my sarcastic mouth." He smiles.

"I never denied that," I say.

His hand reaches around and grabs the back of my neck to pull me in closer. A low moan comes from deep in my chest. His eyes watch me closely. I open my mouth for him and when our tongues meet, I'm swept up amid emotions and heat.

"Zach," I exhale in a desperate whisper.

He hums and stops kissing me to rest his forehead against mine. "Yeah, love?"

It took several months for me to even come close to wanting more with Erick, but with Zach, I want it all as if it's a necessity. I should protect not only my heart but his as well, because of the circumstances of our unknown future, but it doesn't make me want him any less.

"I've never—never allowed someone so close so fast. I want . . ."

He cups my face. "We don't have to do anything you're not ready to do."

"I feel selfish for wanting this, because I'm not sure I'm ready to label this." My smile doesn't reach my cheeks enough for the tug.

"If you're being selfish than I am, too. I just want to know what it's like to have you. All of you." He closes his eyes for a few long seconds. "Even if our time is limited."

"What are you saying?" My question comes out as barely a whisper.

Our foreheads are no longer touching, but I somehow feel the closest I've ever been to someone.

"You're my person." His lip twitches with an attempt to smile.

"Me?" I squeak.

He chuckles. "Yeah. You. What we have now may have an expiration, but something tells me it's only the beginning."

"We'll figure it out, right?"

"Bet," he whispers.

I inhale, then slowly breathe out. Our eyes lock and there's nothing but truth in his stare.

"Tell me what you want?" He narrows his eyes.

"You."

The answer was so easy. I said it without a single ounce of hesitation.

"Hold on a sec, don't move from this spot. Okay?"

He runs out of the room. I lay down and face the door and prop my head up with my hand. He returns in seconds and slides into the doorway, almost missing it completely, but stops himself by holding onto the frame. His pants are gone and he's in boxers and white tee only. He holds up a box of condoms in his hand.

I grin. "Very presumptuous, sunshine."

He strides forward, sights set on me but the second he gets halfway my phone goes off. I sit up and check it on the bedside table.

"It's Sarina."

There's not a hint of him being upset because of our ruined moment. Larry must sense there have been some rocky moments in both of our lives currently. He saunters up behind Zach while pushing his head and then rubbing his back against his legs. Zach jumps in response, probably expecting to be mauled but instead Larry sits beside him and looks up.

I laugh as I grab the phone. "I think you have a new BFF."

He stares at me wide eyed. "I don't know, I think it's a revenge plot." His lips tug up into a genuine smile. "You should talk to her." He nods towards the phone in my hand. "What's that saying, keep your friends close but your enemies closer?"

I answer the phone. "Sarina, Larry is smooching on Zach."

She chuckles. "He's plotting."

"See," Zach says, pointing.

I place Sarina on speaker.

"He knows where you sleep, Zachary," she says.

My cheeks flush and when I meet Zach's gaze, an amused grin dances over his lips. I scowl playfully. For a few seconds, I'm lost in him.

"I'm gonna go chill with my new best bud. Come on, Lar, let's—" He reaches out to pet him and Larry realizes his wrongdoings and hisses along with swiping his paw.

I double over with laughter falling back onto the bed with my phone in hand.

"Did Larry attack?"

"Yes." I hold onto my stomach; it hurts from laughing.

"How are you doing?" she asks.

"I'm okay, minus the fact that Erick texted me, but I ignored it."

"Good. Don't give in."

"Trying my hardest. How are you doing? This isn't just about me."

She sighs. "I'm okay. More worried about you."

"I — I'm sure I'll be okay, but I'm having so much anxiety over what will happen when I go back to California. I haven't had some kind of huge revelation or change in myself. I'm still here running from it. Makes me feel weak."

"You aren't weak, you're human."

My guilt over being the one to win a competition on false pretenses is like a weight that's been hovering and ready to crush me at any moment.

"I don't want to watch it, but I kind of do to see what Lance Greenfield has to say. Some friend of Dad's he is. And Erick probably raves about how he slept his way to the top. God, I was so stupid for believing him. I haven't let anyone in since—"

Finishing that sentence would be a lie. I have let someone new into my life without question. Zach. I promised myself I would keep all men at a distance since, but that has changed

"Penny, what's wrong?"

"Nothing." I swallow hard and decide to change the subject. "I'm a little sad I don't have much t-time—" I'm skirting around my feelings for Zach. The end of my break is almost up. In a little over a week, I'll be back in LA. "I'm gonna miss this place. Now I see why you love it so much. I wish I had spent more time listening to you talk about the love you've always felt here. The friends you made. They are all such beautiful people. The pub. Madeline, Clarice and Mark are amazing."

"They're all pretty cool. I'm glad you and Zach are getting along well. I had a feeling you would."

"I don't know what it is about him, he's been cool about everything."

"Uh-huh."

"Hey, there's nothing . . . okay not entirely true. There's something. There are a lot of somethings, but I'm not sure where it will end up. I'm just living in the moment here with him. And it's nice. So very nice. Sarina, I think I might . . ."

I peer at the closed door. I haven't allowed myself to say it out loud. For the first time in a while I feel like I can take a deep breath. Getting that out there in the open feels right.

"Might be falling."

She makes a teasing *ohhhh* sound.

My face flushes. "Sarina," I chuckle.

"I'm happy for you, Pen. It's so nice to hear your laughter. It's okay if you don't know where you're going with it. As long as you're both on the same page."

My heart hammers in my chest. I think we are. We had a conversation just before she called.

"You keep saying this break hasn't changed you, but can you tell me the last time you truly laughed and smiled before him and the new people in your life. I heard it on the phone the other day when you were cooking together. I'm not talking any laugh, but a real one."

In my heart I already knew without a doubt, everything changed the night I snuck into Wingman's.

"The last time I truly felt happy before this was when my first single hit number one. At least I thought it was true happiness. Then I came here. I met Zach and he brought me into his world and allowed me to catch a glimpse of yours."

"See, you're finding a little bit of yourself and discovering new pieces every day."

I smile and it's a good one. The kind that tugs on your cheeks and one that you can feel in your soul. I'll figure out a way to curb the evil thoughts in my head of this not working. It might take me some time to figure out what it's like to be apart from him and this place after I leave, but a sliver of hope peeks through the darkness.

"Thank you for listening, Sarina."

"Of course. Isn't that what sisters are for?"

"I'm making this promise to you now and I need you to help me, and I'll hold myself accountable for it. I want to visit you more; I want to call and be part of your life. You have this whole amazing and beautiful one that I never knew because I was so wrapped up in my career, the media, what people thought of me, but I'm starting here and now I want to mend our relationship."

"It was never broken. We grew apart. It happens. I'll hold myself accountable as well. I could have reached out too. It works both ways."

"Let's do Thanksgiving together. I'll come and help you cook. You can invite your friends."

"Whoa, hold up. You almost burnt down my house making tacos, what makes you think I can trust you with turkey?"

I laugh. "You're right—I'll buy boxed stuffing."

Her beautiful chuckle touches my heart.

"Can I ask you something?" Sarina's voice is hesitant.

"Anything."

She sucks in a deep breath, waits five seconds, and releases. "How is Maddie? She okay?"

There's something there between them. It's not because she asked, it's how she asked. I may not be looking at my sister, but I know her heart and both she and Maddie are hurting and hiding.

"She's hanging in there. I don't know much about her story, but you can tell she's putting up a front. Pain comes in all forms. Sometimes you can see it in someone's eyes, their posture, their voice. It's written all over her heart and soul. I'm not here to preach to you about what you should do, but if you can, maybe reach out. It might make her day."

"Hey, I'm supposed to be the one giving you advice over here."

"You might be older, but that doesn't mean I can't help my big sister figure out her feelings."

Her alarm goes off. "Shit. I gotta go. Please be kind to yourself, Pen. I know you got this."

"Thank you. You do the same. Okay?"

We exchange goodbyes and hang up. For a moment, I sit on the bed with my back against the headboard and my eyes straight ahead. I'm more comfortable here in this space than I've ever been anywhere else. I don't quite know where this is all headed but my sister called when I needed her the most and now, I have to give myself grace. It's something that doesn't come easy, but if I try hard enough, maybe I'll be able to heal.

Chapter 29

PENNY

Two days left. I want to freeze time. After my chat with Sarina my heart felt a little lighter but as the minutes tick away the anxiety slowly returns. What is keeping me going tonight is the crowd. We're opening soon. We got here early, because Zach wanted to go over the list of open mic performers and test out the sound system.

"Hey, Penny."

I turn from my spot at the bar to find Mark and Zach walking over. I was talking to Maddie and the other bartender Pat about tonight's performances.

"What's going on?"

I look from Mark and Zach to Madeline. Mark has something in his hand. Zach walks around him and settles in beside me, placing a hand on the small of my back.

"Is everything okay?" I ask.

Madeline sniffles. I snap my attention in her direction. Her watery smile is startling. Mark opens his hand. He reveals a golden and green tag with my name engraved on it. It's the one everyone in the pub has. As if my emotions hadn't been running high today, they are bubbling back to the surface. No tears fall but the overwhelming urge to let them free is prevalent.

Zach tightens his grip around me, bringing me closer.

"This is for you. We wanted to make sure you had it before we opened. I know you'll be heading back soon, but we wanted you to know that no matter how long you're away, you'll always have a home here at Wingman's," Mark says.

"I don't—" I look to Zach for guidance. His eyes shimmer and he nods.

"I don't know what to say. I—this means . . . you guys, I've cried enough, I can't again." I laugh, full on laugh with tears streaming down my face.

Zach leans over and presses a kiss on my head. He takes the name tag from Mark and faces me. I lift my chin. We never lose sight of each other as he easily pins the tag to my apron.

"There." He clears his throat. "Now it's official."

"Am I allowed to hug all of you or is that against work policy?"

Mark chuckles. "I think we can make an exception."

I go to him first and he wraps his arms around me. I hug Madeline over the bar and nearly spill some drinks in the process. We laugh it off. The atmosphere has shifted. It might have felt like a place I could call home before but now it's filled with something much more meaningful. It's no wonder Sarina gravitated towards these people. I've never had friends who were true to themselves and true to the relationship.

"This means more to me than you all know. Thank you for giving me the opportunity to know what it's like to have friends in your life that are genuine. You can't get rid of me now."

Zach reaches for me once I've given everyone a hug. His arms circle my waist, and I rest my head against his chest. He takes a slow and steady breath. I focus on us and the way his heart thumps. My eyes wander the space and it lands on the stage first. There's a mic and a stool all set front and center. Off to the left side is a karaoke machine. I smile then move my attention to the table Clarice always sits. My heart breaks. I wanted to say goodbye to her.

I lift my head off Zach and find him staring absently in the same direction I was. I squeeze his hand, and he gives me a sad smile. This won't bring Clarice here or fix his feelings, but I hope for a few minutes it will make him happy.

Zach falls in line beside me again. I take his hand.

"I have something for you. Well, it's kind of for all of you."

I wasn't planning on doing this, but with everything going on, I want him to hear this song. It's about him. About this place. A story of how I was able to find some peace in my life again. I got word from Tanner I'll be recording it the day after my return. It's supposed to debut on the radio right before the awards where I'm slated to perform it live for the first time, but I'd much rather this be my first.

I tug on his hand, leading him to the stage. I reach the mic and turn it on, staring into the space which will soon be filled with guests. I imagine everyone having a good time and saving this beautiful place from possible closure.

Maddie and Mark find a table right in front of the stage to sit.

"You have all made me feel like I belong here, and it truly was the first time I've felt at home." I clear my throat when it becomes dry. "I have loved working here and getting to know all of you. I wrote this song recently about this place, and the person who made me see things in a whole new light."

Zach's eyes soften, and a coy smile flickers on his lips.

"You finished it?" he asks.

I've been working on it all week in between spending time with him.

I nod. "And I thought maybe I could share it with all of you first. Is that okay?"

I'm greeted with love and cheers. The lighting in the room is dim but late morning light leaks in from the large, storefront windows.

"This will have to be just me and my voice, I don't have—"

"Penny?" Mark stands.

"Yeah?"

He takes a deep breath. "I have a guitar. I'm going to perform tonight."

We all stop and stare for a moment.

"Really? That's amazing, Mark."

His usually pale cheeks flush. "Thanks. I'm doing a cover of the song Cynthia and I danced to at our wedding."

I smile. "I can't wait to hear it."

He thanks me and then rushes up to his office. A minute later he comes down with a beautiful shimmering, dark blue Taylor acoustic with a shoulder strap. He steps up onto the stage and I take it, placing it over me. It's not Mom's guitar but it works. I tinker with it to make sure it's tuned and when I'm happy with what I hear I lift my gaze.

I go to strum but stop myself. These people know me. The real version. My heart hammers in my chest, as I tug the hat off my head and remove my glasses. Beside me Zach holds out his hands for it. I guess I'm kinda having a Hannah Montana moment. I laugh to myself. Our fingers brush and a zap of electricity flows through me.

"Thanks," I manage to say, although it comes out squeaky.

I've played in front of thousands of people, but other than my family, none have meant so much to me as these folks do. Nerves settle deep in my stomach, but I can't let it stop me from using my whole heart to sing.

Lost in the key of E,
I'm drowning in the depths of a sharp C.
Searching for a hand to save me from the storm.
I've forgotten who I was and who I strived to be.
Who out there can help me be... me.
I throw it all away
Lock up the key for another day.
Let it go and sing endlessly.
I hide from the pain to feel whole.
I search my soul to find my voice again.
It's strong and hidden behind a broken wall.

The music flows through my fingers to each chord. Zach is the only one standing, he's off to my right, but not on the stage. The first verse and chorus he mouthed all the words. Him mouthing some of the words along with me is everything. My heart is full of an energy I've been missing.

Freedom is close enough to feel.
Unlocked yet forbidden to yield.
The golden tides that greet me
are on edge but tug me back from the sharpness of the sea.
Who out there can help me be... me.

I look at the face of each person in the room. In the very back, the chef, Danny, comes out from the kitchen and leans against one of the large wooden columns by the bar. He's illuminated by one of the lights above him and I catch a smile on his face.

I throw it all away
Lock up the key for another day.
Let it go and sing endlessly
I hide from the pain to feel whole.
I search my soul to find my voice again.
It's strong and hidden behind a broken wall.
A ray of sunshine peeks through the clouds.
The warmth guiding me to the sandy shores.
A hand to hold, to save, and to cherish me unlike any other.
A safety net is thrown, as he stands on shore in the vast unknown.
Who out there can help me be... me.

I use the moment to give each of them my heart somehow. Maddie is first, her eyes are filled with tears. I've loved getting to know her and I hope whatever is happening with her and Sarina that they find their happiness. Mark, he's an amazing man with a beautiful family and I never want him to lose this place.

My heart splits in half when my attention falls on Clarice's table. Her not being here all week has hit me hard, but not as much as Zach. He's focused on me, his heart on his sleeve. Maybe one day I can push past my heart's reluctance to start another relationship. I don't know where I'll be after next week, let alone in a month. I know where I want to be, but I don't know if it's possible.

I throw it all away
Lock up the key for another day.
Let it go and sing endlessly
I hide from the pain to feel whole.
I search my soul to find my voice again.
It's strong and hidden behind a broken wall.

I make sure each one of them understands what they mean to me, and then my eyes land solely on Zach and I sing the last two lines of the song.

No longer bound by the chains that hold me down.
A love that was once lost has now been found.

There were moments when I was off-key. The words aren't perfect, the music itself still needs work, but you'd never know it by the round of applause I receive. They stand and head to the stage. Zach stays off to the side, his gaze burning right into me.

"Wow. Penny, your song. It was great. I mean it when I say, you're welcome back any time," Mark says.

I step off the stage and hand Mark his guitar. "Thanks for letting me borrow your girl, she plays so well."

He grins. "She's a keeper alright." He nudges me.

"Penny." Maddie's voice breaks as she wraps her arms around my neck. "You're so incredibly talented. Fuck all those assholes who think otherwise." She backs away, wiping her eyes with a grin.

I chuckle. "Thanks, Mad. Let's hope I can keep that mentality when I go back to California."

Everyone in the world knows about the documentary. It's not a secret and Maddie and the rest of the crew are no different.

"Now, get back to work you slackers. We have a lunch rush to get through before our big night," Mark says.

With only Zach left, holding my things, I close the space between us and get on my tiptoes and press a closed mouth kiss to Zach's lips. He rests his head against mine and closes his eyes for a second before pulling away. I take my hat and glasses, putting them back on. He lets go of my hand and places both of his on my hips.

"You heard the man, get back to work. Slacker," he teases, but his smile falls short.

"You slack all the time. I mean, it was one dish, Zachary. How hard is it to wash?"

"Hey, now. I've been doing better. Even took the laundry out of the wash instead of forgetting the other day." He squeezes my hips in my most ticklish spot.

I hate the way his smile falls seconds later.

"You alright?" I ask.

He releases a trembling breath and shakes his head. I swallow back the lump in my throat.

"We have a few minutes; talk to me," I offer.

He takes my hand and walks me over to the table beside Clarice's usual one. He's watching it as if she'll appear. We stay connected with our arms resting on the surface. I run my thumb over his rough knuckles.

"I miss her," he says, after a long minute. "It's like there's something missing. I need to know more. I have to know why she didn't say anything for so long. She made excuses at our house but in my gut, I know there's more to it. I hate the fact that she's stayed away from her favorite place because of me."

"If you think you're ready for answers, go talk to her. I think hearing each other out will be good for you."

"I can't go now. I have a shift—"

"I got you covered." Mark rests a hand on Zach's shoulder. I didn't even notice him walking over. "Go. We'll be fine for a few hours. Get her here for open mic and karaoke. I know she'll love it."

Zach lifts his watery gaze up at Mark. It's almost like a father/son moment as they lock eyes, and Mark encourages him with a smile.

"You sure?"

"Absolutely."

Zach takes a deep breath. "Okay. Yeah. I'll go."

He looks between us. "Thank you both so much."

He squeezes my hand and gets up. I follow his lead and stand, pushing in the chair. I widen my eyes and give him a smile before he turns and heads for the door. Mark looks at me with a kind, bright-eyed grin. I almost think some of that advice was geared towards Zach and me.

"He'll be okay," he says.

"I know," I whisper.

Mark puts an arm around me. "Let's open those doors. We have quite the day ahead."

Chapter 30

ZACH

I wait in front of the red painted door of Clarice's white brick ranch home. I spent some time here over the years. Nothing has changed. There is a sense of comfort within these walls. The scent of her famous tomato soup and grilled cheese will always be a memory that sits with me.

The door opens and I jump at the sound even though I was expecting it. Her tired, golden eyes meet mine. She's only fifty-one yet she appears so much older today. An image of a young tween me meeting her for the first time comes to mind. My grandmothers scowl that turned into a fake smile. Back then I had no idea what it really meant and now I do. She didn't want Clarice to have anything to do with me. I clench my fists.

"Zach." Her soft wide eyes speak volumes.

"I'm ready to talk. May I come in?"

"Yes. Of course." Her voice breaks a little as she steps aside.

The large window in the front lights up the living room. The wooden floor creaks with every step I take towards the brown couch placed again the far wall. I turn to her, still standing.

"Can I get you a drink?" She lifts her hands, rubbing them together. There's a slight tremble in them.

"No," I whisper. "I'm okay. Thank you."

Her knitting is on the rustic farmhouse coffee table in front of the couch. I absently run my thumb over the knitted clover she gave me on my keychain, trying to calm my anxiety. Emotions are running rampant inside of me. I should never want to speak to her again. How can I even trust someone who can't tell me the truth?

"I'm not okay with what happened." A mixture of anger and sadness fills my voice. "Was I not worthy to tell? Not good enough? Why?"

I can't stand still so I pace in front of the couch.

"Oh god no, Zach. Is that what you think? That you're not good enough?"

I stop moving and squeeze my eyes closed and make a fist at my side.

"My whole life, Grandma thought I wouldn't amount to anything. Hell, even Macy said I'd never please anyone because my career wasn't enough. Out of anyone in my life, *you* were the one who kept me grounded, who was there on my bad days and good. Growing up you made me feel seen and cared about. But then doubt settled in and I was fucked. How can I trust what you have to say?"

"Sorry will never be enough. What I did was wrong in so many ways. And if you'd let me, I'd really like to explain. You don't have to forgive me, but I would like to tell my side if that's alright?"

I take a deep breath and settle onto the couch. Clarice hesitantly takes a seat at the other end.

"I'm not proud of what I've done. Angry with myself for not telling you. I allowed fear to guide me. I thought by that time it was too late. Grandma said you never questioned what happened to your mom, you just accepted it. And that telling you now would only hurt you. It was best to leave it. And I listened."

"That's a lie," I scoff. "I asked about you all the time. She would always tell me that my mom gave me up to live her own life. You were just one of her friends and that was it. I'm not sure I was better off with her. I'm thankful she kept a roof over my head and kept me well-fed and healthy physically, but I lost out on so much because she never let me do anything. By junior high, I was forging signatures for field trips and sneaking money out of her purse so I could go."

She inhales deeply and exhales shakily. "You're not the only one she did that to. I should have known better, and my age is no excuse. Maybe I should have given you up for full adoption, but she didn't believe in any of that. I'm glad I didn't because I never would have gotten to know you, but I know I messed up and wish I had the courage to tell you who I was."

"Why didn't you come back after college?"

She shifts in her spot and hugs herself. "I was not in a good place. When she sent me away, I rebelled. I spent time with the wrong kids. I ended up in a car accident while a friend drove drunk, and everyone miraculously survived but we were all pretty banged up. I turned my grades around, yeah, but it never felt like enough. I guess like mother like son, huh?"

"And then what?"

I want to know more. I'm starting to grow numb. Unsure of how to react. So, I just listen.

"She said to come back into your life, I needed to have a steady job. So, I went to college. Medical school. I became a nurse. Then she said that I need to prove that it wasn't a phase. I continued to work, and it was easy because she had you, so I didn't have to worry about childcare. Once I was stable, I met a guy who worked with me. The relationship was fast. From meeting to moving in to marrying him. She was not happy, but I thought now I'll be stable to go and be with my son, but he cheated on me. So, we got a divorce. I spiraled into a deep dark depression. It was only then your grandma suggested I could come home. That to you I'd only be her friend and nothing more. Maybe seeing you would fix me somehow."

"And you just let her do that."

She shrugs. "She was my mom, and I gave into the pressure of being perfect for her. She threatened not to let me see you at all. You know how she was. She sweet talked everyone. I had you in my life so that's all I really needed, right? Time passed and it became harder, but you were older, and I felt like the consequences of telling you were worse than not. When she died it didn't feel like the right time either. I'm not proud of myself. I just want to make things right. If we never fully get there, I understand if you want to cut all ties with me."

I grip the soft edges of the couch with both hands and let myself absorb everything she's said. We are alike in so many ways. Holding things back when we should say them out loud. Allowing the voices of others to make us feel like we're not enough. It's going to take so much time for me to feel like I can trust her again, but I hate missing her too.

My leg shakes. I look at her as I think of what to say next.

"That's the thing, Clarice, as angry as I am I don't think I want to cut ties. You were there for me in these subtle ways. I always saw you, always felt this odd connection. I'm pissed at you for hiding it. I don't know how we can get past this but everything inside of me is screaming for me to try. Over the last few days, I could feel your absence in my life, and I hated it. It was like something wasn't right."

She peers up at me with a watery smile. "I know things will never be the same and it will take some time, but I hope we can both learn from this experience. I will do whatever you need for you to process this. We can talk to a professional. I—I don't know else we can do. I think about the what ifs. What would have happened if I passed away and never got to tell you my peace. I mean, you'd never know but how is that fair? Everyone struggles to express their feelings in one way or another. We think our words don't matter or are afraid to be judged or for things to change, but we never know what tomorrow will bring. Zachary, if there is someone in your life you need to say something to, don't wait. They could reject it, could never talk to you again, but what if it turned into the best thing in your life."

I hold my breath for a few seconds and wait until I can't any longer before I exhale. Penelope's face is the first thing on my mind. *What if it turned into the best thing in your life?*

"I can stay away from Wingman's—"

"Please don't do that," I say, almost too loud. "There are people there that would miss you, like Maddie and Mark. I know they've felt your absence too. Even Penny." On her name, my voice cracks. "Tonight is her last night."

I stare down at my nails and pick at them.

"She's going back home? What about the two of you?"

I shrug.

"Zach, if you feel something, you should tell her. Lying to yourself and the person you love will only get you in trouble. I'm the prime example of that." Her tone wavers and I shoot my gaze to her.

"Maddie said the same thing."

Tears are streaming down her cheeks. She's trying to wipe them away, but they are coming faster than she's able to.

"I never told your father I loved him. We planned to run away together. We had it all worked out, as good as two fifteen-year-old kids can plan it. He snuck into my window around two in the morning. Our parents caught wind, and it was not pretty. When they dragged him away, he kept telling me over and over that he loved me, and I loved him back a million times over, but my words failed me. It still haunts me to this day, maybe if I had said it, he could have found me, and we would have been a happy family. I'll never know. What are you afraid of?"

My body tenses.

"We both need to learn to trust ourselves enough to love someone else. You're a good man, Zach. I don't care what anyone else says. I've watched you with her and I've never once noticed her looking at you as if you weren't enough for her. Her eyes sparkle every time you're around. That woman loves you. If you told her how you felt, I think you'd be pleasantly surprised."

"You have so much faith."

"It's not easy, but you're here still talking to me. I have to believe in it a little."

"It's going to take me some time to come to terms with it all. I'm not going to say I forgive you, but your presence in my life was missed and I have to believe it means I have the strength to forgive, but I'm not there yet."

She goes to reach out but places her hands in her lap.

"Understandable. I deserve the anger. I'm glad you came to talk to me. I love you and if you need time I'll be here when you're ready."

"I love you too, Mom." The words come out easily and my heart lightens despite the tug of anger trying to take over. "Don't let this stop you from coming to the pub. You belong there as much as anyone else. You should come tonight. Say goodbye to Penny."

My eyes itch with the threat of tears, but I blink them away.

"Are you sure it will be a goodbye?"

I shrug. "For now, it is."

We talk for only a few minutes longer; she tells me to hold onto the locket until the dust settles. I get to my car and don't turn it on. I stare at her front door waiting. A warmth spreads over me. This was more of a loving home than my grandma's house. Over time I think I'll be able to forgive.

She steps out and turns to lock the door. I can't help the smile that overcomes me. She was getting ready when I stepped out, but I waited just in case. She's coming for a late lunch but taking her own car. Clarice turns to wave, and I return the gesture before pulling away from the curb and heading to the club.

When I pull into my parking spot at the pub only one thing comes to mind.

What if it turned into the best thing in your life?

Chapter 31

PENNY

I can't stop looking at the door.

Our lunch rush hasn't subsided and while it's been a bit overwhelming, Mark has been helping us make sure all the tables are taken care of. It's been good though, because with the uptick in customers I pray it's enough to help Mark. If it's not, I may have to use my resources. This place means way too much to so many.

My heart is here but it's also out there wherever Zach and Clarice are. Since knowing Zach, I've never seen him crumble until this week.

I'm at the bar, waiting for Maddie to fill up a drink for me.

"They'll be okay, right?" I ask.

A soft smile fills her features. There's confidence behind it. She lifts her attention to me.

"It will take time, but I think they will be. It's a lot to process. I'm sure it's not going to be easy."

"You're right." I blow out a breath.

I check the door again. It opens and my heart skips a beat, only to find it's neither of them. I lower my head as Maddie slides over the glass filled with our signature whiskey drink. I'm about to grab it and walk away when I peer at her wrist. Around it is a black bracelet with a silver circle that looks like a knotted rope. I take note of the change in Maddie. Her smile doesn't fade, and she's got this glow about her.

"That's a really beautiful charm bracelet you've got there."

She looks at it for a few long seconds, before lifting to face me. "Your sister sent it. I got it in the mail yesterday."

Maddie's cheeks flush. I knew something was up between them. I open my mouth when a breeze from the door floats through the room. My heart leaps into my throat. It's Zach. I hold my breath, waiting to see if she's with him or any sign that she's coming later. It appears as if he's about to shut the door but then he holds it and Clarice steps through the threshold.

I place my hand on my chest, feeling the emotions build. Zach gives her a smile before his eyes meet mine. He touches Clarice's arm, and she looks over to see me and Maddie. I bite my lower lip to keep it from trembling. Seeing them together and okay is more than I could have ever wanted for my last night here.

They start to head this way, and I put the drink down, going to them. Clarice holds her arms out for me. I step into her embrace, and I'm filled with warmth so loving I don't ever want to leave it. I hold on tight, her laughter comforting me.

"You're here," I say, voice wavering.

"I am. Couldn't miss your last night here, dear."

She rubs my back for a few seconds, my emotions getting the best of me. Her warmth captures me. It's motherly. Something I haven't felt in so long. I sniffle and step out of her arms.

"I'm so happy you came. I'm going to miss you so much."

She sighs and places a hand on my cheek. "You got your clover?"

I nod, unable to speak. "Then darling, you've got nothing to worry about. You'll find your way back to where you belong."

She steps away and turns to Zach. "I'm starved. Wanna get me one of those sammies?"

Zach has been watching our interaction with love in his eyes. There's a bit of sadness in his downturned lips, but it's to be expected with what he's just been through.

"You bet. And look at that. Your table just became available."

"Perfect. I'm ready to get my KAR-A-OKE on," she says, walking away happily.

I wrap my arms around Zach. He grunts from the impact, and I love his deep laughter.

"Whoa there."

"You're good?"

He holds me at arm's length and breaths deep. "I think we will be."

My smile tugs on my cheeks. "Good. Shit. I have a drink to deliver."

❈ ❈ ❈

Tonight has been one of the best nights I've had since I've been here. I'm sad I'm leaving, but this place is packed. The entire staff is on.

Mark played his song, and his wife showed up. It was such a beautiful moment between them. I didn't even know he could sing, but that man has some pipes on him. Clarice signed up for karaoke and sang to "Sweet Caroline". She had the entire place shouting out the "bum bum bum". My heart is the fullest it's been in quite some time. I want to stay, but I can't.

Can I?

I'll figure it out when I get to L.A. because I need this.

I'm leaning against the jukebox, watching two best friends belt out the chorus to a One Direction song, the first song I heard Zach sing.

"Hey, love."

I'm swept up into him from behind. He wraps his arms around my front and holds on tight. We turn to the stage. I rest my head back up against his chest and he lowers himself, so his cheek is against mine. I breathe him all in. He has me questioning everything and contemplating how I can have a life that includes him in it.

I turn in his arms to face him and look up. He peers at me with his adoring, shimmering eyes. I reach up for him and wrap my hand around the back of his head so I can pull him closer. I brush my lips against his and he hums.

"Zach?"

"Yeah?" He nuzzles his face into my neck.

The rowdy guests disappear to the back of my mind and it's only him and I.

"Do you still want me?"

"Here?" He pulls back with a Cheshire grin on his face.

I chuckle and push at his chest. "No, you ass, not here. Tonight?"

His eyes never leave mine. "Nothing has changed. I still do, but you—"

"I want it. More than anything. I was just afraid because we're not ..."

He lifts my chin with his index finger so I'm looking into his golden-brown gaze.

"Fuck what we're not. I'm living in the now because I know without a doubt, I want to experience this with you. Does anyone ever know where the future will take them? We can only be led with blind faith; it all falls into place. I know I want you. To get to know you better, to spend more time with you. I also would like to fuck you, but I want to show you what it's like to have a real man worship every part of you."

I giggle, then lower my own voice. "So cocky."

"You want cocky, then let me rock your world, love."

I shake my head. "Such a cheesy line, but I love it. Should we be talking about this at work?"

His laughter is finally full again and there's a spark of something intense in his eyes.

"No, probably not. I don't know how I'm gonna get through the rest of my shift with this hard on."

I snort, pulling away slowly. "And it's moments like this I'm thankful I'm a lady."

His attention falls to the name tag and mine follows. I stare back up at him.

"I'll leave this in my room when I go," I say, reaching up to grab it.

"Why?"

Our eyes meet and my heart does a double beat.

"So, I know when I come back it will be there waiting for me." I lift on my toes and place a gentle kiss on his lips before walking away to finish my last shift.

Chapter 32

ZACH

The car ride was filled with easy conversation and singing along with the radio until one of her songs came on. She still smiled through, but unlike last time she was tense. The days are winding down and the urge to tell her the three words I feel are strong, but I have to wait for the right moment. She's feeling it, too. I can see it in her sad, confused eyes when she looks at me.

We could have jumped on each other the moment we got home, like they do in books and movies. The tension was there through gentle touches and a few pleasurable ones, but something else hung in the air between us.

When we get back, she says she's going to check on Larry's food and water and I make the excuse that I need to pack. We leave on Monday, and I haven't started yet. Something in my gut has prevented me from doing more.

I pass by her room, about to head downstairs and peek in. She's standing, facing the window with her back to me. Her suitcase sits open and empty on the floor beside her. She's so still. Above us, rain falls heavily onto the roof. It started the moment we got home. The wind outside causes the old house to creak and moan a bit. Some tree limbs hit the window, but it's hard to see in the pitch-black night sky.

Larry runs by me. He makes his little burr sound and jumps into the open suitcase. Her laughter is sad as she kneels and pets him.

"Hey, there, buddy. I can't take you with me," she says, her voice breaking. He headbutts her hand and meows. "I'm gonna miss you, too. You, Petunia, Zach . . ."

Larry makes a low meow-growl, and I smile.

"Oh, hush, Larry. I know you've come to like him."

He burrs again and she chuckles with a sniffle. I want to step inside but stop myself.

"I like him," she whispers. "A lot."

Larry releases a long meow, like he's trying to be part of the conversation.

"Fine, it's more...I've fallen for him."

My heart stops for a second before pounding so hard I feel it against my chest. I've fallen for you too; I want to say out loud. I'd move forward if I could but it's like I'm stuck. I love you is on my tongue, but I can't.

Larry gives her a short meow, then makes himself at home in the suitcase. Her laughter once again is filled with so much sadness.

"I'll come visit—I promise. You have Sarina."

The cat is quiet, but still purring loudly as she pets him. "I miss her most of all. I made a promise that this time would be different.

She's the only family I have left. I need to show her how much I care by being in her life more often than not. I backed away after Mom and Dad died. I can't lose my way again. I have to be stronger this time, Larry. If I surround myself with people who care, maybe I can truly be happy."

What she's confessed to the cat is personal. I retreat downstairs. It was wrong of me to listen. I don't know what I'm looking for when I enter the kitchen. My mind is one big mess. Between her leaving and Clarice dropping this huge bomb, I'm lost. I've always been a little lost in life, trying to find my way. I've been able to, though. Living in my car was never ideal, but Sarina gave me a roof over my head and became a friend I didn't know I needed. Despite Long Island being huge, our town is small enough to where our friends were within the same circle. It led me to Penelope. I don't regret falling in love with her.

"There you are."

Her voice comes out of nowhere, startling me. I drop the plastic cup and it falls to the floor. I don't have a chance to whirl around or pick it up. She's already so close and wrapping her arms around me. My breath catches in my throat as she rests her cheek against my back. Her warmth is all I need now. I turn and she steps back enough for me to grab her waist. I lift her and set her on the counter and stand between her parted legs.

She's wearing one of the black t-shirts with the Wingman's logo I gave her one night after we fooled around. My eyes roam every inch of her in it.

"God damn, you look so fucking sexy in my shirt."

Her cheeks flush and she stares down where my hands find her thighs.

She bites her lower lip and casually looks up at me.

"What's the matter?" I ask in a low growl.

She trembles as I run my fingers all the way up to find she's wearing nothing underneath. I'm rock hard in seconds. Her lips part as she gasps.

"I love when you touch me. Please don't stop."

Lust and love mix in her eyes. I lift the hem of the shirt so I can take in the full view. This woman. Not only does she get my heart rate up, but I also can't be around her without being turned on. She's everything I've ever wanted in someone. Sweet, beautiful, sexy, caring. I see a future with her despite our lives about to go in separate directions. Tonight, I'm going to show her what she means to me, not to force her to stay, but to show her what she'll have waiting for if she ever decides to return.

A thought crosses my mind: if she asked me to go, would I? Leave this life for her? My friends. My family.

Yeah.

The realization stuns me, and I freeze for a moment.

"Penny, while I'd love to have my way with you on this counter, along with so many other places, and fuck you until you're scream-ing my name for all to hear—tonight I want you in my bed."

My reasoning becomes clear to her the second the words leave my mouth. Everything we have done over the last few weeks has been in the bed she was borrowing for a visit. Tonight, I'm inviting her into mine.

We lock eyes and in her soft gaze, I know she feels it too.

"Then take me to your bed, Zach. Please."

I take her into my arms. She wraps her legs around my waist. She's easy to carry up the stairs, even if I trip at the top step. Her laughter settles the growing ache in my heart. I make the turn to my room and allow her in.

Despite no one else being here, I shut the door to close out all the outside noise, although when I'm with her she shuts all of it off like a switch. I put her against the door and press my lips to hers. I love the warmth of her bare lower half against me. I never want to stop kissing her. I'm not much of a make out kind of guy—I like to get right to the action—but with her, I could do it for the rest of our existence and be perfectly fine. With her everything is different. She allowed me to watch her explore and get off while I let her watch me. It's something I've never done before either. I love finding new ways to give her pleasure.

"Zach?"

"Yeah?" I whisper between kisses.

"I want your mouth and hands on me tonight, no toys."

A low, deep growl comes from my chest as I carry her to my bed. I lay her as gently as I can. I've never exactly carried a woman into my bed. In fact, no one has ever been in it.

"Thirteen. You have thirteen toys."

She smirks.

"Aha! Got it! You little tease, making me think you had more."

She giggles and moves so her head is on my pillow.

"Leave the shirt on, but lift it a little, so I can get to where I need."

I massage her thighs. My fingers are aching to touch and please her. She props herself up on her elbows and she's so fucking hot in my shirt that I want her like this all the time for me.

"Zach," she whispers and takes a deep breath. "Taste me. I want you to be the first and . . . only." The last word is released on a whisper.

Only.

"Are you sure?" My voice cracks.

I don't want to pressure her into anything. I'll do what she asks, but I need to make sure first.

"Yes." She pauses to take a breath but doesn't look away. "I trust you."

My heart races. Her confession is huge, and I never want to break her belief in me. I keep my eyes on her as I lower my mouth and roll up the shirt. Her glistening center comes into my view.

"I'm going to show you how it can feel when it's done right."

"You're so sure of yourself, aren't you, sunshine?"

I wink and press my mouth to her clit. Immediately, she arches up and her eyelids flutter. She tosses her head back. I tighten my grip on her legs and tease her swollen pussy. She writhes and moans under the pressure. I swirl my tongue around her opening and she gasps. Her hooded turned-on gaze is everything.

"Zach. More. Keep going."

I slip inside and her feral cries make it all worth it. She grabs the comforter, bunching it in her fists. She tastes so fucking good, I need to come along with her, but I want her to experience this first.

"You are so good at that," she sighs.

My mouth stays firmly on her clit. I run my fingers along her swollen lips, then carefully push one inside of her. Her hooded gaze is hungry while she watches what I'm doing to her.

"Oh!" Her moans are music to my ears.

I find the spot that makes her clench around me.

"Keep going, Zach. Please—oh, fuck."

I add a second finger. Her moan nearly takes me out.

"You taste so good, love."

She's close. Her thighs squeeze together. She bucks her hips and calls out my name. She tightens around my fingers and comes undone. Her eyes don't shut, instead remaining on me, as mine stay on her.

"Are you ready, Pen?"

"But you . . ."

I shake my head. "I want in."

"Okay, but next time we start with you," she says.

I've never once understood when people said their heart did flips over someone or it gave them butterflies. I thought it was always made up, but they are more real than anything I've ever felt before. What does it for me is how she doesn't look away when she says *next time*, letting me know there's a possibility we're not over.

I hesitate to get up and grab the condoms but do because I can't stand another minute without being inside of her. I throw it at her, and she chuckles, lifting one of her legs up and staring at me with eyes ready to devour.

She places the condom on the gray comforter and gets on her knees. With a crook of her index finger, I walk forward.

"You still have your clothes on. We should do something about it."

She teases the hem of my white shirt. She kneels before me on my bed in only my t-shirt. My cock grows harder against the fabric of my gray sweats. What she's yet to discover is I'm not wearing boxers. Her fingers dance along my stomach. She bites her lower lip, and I lean forward to kiss her. She continues to fidget with my tee and shifts rubbing her thighs together.

"What's the matter?" I whisper low and deep.

She grabs my hand and moves it so I'm cupping her fully. I can't love this woman any more than I do now. I'm at max capacity. She's dripping for me.

"So impatient."

She reaches back, keeping her sights set on me, like I'm the prize she wants to win. She grabs the condom and tugs at the waist of my sweats. They fall to my feet, and I try to get out of them without fumbling.

Score! Got it.

She giggles like she knows I'm celebrating the victory in my head.

With a sexy confidence, she keeps her focus on me while sliding the condom on. Her breathing has become faster and mine follows suit. I push gently at her chest, and she leans back until she's laying down staring up at me. Her legs open for me. I crawl onto the bed, pushing them apart to kneel between. I've never wanted to use the term make love and fuck at the same time, but I want to do it all with her.

I tease her a little at her entrance with the tip before slowly filling her. She's tighter than I imagined and so fucking perfect. She's slick already and her walls tighten around me. Her mouth falls open. Her soft whimpers do me in. She lifts her hips, and I lower my body to get closer. I go in for a kiss, but she turns to suck on my neck. The sensation ripples through my body, making me pulse inside of her. I sit up a little and she grabs my hands and places them under the shirt and over her breasts. They fit so perfectly in my grasp. She once again pushes her hips up and into me. I let go and put both hands on either side of her, lower myself again and this time score her lips. We kiss and meet each other thrust for thrust.

I lift only slightly so I can watch her. I want to look at her while she squeezes me so tight. I groan, trying my hardest not to come to a climax yet.

"What are you thinking?" she asks.

"How I'll never be able to get the way you look in my t-shirt while underneath me moaning my name out of my head."

A blush crawls up her neck and covers her cheeks. The ends of her lips tug up into a sexy sweet smile and I press a kiss to her mouth before she can say anything more. And then, I lose myself in her.

Chapter 33

PENNY

I've never been with someone who wants to take his time with me. Who gives me everything I'm dying to feel and more. He's the perfect size and the movement is like a gentle massage. My heart and emotions can't keep up with each other. One moment I want to cry then next I'm so turned on and grow wetter by the minute. He watches me in awe as he gently rocks back and forth. Occasionally, he'll push harder. I've come close to the edge so many times, but I'm holding back. I want to experience the moment together.

I push on his chest. I want in on the action too and to make him feel good.

"What's the matter?" he asks.

"Trust me?"

"Yeah," he says without any sense of hesitation.

I've never had any sort of control in this part of a relationship. It was always what he wanted or helping him get there. Never about me, but even though I'm about to turn the tables and make him feel good, I'm still going to enjoy doing it.

"Get on your back," I say, half demanding but a little sweet.

He grins and pulls out. There's a slight resistance, but I quickly remedy it for him as I straddle his legs and turn my back to him.

"Pen," he groans.

I start moving, grinding slowly at first. I've seen this done before but have never tried it. I'm human and I've done some incognito searches on my phone. He puts his hands on my hips and squeezes. Normally this would tickle but right now the deep pressure of his fingers digging into my skin is turning me on and making me shudder with an impending release.

He's able to sit up and his lips trail down my back. He kisses up and down my spine while I pleasure myself, not only by grinding but touching my own body in ways I know will help me.

"What are you doing with that hand?"

"Thinking about how good you feel inside me."

"I love watching you give yourself pleasure while getting off on me," he says.

I glance over my shoulder at him and smile. In his eyes there's a bit of a haze filled with emotions. One I've never seen in a man before directed towards me. It hurts to keep my neck like this but I'm so close.

"Zach. I'm coming."

My stomach muscles tighten as the pressure builds. Playing with my clit while rocking on his cock intensifies my pending orgasm.

"Let it go, Pen. I want to feel you orgasm on me."

I'm tight around him as I cry out. I feel myself grow wetter with each ripple through me. I tremble as the release rocks my whole body. He holds my hips to steady me as I come down from the high.

I slide off him and face him. He gets on his knees and twirls around his index finger with the most intriguing devilish smile. I know exactly what he's asking. I get on all fours. He runs his hand up and down my back before giving my ass a slight tap. I groan.

He's back inside of me in seconds and presses kisses up and down my spine. After a minute he reaches his hand around to give me some extra attention. His hand is so much better than mine. His fingers are thicker, enough so he's able to cover more of me. The tightening happens so fast I've already almost reached my climax again.

"Don't stop, Zach. It feels so good."

I tilt my head back and grip the comforter.

"More, please. Oh, God, Zach. I'm coming again."

"I could keep going like this all night, love," he groans.

"Keep calling me that," I say.

He chuckles and the sound alone does me in. I yell out for him again.

"I'm gonna need you on your back, love. I need those lips on mine."

I moan at the name. I don't know why I ever told him no nicknames, but it slowly became something I loved hearing. I move quickly so our connection is only apart for seconds. This is it. The moment he is back inside of me I know I'll be a changed woman after this. No one will ever come close to giving me the same sensations he has.

"You gonna kiss me or not, sunshine?" I tease.

It's his turn to moan, but it's silenced quickly as he kisses me again. His mouth is warm and inviting. His whole presence is. He slows his pace, and we enjoy each other with minimal movements. His hand cups my cheek and I wrap my arms around his neck and play with his hair.

We remain like this for several minutes, kissing each other while he slowly moves in and almost out. It's a slow build up and with each push inside I grow further needy for the big finish. I don't want it to end but I want to know what it's like. I've fantasized about it since the first time we watched each other climax.

I hate not knowing if we can make this work. I have to make sure I can curb the fear of being far away before I can commit. I've been trying to keep my feelings at bay.

He buries his face into my neck and kisses me there. The sensation drives me wild and vibrates through my whole body. I squeeze him and my name leaves his lips again in a desperate moan.

Aside from the heavy rain drops battering the roof, I'm at peace and the rest of the noise is all drowned out. In his space, in his arms, is the only place that makes it all go away. There's no denying that I've fallen irrevocably in love with this man.

"I'm so close, Pen. I want you to look at me when we climax, alright? Just look at me. It's only us . . ."

His entire body tenses above me. The haze in his eyes turns misty and I feel everything and nothing all at once. There's a future with him but not now. I have to let go for a bit, because I need to see how I'll feel when we're apart for so long. I don't want to be the girlfriend who is checking in because she's paranoid. I need to learn to trust before I dive into the deep end. I'm scared. What if he can't wait? What if all of this will be a distant memory some day?

"Pen," he cries out for me and I for him as we both come undone.

He's quiet, but the first thing he does after is kiss me. It's passionate but it's not gentle either. It's somewhere in between. I reach behind his neck and run my hand through his wavy hair. My name is whispered against our lips, and then I'm not sure if I hear him right, but I swear he whispers, "I love you, Pen."

I stiffen and he pulls away, eyes wide, cheeks flushed. As we finally come down from the emotional high, he stops and pulls out. He gets up but only for a second to use some paper towels on his desk and tosses the condom into his wastebasket across the room. He comes back and relaxes beside me.

"Come here," he says.

A lump forms in my throat as he pulls me against him. I rest my head on his chest. I try to hide the tears, but they fall anyway. He can't see because I'm not facing him. He interlocks our hands together. I'm grateful there aren't many that fall, it's short lived.

I love you.

Did I imagine it?

He's supposed to come to L.A. with me, but what if it was a goodbye? I listen to his breathing and there are moments where I swear it sounds as if he's upset, but I can't bear to look. His soft touch on my arms warms me, yet my body still shivers from the touch.

"You're the only one." He rubs my hand with his thumb.

"Only one?"

My brain is scrambling for what he's talking about.

"That I've had in my bed."

I lift my head and adjust so I'm facing him. There's not any hint of a lie on his face. He doesn't look away from my curious stare.

"What about . . ."

"We always went to her place. Mine was never"—he huffs—"never good enough. It's only been you." He pauses and waits, but I'm not sure how to respond. "You don't have to say anything. I don't know why it matters. I—"

I kiss him and rest my head back on his chest. I go over what he confessed to me. He's had women but never in his bed. Only me. He's making it so much harder to walk away. I almost despise him for it but can't find it in me.

"Penny?"

"Yeah?"

"Will you be my opening act in our last—in our shower concert?"

I swallow hard before my response. I lift from my position so I can see him. He's smiling but the light doesn't reach his eyes.

"So, you're the main act now."

He chuckles. "Always have been. It's my shower."

I laugh. "Has anyone ever told you that you're cocky?"

"Some would say I have a big head."

I snort and shake my head. "I'll be your opening act if I can—"

He doesn't let me finish, instead he tickles me, then stands and lifts me up off the bed to carry me to the shower, our laughter trailing along with us all the way there.

Chapter 34

ZACH

As I go through the motions of making our last dinner together in this house, I can't help the nerves nestling inside me. She's been out with Maddie for the past three hours; said she had last minute shopping to do and wanted to have some time with her. Penny spending time with one of my friends makes what I'm about to say to her so much more real.

I said the words, but maybe she didn't hear them or she's not ready. I can't think of the other option.

I've decided to be funny and make dino nuggets with French fries that are smiley faces. For dessert we'll devour the last two strawberry eclairs. Clarice's words hang in my head, and I need to let her know how I truly feel. I don't know if things will change between us and I know we still have another week together before the awards, but if I don't get it out now I might never.

My heart jumps at the front door opening.

"Honey, I'm home," she calls, and I snort-laugh.

"In the kitchen," I say, the words flowing out as if this was our reality.

I take a deep breath. She once told me I was good enough and I'm choosing this moment to believe I am. I keep replaying last night in my head. How good it felt to be inside of her. Sex with Penny has made me understand the term making love. I always laughed it off, thinking it was something written by women in romance books.

The oven beeps and I take out the nuggets, placing them on the stove top along with the fries.

"Hey there, sunshine." Her voice is brimming with lust.

I whirl around dropping the oven mitt on the floor in the process. My jaw goes slack at the sight of her leaning against the wall, hair a little wild from the windy day. Her tight black jeans show off every curve I love to devour. What has me almost bursting a load in my pants, is her see through black and white striped blouse, with a matching lacy bra underneath. I try to speak but nothing comes out.

She pads across the kitchen, barefoot and so sexy. She gets up on her toes and wraps her arms around me. I lower my head and sigh into her neck. My lips are grazing her skin. She groans and slowly tilts her head back to make it easier.

"What are you doing to me, love?"

I pull back in time to see a sly grin forming on her lips.

She gasps. "Oh, dino nugs!"

She unwraps herself from me and steps to my right to reach for the pan. It takes me a second before I say, "It's hot!"

She hisses at the contact and pulls back.

"Penelope." I shake my head, and she whips her attention to me while releasing a *fuck* under her breath. "Again? Really?"

"Ow," she chuckles and whines at the same time.

I laugh. "Come on you. Under the faucet."

I bring her to the sink and stand behind her, while turning on the faucet and help her to put her hand under the stream of water. She breathes in deep and leans into me.

"You made dino nugs," she says, her voice breaking.

I run my fingers just below where she grabbed the nugget.

"I did," I say with an amused tone. "And for dessert we're having—"

"Eclairs? You'll share with me?"

"Always, Pen. Always," I say, kissing her neck, while continuing to run her hand under the water.

After a few minutes I shut the water and help her to dry her hand. I peek and it's only a little red. She probably just barely touched the nugget, not the pan. I want more than anything to have her, this time right here in the kitchen, but her growling stomach interrupts, so I suggest we eat instead.

She animatedly tells me all about her shopping adventure with Maddie. Her disguise seemed to have worked. No one bothered her or stared too long. I love the way her face lights up when she says it was the first time she had done that and wasn't bombarded by press wanting to know every detail about what she's buying.

We clean up together and then snuggle on the couch in the den despite knowing Sarina wouldn't be too happy with us eating ice cream there. Our flight leaves early, so it's nearing bedtime.

She sits up after an episode of some home makeovers show we were watching is over.

"I have something for you," she says at the same time I say, "I need to tell you something."

We laugh.

"You go first."

"You go"—she pauses and grins—"Okay, fine." She rolls her eyes and gets up from her spot, heading towards the main room.

The closet in the main room where Sarina keeps some extra jackets and sweaters opens and closes. Larry comes in trotting beside her. In her hand is a tan garment bag. She holds it out to me.

I narrow my brows at her. "What's that?" I ask, starting to tense up, but full well having a good guess of what it is. I already had one and it fit fine.

"Open it. Please." She tilts her head, one side of her lip quirking up.

I turn from her hopeful stare. I can't let her get wind of my emotions. It's not her fault, it's my own, but I can't stop it. I get to my feet and walk across to where she's still standing a few inches from the entry way. She holds it out with sparkling excitement in her eyes. I grab it, keeping my eyes on the floor. I unzip it to find a brand-new tuxedo. I swear I hear the blood pumping in my ears.

"Penny," I start to say.

"Look, I know you had one, but I wanted to because I—" She pauses. Her eyes are glimmering with hope. "Look, I even got a tie to match my golden—"

"Penny, stop." I close my eyes to try and talk myself down. I heard what she said but I can't register it over the loud thoughts.

"Zach?" Her voice goes high. "What's wrong?"

If I open my eyes, I know I'll see the disappointment on her face. I don't want to hurt her, but I can't accept this. Groceries were one thing, but this is a whole other ball game. I've tried not to let it bother me, but it does and maybe that means I'm not ready for whatever is happening between us.

My hand touches what I think is the price tag. My jaw drops at the additional zero. It's well into the thousands range. My stomach churns.

"Christ, Penny, I can't take this." I push it towards her. "Almost five thousand? I can't. You need to take it back."

Her face scrunches as if she's in pain. "Wha—why? I don't understand."

"You can't buy me shit like this!"

"Why the hell not?" She fights back, clutching the bag to her.

Her forehead wrinkles and her lips start to quiver.

"Because!" I pause and try to breathe. I don't want to fight with her. It's the last thing I want to do. I'm supposed to be over here confessing my love to her, but now I'm caught up in this and it's ruined.

"Zach," she hisses.

I throw my hands down at my side. "Because I'll never have enough money to keep you happy. To buy you four thousand-dollar dresses and jewelry. To be the man you need me to be."

Her face turns red as she holds the bag tighter. I hate how upset I'm making her but what I have to say has been festering like hot lava with nowhere to go but up and out.

"And I want to be." My voice hitches. "I want to do those things for you, Pen. I'd buy you the world if I could, but I can't. I won't ever be able to give you the life you deserve."

"Have you not been paying attention this entire time? I thought you understood and knew me, but I'm beginning to think maybe

I was imagining it all." Her voice shakes and brows furrow. Her watery gaze hits me dead on.

She twitches her nose and sniffles. I wish I could take it all back. I want Macy's words to vanish from my head. It didn't help that growing up I had a grandmother who never believed in me. Tack on the betrayal I'm still working through with Clarice, despite our conversation. It's all so much and I know I shouldn't be putting it all on Penny.

She's trying to hold back tears, but a small sob breaks free and lets them lose. "Have I ever said I need someone with money to make me happy? If I have, please tell me when because I'd really like to know. Is this because I bought groceries every week and replenished your ice cream? If so, that's the most ridiculous reason I've ever heard."

She pauses. "Is it, is it because of that woman? The one you told me about? Your ex?"

I suck in a breath, realizing I've fucked up. She's been open and honest with me and it's my turn to return the favor.

"Yeah. My ex left me the day I was going to propose. I saved up for the ring; it took me a long time to do. When I went to her, she'd already found someone else. A doctor. And do you want to know what she said to me?" I don't let her answer. "She told me, I'd never be able to find a woman and make her happy because my job wasn't good enough. That kind of shit sticks with you. So, when you came here and turned my world upside down, those insecurities reared their ugly head. What would a sweet, beautiful and sexy famous musician want with a regular old guy like me? I'm renting a room after living in my car and working at a job I love despite the pay. There's no way I could make the woman I've fallen in love with happy."

Penny gasps, her glimmering eyes widening. A soft murmur falls from her lips. "What? What di–did . . . Z-Zach?" She's frozen in place.

I back track in my mind until I realize what I've said. My heart hammers in my chest as I try to read her facial expression. She heard me loud and clear this time. Penny takes a step back and gives me a once over. She presses her lips together and when she goes to open them my phone goes off. I check behind me on the table and notice the pub's number on the screen. I let it go to voicemail. It dings with the notification of one, followed by a text. Her phone is next to go off. It vibrates beside mine while it rings. Neither of us move. I stare at her. We're lost in a contest of who is going to speak first. I blink as if to clear the mush my brain has turned into.

"Zach—"

My phone rings again.

"Who keeps calling?" she finally asks.

"Uh—" My eyes narrow as I walk over. "It's the pub."

My gut tells me to answer.

"Hello?"

"Zach?" It's Maddie and she's sniffling. "It's—it's, Clarice."

My knees grow weak, and I feel for the couch, my vision a little gray. As I sink down onto it, I feel Penny's touch.

"Mads? What's wrong?" My heart sinks.

"We h-had to call an ambulance. She wasn't feeling well and almost passed out. She didn't look good, Zach."

I clutch my chest and grip onto my T-shirt. Please let her be okay.

"Fuck. Okay. Tell me where she is."

Chapter 35

PENNY

He's in love with me. He really did say it the first time.

Zach is pacing the waiting room. The stench of alcohol and strong cleaners waft around us. There are a lot of people here despite the late hour. It's almost one in the morning and our flight leaves in a few hours. They haven't let Zach back. They are running tests, and she hasn't gotten to her room yet. My leg shakes as I sit on a bench seat against the window.

I've barely had time to process the fight Zach and I had. I'm not going to bring it up now. I'm honestly surprised he let me drive him in his car. It's been a while since I've been behind the wheel, but Zach wasn't in a state to drive. I almost thought he was going to fight me on it with how upset he was over me doing things for him, but he didn't.

He walks past me and this time I reach out and grab for his hand. His attention snaps down to where we're connected. He doesn't pull away and takes the seat beside me with a sigh. I'm not sure what to say, so I stay quiet.

With my hand held tight in his, he says, "You should go. You'll miss the flight." He stares at the scuffed up tiled floor.

"But Zach, I can take another flight . . ."

A lump forms in my throat and I grip the edge of the hard seat.

"I think it's best if I stay just in case Clarice needs me."

He leans to the side and pats his pocket. I had given him his keys when we arrived. He lets go of my hand and places them into my palm. The world blurs but I bite back the tears.

"Take my car back to the house. Your limo is coming in an hour or two."

"I don't want to leave you or her like this. I have to know she's okay."

He breathes in deep, still refusing to look at me. His eyes are back on the floor.

"Thank you, but we'll be okay. I'm here, but you have a job to do. You got this, Penny," he whispers. "I believe in you. Go back there and show them who you really are."

I don't feel like I have a right to be upset. Tonight is about making sure Clarice is okay. I have to suck it up. I don't want to, because I'm worried about her and Zach. He closes his eyes and I'm guessing internally he's beating himself up.

His keys dig into my palm as I hold them tight.

"Okay." My voice is meek. "I-I'll go then." I blow out a breath.

"I'm sorry." His voice is so soft I barely hear it.

I stand and he doesn't follow. He lifts his chin to find my eyes but there's no light in them. The worry in his creased brow makes me want to call Tanner and tell her fuck the interviews, but I don't think he wants me here.

"B-bye, Zach," I say, trying to hold myself together.

His lips part. "Pen, I—"

"Zachary Cullen?"

I move aside and he shoots up. "That's me."

"You can see her now."

He nods his head and runs a hand over his scruff. He looks like he has aged a lifetime in only a few hours. His shoulders are slumped. He starts to walk away and gets quite a few steps before stopping. His hands ball into fists at his side and he turns.

His eyes are misty and with each swallow his throat bobs. His breath hitches. "Bye, Pen. Good luck with your award." His voice breaks and his shoulders rise and fall. He turns and heads towards the double doors where the nurse in green scrubs stands.

I've lost my voice and hold my throat as I watch him walk away without looking back.

🐾 🐾

The whole ride home I'm trying my hardest not to cry while I drive. The headlights of other cars on the road make it hard to see. I wince at the glare. I turn onto Sarina's block and catch sight of a familiar black Lexus in the driveway, one I haven't seen in so long. The sight of it breaks the dam and my tears start to fall.

I pull in behind her and before I shut the car the front door opens. She steps out onto the porch dressed in heels, tight back skinny jeans, and black and white plaid button down.

"Sarina," I whisper, turning off Zach's car and getting out so fast I'm almost dizzy when I stand to my full height.

"Penny?"

I break down at the sound of her voice and swiftly go to her. She meets me at the bottom step. Her heels clicking as she walks. I wrap my arms around her, enveloped by her warm vanilla scent and let go, sobbing into her red and black plaid shirt.

There isn't much time to explain. As we part Charles pulls up in his black stretch limo to bring me to the airport. I step back and her dark eyes meet mine under the porch light.

"You're here," I say.

"Wasn't gonna miss my little sister's big day. I wanted to surprise you, but when I got here no one was here. I tried to call."

I wipe my eyes. "Phone was on silent. I'm sorry."

She touches my arm. "It's alright, Maddie told me what happened. I hope Clarice is okay."

I smile through my tears. "You talked to Maddie?"

She nods. "Yeah. All is good."

I sniffle and place a hand on my chest. "Good. That's good."

"Come on. Let's get our things. I see we have a lot to talk about."

I can't help myself. I hold on tight, nearly knocking her over. Sarina chuckles and rubs my back. "I got you, Pen."

Chapter 36

ZACH

C larice slaps my hand away as I open the passenger door.

"Oh, stop fussing. I'm fine."

Mid-morning sunlight dances overhead. There's a slight chill in the air, but today is the warmest it's been in a while. A winter jacket or heavy sweater is still needed but you can tell spring is coming.

The doctors ran a bunch of tests, and all were inconclusive. Other than being a little dehydrated and some low iron, they gave her some infusions while there, things seemed mostly normal. She said she woke up Sunday morning with some chest tightness and by the time she got to Wingman's, she felt pain. They did a cardiology workup, but recommended she follow up with her cardiologist, which she already has an appointment for later this week. I told her I'd be around to take her. She also has a follow-up with her primary doctor on Wednesday and I'm taking her to that, too. It didn't come without some push and pull. She wanted to do it on her own, but I wasn't backing down.

When we get inside, she hangs her jacket on the golden coat rack and turns to me as I shut the door.

"Zachary, you can go. I'm fine. I'm going to take a shower, get into my own clothes, and knit for the rest of the day. Really, I'm okay."

I stare at the woman in front of me. I'm still getting used to the idea of her being my biological mom. I linger by the door. She turns to me and tilts her head with a sigh.

She says, "My boy," and the name has emotion clogging my throat.

The last few days have been exhausting. I've been worried about Clarice. She's young, but it doesn't mean something can't happen to her. There's some lingering anger and resentment for her keeping who she is a secret all these years, but when I got the call from Maddie, I think it morphed those feelings into fear. What if it was something worse and I was still mad at her? She had said something similar when we spoke.

Then I feel guilty for yelling at Penny over something she didn't even know. I have mentioned it before, but not in detail. Going back to L.A. was already something she had been dreading and she had to go back upset. I hate that I allowed my insecurities to hurt her. Then when I told her I loved her, she froze. I'm not sure if she heard me when she was coming undone underneath me, so it slipped during our fight. What terrible timing I had.

Clarice touches my arm, pulling me out of my head.

"Shouldn't you be in L.A. with that sweet woman of yours?"

I lower my head and stare at the clean wooden floor.

"Zach. What happened?"

"Nothing."

"It's not nothing."

I lift my head and find her eyes. They are soft and warm. She's never given me a reason to believe she doesn't care for my well-being. Even with the huge lie buried deep.

"I fucked up."

"We all do that from time to time. Did you tell her how you felt?"

I nod and she leads me over to the couch where we sat the day I came to speak with her. She's closer to me this time. I don't want to burden her. She's been in the hospital, but I also know she's not going to let up until I talk to her.

Clarice doesn't take her eyes off me but remains silent while she listens. I tell her about the fight and the tuxedo, and how the I love you slipped. I vaguely mentioned the first time, but didn't say the sex part, just that I didn't think she heard me.

"You want to know what I think?"

"I'm pretty sure I already know," I say, with a half-smile.

She chuckles. "Good. Let it all sink in then. Our past doesn't define us. We've all made mistakes, allowed others to belittle us and make us feel bad for who we are and what we love. But we're here in the now and what we can do is make each day count towards a better future. I'm not telling you to hop on a plane this second, but what I am saying is to take this time to yourself to think about how you can help yourself to have a better tomorrow. If it's a simple apology and moving on or if it's getting on that damn plane and sweeping that woman up into your arms and never letting go, the choice is yours to decide. We can't predict tomorrow or the day after or years from now, but we can do better than the day before."

I let everything she said sink in. We sit in silence for a few long minutes. I peer over at a sleepy looking Clarice. She rests her head back on the couch. Her breathing is slow and steady.

"I'm fine," she says, a smile tugging on her lips.

"Good. Not ready to lose you just yet."

She rolls her eyes and laughs. "Can't get rid of me that easily. I'm still a young chicken."

I leave to let Clarice get some rest. The ride home is quiet. I reach for the radio and fidget with the dial while waiting at a red light. I'm not a big fan of top 40 radio but happen to land on a station playing "I'll Look After You" by The Fray. The light turns green, and I can't help singing along. My voice falls in line with the range of the lead singer. A lyric I used to graze over hits me square in the chest; it's the line about feeling like a person in your life is home.

I grip the wheel and stop singing, allowing the song to end and the DJ's voice to take over.

"Coming up this Friday, if you haven't heard, Penelope Clarke has a new single debuting, and we are going to premier it on our morning show at nine sharp. Don't miss out to hear it before her performance at the Great American Music Awards next Monday. In the meantime, here's an oldie but goodie, "Make It Last", right here on the tri-states number one hit station."

As Penelope's voice fills my car I pull into the driveway. It's not the same as having her here. There's something so raw about her voice when it's not backed by a track from the studio. I look over at the passenger seat as if she was there. With the empty space beside me, it feels as if something is missing from my life.

My phone screen lights up and my eyes flicker to it on the dash in its holder. A text from Mark comes through. I unbuckle and lean forward to check it.

> Mark: I hope Clarice is doing well, please let her know we are thinking about her. I have something I want to talk to you about. Are you free Friday?

They all know I'm not in L.A. Maddie picked me up from the hospital early Monday morning so I could get my car. When I pulled in and saw Sarina's Lexus, I was relieved to know at least Penny had someone. She left a note stating she went with her to L.A., which means I'm here alone with Larry and Petunia.

I grab my phone from the holder and let Mark know I'm available and give him the update on Clarice. I stare up at the house that feels so empty right now. I swallow past the lump in my throat and finally force myself to go inside. The silence is deafening. Larry meows and unlike before Penny's presence graced this house, he struts towards me. He yowls like he's sad, and then smooches on my leg. I leave my shoes on the mat by the door. Larry follows me upstairs. I didn't sleep well last night. Tossed and turned, then got to the hospital early to make sure Clarice had a ride. Maybe a nap will help.

In the hallway, I pass by Penny's room and stop. The door is partially open. Everything is gone. The air feels like it's been ripped from my lungs. I grab the door frame and hold on. Larry sits beside me. He meows again. Not a normal one. He hasn't left my side. He tips his nose up towards me. I give the room one last glance before heading to mine.

I undress down to my boxers and place my phone and keys on the bedside table.

Larry meows.

"I know buddy, I feel it, too."

As I climb into bed, he does right along with me. He's never been here. Maybe only to hiss at me, but the last two days it doesn't seem like he has the energy to be an asshole. He must sense something is off. Maybe he doesn't want to be alone, and for once I'm grateful for the devil cat's company.

Chapter 37

PENNY

A room full of strangers, and Sarina, all sitting in rows of chairs in an enclosed space as part of a radio station gig. Using my own guitar for this song should be a special moment, but as I take in each face both young and old, my heart isn't into it.

There are no windows here. The walls feel like they are closing in, but I continue to play and sing.

I throw it all away
Lock up the key for another day.
Let it go and sing endlessly
I hide from the pain to feel whole.
I search my soul to find my voice again.
It's strong and hidden behind a broken wall.

The people before me are radio winners. They either called into the station or are friends of the DJ's. I'm not sure if they notice my heart isn't here, I left that back in New York. Everyone continues to be mesmerized by my performance. Am I the only one truly listening? It doesn't sound right. I'm not off key, so that's not the issue.

I smile and sway back and forth while sitting on a stool. There's no stage here. I'm on the same level as them.

I think about how a few nights ago I was on stage at Wingman's. I remember how it felt to take off my hat and glasses and play from my heart. How when I met Zach's eyes during the chorus he sang along, and I finally felt whole. Here with all these people, I appreciate them and their love for my music, but it's not the same.

The ending of the song feels like a dream.

My voice cracks on the last word, but without a second thought the small audience applauds. DJ T, comes over. He's holding a mic in one of his large hands. The man towers over me, possibly over six feet. He's built and muscular and his shiny bald head twinkles from the lighting above.

"Ladies and gentlemen, you heard it here first. "Lost and Found" from our very own Penelope Clarke. Penelope, how does it feel to play your newest song in front of your hometown audience?"

I almost scoff but hold back. Hometown? I may have been born here, but it's not home. Maybe it never was. I clench my jaw and try my hardest to battle with the wave of sadness stuck in my throat.

"It feels wonderful. I am so thankful to all of you who came out here today to support me."

DJ T stands beside me and from my seated position I crane my neck to look at his face. His large smile is all an act. His eyes fall heavy and are vacant. I know that look all too well. It's one I noticed in videos of my last tour, towards the end when my battery had run out.

"Now Penny, we are all eager to find out on Monday if you're going to win Artist of The Year. I know you released a statement on your social media, but tell us how you really feel?"

I forget how to breathe, and a wave of dizziness hits me. Thank God I'm sitting. I stare out into the crowd of eager fans. After this they will each come up one by one for a picture and autograph. I have to get myself together or else the tabloids will have a field day with not only me being fake, but a bitch too.

"I'm nervous," I let out a fake laugh. "But most of all I'm excited to just have been nominated. It's an honor. My dad was—" I suck in a breath and stop, but no one seems to notice my turmoil. "He won the same award about thirty years ago. Even if I don't win, I'm happy to have been amongst so many amazing musicians."

"Including Erick Platt?"

The blood rushes to my face. My cheeks heat and my ears feel like they could blow steam any second.

"Of course."

My pulse races and I brace myself for him to question me about the documentary. It's gotta be coming. Not a single interview this past week as skirted around it. I've been polite even when I didn't want to be. Once or twice, I had to tell them no comment, but I went through the motions mechanically. Bracing for the blow, I hold my breath.

"Well, that's all the time we have. Thank you for performing and answering some of our questions. We're going to do some autographs and pictures."

I exhale and my shoulders sink.

DJ T and the other station workers are getting all the fans lined up to meet me. Sarina comes over to take my guitar. She grabs my hand with her free one.

"You alright?"

"Yeah. I will be."

I go through the motions of singing and laughing with my fans. They are all so sweet. None of them bring up the documentary or the awards. I have simple and fun conversations with each one. There are maybe fifteen, so it doesn't take more than an hour to get through them all.

Their security begins to escort me from the stuffy yellow painted room when I hear a small voice say, "Excuse me, Ms. Clarke."

I stop and turn, taking note of a young girl with her brown hair in braids. She's got a guitar over her shoulder.

"Hi. I don't believe we met during the meet and greet. What's your name?"

Her eyes water and tears spill over onto her pink cheeks.

"Suzie."

It feels as if all the air in my lungs has escaped. My knees tremble slightly. I touch my locket to ground me.

"That's a beautiful name. It was my mom's too."

"I know," she whispers. " 'My Butterflies' was the first song my mom taught me how to play."

She glances over her shoulder at a woman with similar color hair. I lift my gaze and nod at the hazel eyed woman.

"I had Suzanna's record. I loved her music. It saved me from a dark time in my life. I wish she had continued singing. I would have loved to meet her. I've been playing it since Suzie was a baby and it's one of her favorites. She really wanted to learn it, so she's been practicing for months."

"Sarina, can I get my guitar for a sec?"

Sarina shifts the bag and brings it to me. A proud, beautiful smile dances along her lips. It's moments like these that don't make me want to quit. When I can see the difference I've made in a person's life, it makes all the other shit worth it. I take the guitar and begin opening my case.

This is the first time I've met someone who has ever mentioned Mom's album. Not many people remember or know about it. When it flopped it was like it didn't exist. An energy buzzes through me at knowing someone is still a fan.

My lips quiver and I nod. "I'm so happy to hear her music was a big part of your life." I sniffle and turn to Suzie. "Do you want to play the song with me?"

The smile on her face makes all the pain vanish.

"Really?" Tears fall down her pink cheeks.

"Yeah."

She holds her guitar as if she's been playing her whole life.

"Ready?" I ask.

The first chord hits and I'm lost in the lyrics.

Your wings are soft and delicate,
but don't let it fool you.
Your strength comes from within.

Suzie belts out the lines as if she's using the words to help her through something big. It's like Mom knew one day someone would need to hear these words. She's here with me. I feel her. It sounds crazy, but I do.

I almost miss the beat with how good she is. We start singing together and the girl watches me, never once letting her eyes stray. It's a moment I want to frame. She hits all of mom's low notes along with me, her voice matching mine.

The last two lines almost manage to make me cry but instead, make me feel stronger.

> *Tune out the darkness and spread your wings.*
> *Show the world the light in the darkened springs.*

We strum the last chord together and I lift my gaze to the mom who has tears streaming down her cheeks.

"That was beautiful. You're so incredibly talented."

Suzie's cheeks brighten and her eyes light up. "Thank you for making my dream come true."

Her words echo in my head as we leave the building. It's the first day since I returned that I am feeling a sense of relief, like maybe things will be okay. When I'm finally back in the limo and its only Sarina and I, sitting at the very back, I turn to her and blow out a breath. Something about Mom's song triggered the urge to do something I haven't done in a long time.

"We should go visit them."

Her hand slips into mine and she squeezes. She doesn't have to hear their names to know I mean Mom and Dad.

"Hey Charles," she yells.

The divider is down, and he peers into the rearview mirror. Our eyes meet his and it's like he knows.

The grounds are beautiful and well-kept. While you can still see the city from inside the gates, in here is peaceful. I can't remember the last time I came here. It's been a long time. Sarina and I wind through the stones until we come up to two that are under a giant tree. The late afternoon sun is shining through the green leaves, leaving shadows on the ground. The weather is warm with a breeze. Our hair blows around a little. She and I take a seat on the manicured lawn. A sense of calm washes over me and I allow myself to be present and open my heart and mind to everything I've been feeling the last few months.

"Do you remember when they told us about how they first met?" Sarina asks.

"Yeah," I say, picking at the bright green blades of grass.

I can't help smiling. The memory of it makes my heart yearn for a romance like theirs. Only to realize, I think I may have had it with Zach. Like any couple, they went through a period of doubt right before their accident, but their love was what won in the end.

"Dad said he knew the moment he laid eyes on her that he was in love, and she was the one."

I laugh. "He was such a sap."

"Every song was about her."

I lower my gaze to the ground. "Do you think it's possible to love someone so fast?"

"I think it's more than possible. Love works in mysterious ways. It brings people into our lives when we least expect it."

I close my eyes and allow the peace of the cemetery to take over my senses. I breathe in deep and count to four before letting go. I feel closer to Mom and Dad when I just allow myself to feel.

I sigh and open my eyes. "When they separated for a short time, I used to hear her crying in their bedroom. The distance was so hard on them when we weren't on the road with Dad. How did she keep it together all those times? So many women threw themselves at him and yet he stayed loyal, even through their messy time."

"What you're really asking is, how can you make a relationship with Zach work without allowing what asshole Erick did to affect you?"

I scoot closer to her, bridging the gap and resting my head on her shoulder. A trembling breath releases from my parted lips.

"Have you heard from him?" she asks.

I shake my head. "I'm giving him space. I think I needed it too. Maybe it will help me to see I've got nothing to worry about."

"It doesn't hurt to take a step back and evaluate your relationship with someone. How are you feeling now that you've been away for a few days?"

I think back to this past week. My mind has been all over the place. From preparing for the awards to the interviews. Despite our little argument before I left, I never once felt as if Zach would do anything to destroy what we had. I've wanted to check in, but not to be paranoid girlfriend, but because I want to make things right. My heart has known since the moment we kissed what we had was different, but my pesky brain wanted none of it.

I lift my head and stare at the gray stones with a beautiful black plaque attached. Their names are carved in golden lettering. I trace the letters with my eyes. I lower my gaze, and something flutters in my peripheral. I focus to my right and a beautiful orange butterfly flaps its wings and lands on top of mom's stone.

A breath gets caught in my throat as I choke down a sob. My hand reaches for my locket. I run my fingers over the bumpy outline of the butterflies.

"Mom knows we're here," I whisper, pointing to the butterfly.

Sarina smiles. "They both do."

We remain quiet and watch the butterfly until it flies off through the cemetery. My heart knows there's only one place that feels right to me. A place where I'm surrounded by people who aren't using me for my fame. Ones who don't go behind my back making documentaries about my life. I miss not only Zach, but Maddie and Mark. Clarice. Wingman's, as a whole. Could I make this life work while living there instead of here? I've never planted roots anywhere but California. That in and of itself scares me. Zach and I need to be more open with each other. We only scratched the surface of talking about what we wanted. Casual could have worked if I hadn't fallen in love.

When I think about where I want to be, I close my eyes and swear I smell a pulled pork sammie. There's a murmur of voices, and shouts when a beloved hockey team scores. Clarice at her table, knitting. The warmth of her smile, and Maddie with Pat behind the bar cracking jokes and having fun. But mostly it's the comfort of being in Zach's arms and locking eyes with him when we make love.

"I want to go home."

She scrunches her dark brows and doesn't speak for a few seconds.

"Oh. Okay. I'll get Charles—"

She starts to stand, and I grab her arm. "No. That's not home."

Sarina's gaze flickers to mine. Her misty eyes releasing a few stray tears. "Home." Her lip quivers. "With me?"

I nod. Feeling my tears fall. I wish I had done and said things differently the other night. I was angry because he didn't want to take a tuxedo from me. I should have understood where he came from, but instead I got offended. After the awards I need to go to him. I'll get Tanner to book me a flight out that night. I don't need to go to some stupid after party just because. If I win, the only people I want to celebrate with are the ones who made me feel alive again.

"I've got an idea. Hear me out?"

"I'll take any advice you have," I say, voice breaking.

"What if you recorded your next album at the studio in Manhattan instead of here. It would give you time with Zach to get used to your busy schedule. At the end of the day, you get to come home and be where you belong. When it comes to touring, maybe take a small break. The album will take a bit to come out. Put your foot down about what you want from your career. You don't have to be on the road all the time. It's your life and while Tanner is your manager, you can always say no. You don't owe the press anything."

I think deep down I thought saying no would make me a failure. I was scared Dad would give me a cold shoulder, kind of like he did to Sarina when she wasn't coming back. He was a flawed man and the world knew it. I was blind. I hate being angry at him since he's not here, and although he was trying to help, he made things harder for me in the long run. I'll always love him and appreciate all he did, but it's time I take my life back one step at a time. First, I'll need to talk to Tanner about the album and maybe come to an agreement with the label regarding what happens after.

"It's the last album to fulfill my contract . . . maybe that's a sign, it's time for a break."

"Nothing wrong with that."

I'm done letting people and the media walk all over me and my life. I don't have any doubts Zach and I would be okay with any scenario. I love him with all my heart. He brought back my spark and all I want to do is run into his arms and tell him the words I didn't say back.

Chapter 38

ZACH

I didn't have any shifts this week, but tonight Pat called out sick and since I'm going in anyway, I'll take over behind the bar for tonight. It's been a while since I've bartended, but I love the rush of it, especially on a Friday night.

I'm in awe as I pull into the parking lot of Wingman's. My usual spot under the brightest lamp in the lot is taken along with all the others around it. I swing around and head back out to the street. It's a residential area but the overflow of cars are parked all along the curbs for two blocks.

Tonight is our second karaoke night and tomorrow is open mic. When Maddie picked me up earlier in the week at the hospital she and I came up with an idea for our next karaoke. A little friendly competition couldn't hurt and so we are giving away a hundred-dollar gift card to Wingman's and a basket of goodies donated by some local business who Mark is friends with.

The energy of the crowd hits me the moment I walk through the doors. The tables are filled, the bar overflowing with patrons. I stop and take it all in. When Mark asked to meet with me earlier in the week, I'll admit I was worried that it was going to be news I didn't want to hear. With all the liveliness here, I don't think it's the case anymore.

Mark is on the stage setting up the karaoke machine. I weave through the tables and over to him.

"Hey, what a great turn out tonight," I say, having to speak a little louder than normal.

He lifts his gaze from the machine, and I'm met with a wide smile I haven't seen from Mark in some time. It's a complete turnaround from the night he told us things weren't looking so good.

"Oh great, you're here. Let's talk in my office real quick. Then Maddie needs you at the bar."

He hops down from the stage with a bounce in his step. I follow him to the stairs. He holds the door open when we get to the top and I throw one last glance behind me at how much of a difference this all has made.

"Grab a seat," he says, gesturing for me to sit.

The noise of the crowd is muffled by the closed door. My stomach knots as Mark relaxes in his chair. This has to be good, right? He hasn't given me any signs of something being wrong. My heart is close to bursting in my chest over the few seconds of silence. I grip the cool metal of the chair and wait for his news.

"I wanted to talk to you privately for a few reasons. First, the pub is doing well enough so that we will be okay for the foreseeable future. I have full confidence we can keep this all going. You have all put your heart and soul into this place and we wouldn't be here if it wasn't for you. That includes Penny. Maddie said she spoke with her and Sarina today and she's donating a signed collection of her CDs to tonight's winner. Which I think definitely brought the crowd."

My chest constricts at the mention of Penny, but at the same time I smile, because it's so like Penny to continue to help despite everything that went down. Through the hurt of our fight, all the pressure and tension from my body releases. My home is safe and so are the people I consider family. It doesn't mean we can't slide back down into the negative, but it means we have the time to find ways to continue to prosper.

"With that being said, I have an offer for you."

My knuckles turn white from the force I'm grabbing the chair with.

"Okay, I'm listening."

Mark's smile doesn't fade. My leg bounces as I wait for him to continue.

"This is a decision that has been a long time coming. The only reason I've waited until now is because I didn't know what was going to happen with the pub. You've put so much of your heart and soul into this place. Last year when I went on vacation with my family, you took over for me and really showed so much potential. I didn't have to worry with the pub in your hands. I need a manager. I'd like to have more flexibility in my schedule for Devin. With my wife's new venture into being a NICU nurse, I want to support her the best I can. In order for me to do that, I need someone I can trust to step into my shoes."

I suck in a breath as emotions clog my throat. I let go of the chair and get to my feet so fast I'm dizzy. I put one hand on his desk.

"A-are you kidding me?"

Mark chuckles. "No, definitely not."

"W-what does that mean for me?"

"It means a significant pay raise, about twenty-seven an hour as opposed to server salary."

I blink several times trying to do the math in my head, but it's a jumbled mess up there. I am making seventeen and change now. This would change so many things. Mark stands and walks around the desk. I've started pacing because this can't be real. He stops my movement by standing in front of me.

"Zach, what are you worried about?"

I wait for Macy in my head to tell me this raise still means nothing. That I'm still not fulfilling my potential. That I'll never make a woman happy with my earnings. Instead of Macy, all I hear is the voice I miss most.

"But you are good enough, Zach. You matter to so many people."

I swallow and go through all the time I spent with her. From the moment she found me squatting on the chair to our first kiss in the car to the bright smile on her face when I'd tease her about her sex toys. I remember the broken-down woman with tears as I walked away from her. Never once did she ever belittle who I was. She might have bought me things, but it wasn't to make me feel less like a man, it was because she did it out of the kindness of her heart. I fucked up so bad. I hate how nasty I was to her.

I close my eyes and grip the desk and Mark steps closer, his forehead wrinkling.

"Zach?"

The only thing I want to do now is tell Penny I got the job. I imagine her excitement and encouraging words. When she was at some of her lowest moments, she still made me feel like I was on top of the world.

It takes me a few good deep breaths before I can face him.

"Nothing. I'm worried about nothing. I'm all in, Mark." I stand straight. "I'm all fucking in." I laugh. "When do I start?"

Mark's worried frown shifts to a smile. "How does after you get back from L.A. sound?"

I narrow my eyes. "L.A.?"

Mark has always been a father figure to me. With his arms crossed, it feels almost like he's about to give some father-son advice. He changes from boss mode to dad mode with the flip of a switch.

"It's where you're supposed to be, right? With her?"

"Yeah," I say, breathily. "But I fucked up."

"So, fix it," he says, as if it's no big deal. "Get your ass on a plane and fix it."

I run a hand through my hair. Contemplating his words. If I go and she pushes me away it's my own fault, but if I don't go and we never talk about what happened, I'll be wondering what if for the rest of my life.

"What about Clarice? What if she needs . . ."

He holds up his hand. "Don't you worry about her, we can all check in."

"And Sarina's cat and axolotl. Someone needs to feed—"

"All I'm hearing is excuses. What are you waiting for?"

"My shift to end?" I smile, realizing how much lighter I feel thinking about flying to her and apologizing. The money doesn't even matter, all I know is I need to get to her.

Mark snorts and places a hand on my shoulder. "Alright, you got me there, but Zach, if she means something to you, don't just let that go. I can't imagine life without my wife. Sometimes we don't always see eye to eye but coming home to her every night is a blessing."

Mark and Clarice have both said similar things to me and they are right. It's time to stop living in the past and focus on what I have in front of me. Penny and I could have a future together. I understand her fear of being away, but if we don't try how will we ever know if it could work or not. I have to know.

"It's about time I start some karaoke. After tonight, I don't want to see you back in this pub until you've talked to her. Got it?"

"Yes, Dad," I tease.

He chuckles. "See you down there."

When he shuts the door and leaves me alone, I lean my backside against the desk and stare at the wall. There's no other place I want to be but here at Wingman's, but there's also no other person I'd rather share that with than Penny.

I can't help the smile when what Mark said fully plows into me like a running bull. I'm going to be the manager of Wingman's. It's been a long time coming and a goal I've always wanted to accomplish. I push myself off the desk and stride across the room. My hand turns the knob and a familiar song about a girl named Penny fills the pub. I reach for my phone in my back pocket.

Sarina, I need your help.

Chapter 39

PENNY

My phone shakes in my trembling hand as I watch it all play out on screen. The moment I won Talent in America was one I'll never forget. It's here in the documentary. I should be getting ready for the award show, but I felt like I needed to do this first.

I'm sitting on the edge of my bed in the bedroom of my house, and I've hated every night I've slept in it. I've gotten next to no sleep and I'm running on fumes. The wooden floors were freshly polished when I arrived. The bed was too perfectly made. The white comforter tucked into the black framed canopy bed as if it was a display model. Picture frames of random places hang on the plain white walls. Images I could care less about but hung them to give the space life. It's cold and uninviting, but I only needed to stick it out until today. Tonight, we're going back to New York.

A round of applause pulls my attention back to the phone screen. I've already watched countless interviews after interviews of people

I've either known most of my life or ones that were just in it for a short time.

I've managed to not shed a single tear throughout. The documentary started out with my dad's life. They showed old video footage of him in various stages of his career along with a few from childhood that was dug up. Sarina and I ended up in quite a few of the ones during his tours or even out and about. Lance Greenfield was not only the creator but the narrator. I'd know his nasally voice from anywhere. He spoke about dad as if their friendship never mattered. It was disgusting. They had grown up together. Played in high school bands and Lance even played bass for dad a while, which of course was noted.

Erick's interviews shed light on our relationship. All the bad, nothing of the good, because there were moments where it was. He made sure to talk about all of the times I'd call him or leave him voicemails while I was on the road, or he was. He made me look as if I'm needy. I cringed all the way through, but something inside me didn't allow me to cry no matter how much it hurt.

They saved the show for the last fifteen minutes. Seventeen-year-old me stood on a stage lit from the bottom. The host Bryan Riverbend stood between me and the other contestant. Bryan's blonde, messy hair was styled to look amiss. His blue dazzling eyes always wowed the audience, and each one of his tuxedos was specially crafted for him. Julie St. Cloud, the other contestant, rubbed her arms nervously. She had almost Taylor Swift vibes with her blonde, crimpy hair, a pink dress, and brown cowboy boots. I'm not sure whatever happened to Julie; she and I got along well.

"Julie, Penelope congratulations to both of you for getting to this moment. One of you is about to make history."

Bryan looks back and forth between us. My heart hammers in my chest the same way it did while I stood there. The screen behind us swirled with colors, lights. The cameras are holding steady. Bryan opened the envelope with ease, taking out the golden ticket.

"And our winner is—"

"Penny?" My sister's voice cuts through, and I fumble with my phone to shut it off.

It falls to the wood flooring below. "Shit. Come in."

Sarina peeks her head around the white painted door. Her eyes narrow at me. Her long, brown wavy locks are already done up nice for the awards. She steps into the room, dressed in a beautiful strap black dress that ends at her knees. Her matching heels click along the floor. She purses her red lips as she takes in my appearance.

"You're not even dressed?"

I hop off the bed and grab my phone. I toss it onto the mattress, stand straight and gently pat my hair. It's down. The right side in waves over my shoulder and the left behind. There's a golden bow holding back some of the hair on the left.

"I'm all done up. I just have to put it on."

My cheeks heat under her stare. My makeup is all set too. I honestly don't love lipstick. I hate the waxy texture and taste, but tonight it has to be done. I've decided a matte red. My eyes are decorated with a warm brown that shimmers in the light.

I reach for my necklace and hold onto it. I don't care if it doesn't match, it's coming with me.

She crosses her arms. "What were you doing?"

I blow out my breath. "Watching the documentary."

"Pen." She tilts her head and raises a brow.

"I'm fine."

It's not a lie. I am. It will take some time to process, but I did it. I got through it on my own. No matter what happens on that stage tonight. If I perform and then lose, perform and then win, it doesn't matter. I know what is going to make me happiest. I'm worried it might not work out, but after my moment with Suzie, and the butterfly at the cemetery, I know it's the right move.

"Ladies?" Another knock at my door and the sound of Tanner's raspy voice has us both eyeing the entryway.

She steps in and like Sarina is already dressed and ready to go. She's in a tight red sequin floor-length dress that matches. Her hair pulled back into a tight bun. A mixture of Sarina's vanilla perfume and Tanner's bitter one fills the room. Tanner lifts her index finger, her lips part, and not even one sound comes out before I stop her with my hand up.

"I'm getting dressed now."

"Okay. I was only coming to let you know it's all taken care of. Everything we signed this morning is good. This will be your last record with Paradise Entertainment Group."

I was contracted for four albums, the one I'm set to record in the coming weeks, is number four. On top of that, I will be using their Manhattan based studio to be closer to home like Sarina suggested.

I can't help the smile on my face. It's the first, I've really given it my all since I've been back here. This doesn't mean I'm going to fall off the face of the earth and never record another album again, this means I can control my own future. I've got some ideas, but I've yet to look that far ahead. First thing is first. Get through tonight and make amends with Zach. I feel my heart beating hard inside my chest. This is only the beginning. After tonight, my new chapter starts.

My phone beeps with an incoming text.

Zach: You got this, Pen!

※ ※ ※

The moment I step out of the limo in my golden dress a thunder of voices and the shutter of cameras start going off. At my side is Sarina and on my other is Tanner. My dress shimmers in the fading L.A. sun as I walk forward. It's a beautiful evening. I can't stop smiling from the text Zach sent earlier. Nothing will stop me tonight.

Across on the other side are the fans. They are behind a short barrier. Their cell phones are held out and they reach for artists as they pass by. A few shout my name and I lift my golden dress to head in their direction. Tears run down a few of their cheeks. They are first on my path, and I stop. Their faces are flushed as one girl with black hair hands me her phone. I lean back and take a selfie with her and some others. This is the one part I'll never get tired of. Making my fans day.

We're being moved along so I do what I can for each one to make them feel special. Unfortunately, I don't get through them all before Tanner is pulling me in another direction. Sarina follows behind me and I catch her waving and smile. She always says she's not natural at being in the spotlight, but once we're here she owns it.

Ahead of me someone with familiar blonde hair bobs through the crowd of photographers and press. It's hard to get a visual but I'd know his stride anywhere. He's got a swagger about him that screams confidence with straight and perfect posture. He throws his head back when a woman beside him in a navy-blue A-line gown and blonde hair touches his arm.

I square my shoulders and continue forward.

"Okay, we're about to head for the media," Tanner says taking my arm. "You don't have to—"

I step out of her grasp and turn to her. My pulse is racing, and my chest is tight with fear, but a voice in my head causes me to pause. Knots form in my stomach. It's all too real now. I haven't seen Erick in person since we broke up. It's a shock to my system, that's all I keep telling myself.

Don't let the outside world get in your head. Don't let him. Zach. *You should be celebrating this victory. You did this!* The anxiety is starting to diminish as Zach's voice in my head drowns out everything else around me. *No one should make you feel like you don't deserve every ounce of recognition you've gotten.*

"I deserve this," I say, quietly to myself. "I deserve this. I deserve it."

I swallow hard and take a step as the photographers and media point their attention directly at me.

A woman dressed in a black suit holds out a mic to me. "Penelope. Congratulations."

Deep breaths, I tell myself.

"How are you feeling tonight, sweetheart?"

Her voice is smooth and sweet, but it doesn't mean she's not about to grill me. I've been here before.

"I can't wait for the show to start. Looking forward to seeing the other nominees and performances."

Her bright red lips tug into a smile. My pulse races as the flashes from the cameras start to create spots in my vision.

"Your new song "Lost and Found" is incredible. Could you quickly tell us where you drew your inspiration from?"

Her question catches me a bit off guard. I haven't been asked this yet. Not even by the radio station. I stare at her mic. Images flicker through my mind like a movie montage. Zach on the back of the chair, Larry and his love for sex toys, our candy adventure . . . I could go on. My cheeks pinch from my smile, and I lift my gaze to meet the interviewers bright green eyes.

"It's about a man and a community who saw me for who I was when I was drowning in my own self-doubt."

"Can you—"

Tanner's hand grabs my arm, and she politely tells the woman we need to move on. I wave as she brings me over to where the large white back drop with the music award logo on it. A red circle, white middle, with a red microphone and the words *Great American Music Awards* written in gold.

It's time for pictures and I have no problems smiling because I know when I'm done here, I'll be on my way home. It's what keeps me going.

"Well, well, well. She comes out of hiding." A voice so sinister its almost villainous says beside me.

"Erick, Penelope, get together for a photo." A photographer shouts.

In the corner of my eye, Sarina is about to go all big sister on them, ready to step forward but Tanner stops her. Sarina yanks her arm away and I whip my head to Sarina, take a deep breath and mouth, "I'm okay," despite my trembling lips.

"I don't have to explain anything to you."

He chuckles, low and deep from his chest and I roll my eyes as a flash goes off and I'm sure they've caught it. Erick is standing way too close. His musky scent clogs my nose and makes my eyes water.

"Erick, Penelope, do you think you'll ever get back together?" A man in the crowd of media shouts.

There goes my heart again, beating so fast it's like running a marathon. My stomach is in knots. I try to stop myself from wrinkling my nose in disgust at his question. I don't have to answer any of them. Erick is quiet as he stands beside me posing for the photos. I follow along and do the same, keeping Zach's voice in my head. I owe them *nothing*.

"How did you feel about Erick's interview in the documentary?" another asks.

That question hits me square in the gut. The documentary is fresh in my mind after watching it. The lump in my throat threatening tears is hard to swallow, but I keep my eyes on the camera.

"Yeah, Pen. How'd ya feel about exposing what a fraud your father is." Erick elbows me and I whirl to him, so close to knocking him out.

I clench my fists but relax as Zach's words repeat in my head. I pump my hands to relax my tense fingers. There is no reason I should fight fire with fire. It only leaves you burned. I play with my necklace and run the pad of my thumb over the engraved butterflies.

I lean but not too close and whisper, "Say all you want about my father, at least he didn't need to sleep his way to the top."

Pulling back, I tilt my head and stare into his icy gold gaze. His jaw twitches and that's how I know I've got him. It always ticked when he was embarrassed or knew he got caught doing something.

I grin. "I guess we're both frauds then."

I could go and spill the tea on what was the last straw for me. It was his secret affair while we were still dating, with a record exec, who was married, but I'm not that cruel. I've told absolutely no one about this. It was the reason he was signed. I found out on the road one night and it was how our breakup became official. I'm not that person. It's his burden to live with. Not mine. I'm taking the higher road.

He says nothing and I wave politely to the media before glancing over my shoulder at Sarina and Tanner. I don't wait for them, I start walking, leaving a stunned Erick in my wake.

※ ※ ※

Last year, the rock band, Seconds to Midnight, won artist of the year. It was a huge deal for someone in the pop/punk world. Most of the nominations are pop artists. They were all fans of my dad and when I met them backstage, they had nothing but nice things to say. Sam, the lead singer, his dad is their manager, and dad and him were friends.

The three of them walk forward towards the fancy acrylic podium in front of me. It's lit reddish from the lighting illuminating it. Sam steps forward first. His usual dark emo cut is styled so its slicked back. Chris stands to his left, tattoos showing on his arm from his rolled-up cuffs, and Nate on his right all curly haired like a Jonas Brother.

The audience applauds for a few seconds. For this event, they have an area to the left of the stage with small round tables set up for the nominees. It's kind of cozy, and each seating arrangement has a flickering battery lit candle.

It's time for the award. Either outcome, I'll be the closing performance of the night. Erick's was in the beginning. From an industry standpoint it was good, but for the first time since our breakup it had no effect on me at all.

My heart starts racing and Sarina takes my sweaty hand in hers.

"Good evening, all. It's been a night," Sam says, his voice raspy. The audience cheers and whistles. "So many great artists have performed on this stage, and so many others will each year. Last March was special for us as we walked away with artist of the year."

He places his hands on the podium, showing off his muscular build.

"Tonight, we get the honor of announcing this year's artist of the year."

Chris leans into the mic. "Let's take a look at our nominees."

In sync the three of them turn behind them to a large screen. My leg starts to shake under the table. I've begun to tune out the names they are saying and the videos playing. Sarina squeezes my hand. I stare at the fake, flickering candle. My vision blurs and I close my eyes as Sam says my name. I reach for my necklace and trace the butterfly.

Mom. Dad. A tear slips down my cheek and I let go of a trembling breath. *I love you both so much. I wish you were here.* Another tear. Erick's name. My leg keeps going. Sarina leans into me and my eyes flicker open. On the screen as it fades out are the outline of white butterflies before it reverts to the swirls of gold and red like a screen saver. I gasp and beside me Sarina does the same. I peek over and see her tears too.

"And this years, artist of the year award, goes to—"

Chapter 40

PENNY

The audience erupts in cheers. From a low rumble to a deafening roar. People get to their feet. Spotlights dance around. I'm frozen in my chair. Stuck in a limbo between reality and not. Music plays around us. First, just a familiar melody. It's hard to hear over the thunderous applause.

Warmth fills me and air enters my lungs as I take a breath for what feels like the first time in hours. A comforting hand touches my shoulder. I lift my gaze to Sarina's dark tearful eyes. She's saying something to me. Yelling. But my ears and my heart still aren't registering anything. I continue to stare at her for what feels like a lifetime trying to sort through the chaos inside my head and around me.

Butterflies dance in my stomach as if they're alive. Sarina sits in the chair beside me and this time her voice breaks through.

"You did it!" She yells and gets to her feet and pulls me up along with her.

In my head, I hear Sam say my name. It plays like a broken record but it's the best one I've ever heard. I rise and Sarina pulls me into a hug. Across the table Tanner has a proud grin on her face. She tilts her head, widening her eyes to get me to go. Holy shit, I have to make a speech.

I turn and am greeted by nothing but love. Reporters aren't digging at my father. The keyboard warriors are hidden away. I don't bother to look at Erick because there's no reason to. I weave through the tables and Chris meets me at the first step. He has his tattooed arm outstretched to me and I take it, while lifting my dress with my other.

Sam has the award in his hand. It's a golden microphone. He gives it to me and leans in.

"Congratulations, Penny. Your dad would be so proud of you as we all are. Thank fuck you beat that asshole, Erick." He pulls back and winks, and I laugh.

I touch his arm and mouth *thank you*. The guys step aside giving me full access to the microphone. I place the award on the surface. There are still a few lingering cheers. In the crowd I look to my right where my sister is. She nods her head with a smile, wiping her happy tears.

"Wow. Thank you so much. I—" I pause and for a second my eyes land on Erick's scowl. I shake my head and focus my attention to the whole audience.

I clear my throat. "I had a speech in mind, but I think I'm going to go rogue tonight, if I can. Cut to commercial at any time."

There's laughter out in the crowd. I smile at the sound. My hands are trembling but not in a bad way.

"First, I'd like to thank my parents, for never letting me give up. Although they aren't here their presence is strong in my heart. My sister, for being there always, even from afar. She is my rock. We've been through a lot together, and I can't wait to spend more time with her soon."

I look at her, and she wipes her eyes.

"To Tanner, my manager, for staying on top of things and being organized, my record label and to all the fans who have made my dream become a reality. The last few years have been so hard. I lost two important people in my life, went through my first public breakup, and then had a documentary made about my family. I'm not going to lie, it's been a bit taxing on my mental health. I recently took a break, which some may have noticed. I vanished off social media and gave myself time reflect on it all."

I take a deep breath, waiting for someone to boo or Erick to yell out I'm a fraud but none of that happens.

"During that time, I learned some things. Not everyone is going to like who I am. They aren't all going to like my music or how that music was made. People will always talk. We're human and not perfect. And you know what. That's okay because at the end of the day it's about you being happy with you. My father, who I love dearly, may have done something I'm not proud of and I would never condone his actions, but he and my mother, along with my sister Sarina, supported me throughout my career and gave me the courage to sing on that stage. Without him I wouldn't have had some of the greatest experiences of my life."

I scan over the audience and my heart sinks as I stare at each face searching for the one person I know isn't here, but somewhere deep in my heart I know he's here with me. I release a shaky breath.

"If I may, I'd like to thank someone else. Zach Cullen." I smile and shake my head and stare directly into the main camera. "He helped me to believe in myself again. I'm human. I'm flawed. I make mistakes, but that's the beauty of life. We live and we grow. He taught me how to love myself again. I can't forget the Wingman's crew. When I was at my lowest, they never once treated me like a puppet on display for the world to criticize. I found a family that isn't blood and if it weren't for them, I wouldn't be in the good headspace I am now. Thank you all again for supporting me."

I step back. "I promise I'm done."

The audience laughs and once again without hesitation they get to their feet and clap. I can't stop the tears as I hold the award up. I turn to the three guys and I'm greeted by a group hug as they escort me backstage for my song.

Closing out the award show was something I never imagined I'd get to do. Most artists put on an elaborate show, but me, it's just me and mom on this stage. Her guitar brings me warmth and joy like she's here performing with me. I sing my heart out and hope to God Zach hears it in New York. The performance is one of my best. I'm on key and hitting every note the way it was intended to be. I take in the faces of the people I can see and absorb this moment in time. My career isn't ending, it's just getting started.

Chapter 41

PENNY

I don't waste a minute. The second I'm back in my bedroom I go for the opened suitcase I left in the corner. I toss the clothing I never put away onto the floor and then drag it to my bed. As I'm about to walk to my closet there's a knock at my door.

"Come in."

A few seconds pass and no one enters the room. Maybe I was hearing things. I shrug and start to walk but am stopped by the door creaking open.

"Took you long—"

"Hey there, love." Zach cuts me off. There's a hint of laughter in his sad tone.

A sound resembling a gasp mixed with a sob comes out of my mouth. The closet door is closed and on the back is a mirror. I haven't even changed out of my dress and it's dragging on the floor a bit without my heels. I lift my gaze to meet his soft golden eyes.

"Wa– wa– why are you wearing that? I thought you—I thought . . ."

It's not what I wanted to say but it's the first thing out of my mouth. I hold in a sharp breath to keep myself from breaking down. He takes a confident steady step forward. His hands rest at his sides. I try not to allow myself the pleasure of enjoying him in the tailored suit I bought for him. The black jacket sits well on his small, yet perfectly framed shoulders. Black tie, white button down, black slacks and dress shoes. His hair curled to perfection, slicked back with not a single strand out of place.

"Well, you see, it was a gift for this special occasion. A gift that I should have said thank you for instead of acting the way I did. Being in my own head because of my past, is not an excuse for my outburst. I'm sorry." He peers at himself then locks eyes with me. "The woman I've fallen in love with is nominated for this pretty big award"—he swallows—"I was cheering her on from afar, downstairs on the big screen TV. She gave quite an impressive speech. Also, the television is massive." His lips turn up into a smile. "Could catch an unwanted nose hair on that thing."

A watery laugh escapes my trembling lips. "Yeah," I squeak. "It-is rather large." I sniffle. "Wait. Back up, sunshine, can I hear what you said again?"

"It's big?" He grins.

I shake my head.

"Nose hairs?"

An unpleasant snort flies out of my nose. His grin kicks up the butterflies that were dormant in my stomach, waiting for the moment he flipped the switch. We're still eye to eye in the mirror. He steps forward and my heart does one of those double beats.

"Massive? Big award?" He wiggles his brows.

"The other part?"

He keeps himself at enough of a distance but close enough to feel his warmth. There's a sob building in my chest.

"You can say it," he whispers.

My words catch in my throat as his hot breath dances along my bare neck.

"Y-you've fallen i–in love with this woman?"

We never break eye contact. I so desperately want him to close the gap, but he's waiting for me to allow it.

"Irrevocably. And I was kind of hoping she felt the same. I tried to tell her, but I think I might have done it at all the wrong times. I'm not so sure she got my message. I also wanted to let her know that I want there to be an us. If she said look, I have an album and a tour to do and I'll be gone for a while, I'd be okay waiting. I've waited my whole life to find someone who I could call my safe haven and there's only one person who has ever made me feel it and it's her. I think––no, I know, it always will be."

"She's a lucky woman."

"No. I'm the lucky one, because I have her whole heart."

He says those words with confidence, and I can't help allowing myself the grace to smile.

"You're so cocky and sure of yourself aren't you, sunshine?"

The grin on his face zaps me into a new reality.

"Your damn right I am."

I laugh. I wipe some tears and find mascara on my fingers. I'll have to reapply my makeup but honestly, right now I don't care how I look.

"I'm here because I wanted to show my support and show her, she can have her career and me all at the same time. I'd love for her to trust me. I want to support her in any way I can. As a man in love should do. Relationships take time and patience. When you see your whole future flash in front of you with that person, you hold on because that's when you know it's the real deal. She's it for me."

"You didn't give up on her?"

"No. And I know for a fact from a little birdie with a big mouth that she didn't give up on me either."

I groan and mumble Sarina's name under my breath.

"It was Larry actually." He grins.

I snort out a laugh.

"I gave her space because I know she needed it, but I couldn't go another day without telling her how much . . . without telling *you* how much I love *you*. If you need more time . . ."

I whirl around, and I'm met with his shimmering eyes. They are so much more striking now that they aren't a reflection. His hands are fidgeting at his sides as if he wants to reach out but still waiting for me to say okay. I don't have the patience to wait another second for his touch. I lunge at him, closing the space and wrapping my arms around his neck. He stumbles back with a bellowing laugh.

"She—damn it, Zachary, you got me doing it too!"

Our laughter sounds magical, and I want to hold onto it.

I put a hand on my chest. "I love you. I trust you with all my heart. I shouldn't have ever doubted that we could make it work. During our week apart I realized I wasn't worried. I trust you. I was scared to feel again, but the moment I was singing my song and realized you weren't there with me, I knew I didn't want a life without you. Deep down I knew from the moment you were crouched on a knocked over chair."

We laugh together and I love how joyful it sounds.

His lips quiver with a hint of a smile. "Say it again, love."

"I love you, Zach."

My words are cut off by his intense lips crashing into mine. My knees weaken, and I melt into him. His arm snakes around my lower back to keep me from falling. He pulls away only slightly and I stare up at him and his soft gaze says it all.

"Keeping an eye on you started as a favor to your sister. She gave me a roof over my head, because my stubborn ass was too prideful to take the help of others. Spending time with you quickly turned into something more. I fell for the person I came to know. The terrible cook, the one with eighty-seven vibrators . . ."

I push at his chest and laugh.

"The one with a strange love for evil cats, and weird sea creatures. But mostly I fell in love with a woman who saw me too. The fear of not making enough money to support you made me think I wasn't good enough. Like you, I allowed my past relationship downfall to come between us. I'm sorry I got mad. I never should have talked to you the way I did. You have never once used that against me or made me feel bad for what I do for a living. I enjoy what I do, and I want a partner who can respect that, and you did from the start."

"Your love for your career is one of the things I love most about you. You have always been good enough for me."

His lips meet mine again in a searing heated kiss. I wrap my arms tighter around him as he grabs a hand full of my ass and squeezes. I sink into his touch and moan. Our tongues tangle as he backs me into the bed. We don't collapse onto it but keep kissing.

I gasp "Wait! Who is watching Larry?"

"I spilled all of my feelings, and your first thought is the cat."

He touches my waist and squeezes, tickling my sides. Laughing with him gives me the sense of calm I was searching for.

"Squirrel brain. You have to admit it's on point for us."

He chuckles. "It sure is."

"Maddie is taking care of them."

"Larry likes her?"

"Hold on."

Zach reluctantly removes his arm from around me, but before he has fully pulled away, he leans forward and kisses the top of my head. A soft blush dances across his scruffy cheeks. For a moment we stay like that before he reaches into the front pocket of his slacks to grab his phone.

"Look at these two."

He pulls up a picture of Maddie and Larry lounging on the couch. Larry is on top of Maddie's stomach and curled into a ball.

I laugh. "Seems Larry found a new BFF."

"Yeah, but that's okay." He slips the phone back into his pocket. "Because I got my girl."

He wraps his arms around me and tugs me closer to him. With his free hand he lifts it to my face and runs his thumb across my lips. I close my eyes and take in the moment with him. I hum and his thumb is replaced with his soft lips. I open my mouth for him. Our tongues collide and I shift to throw my arms around his neck.

"A job or career doesn't make a person, it's what's inside their heart. And you have a pretty big one."

He grins and I side eye him with jest.

"That I do."

I roll my eyes, and he holds me tighter.

"Mine," he growls, all low and possessive and it does something to all of me.

"Zach, I—"

"Holy shit, did you two make up already? I'm dying out here." Sarina whines from the other side of the door.

Zach chuckles and backs away. He sighs. "You can come in."

She rushes in and heads straight for us. We step into her open arms, and she squeals.

"ROOMIES! I can't wait till we all go back home and—"

"Home?" Zach asks.

Sarina lifts her hands in surrender and slinks back as if she's been caught doing something wrong. "Shit. You didn't tell him."

I shake my head and look at Zach. "I'm coming home." I pause. "Wait! You knew he was here?"

Sarina has a sly grin on her face. She shrugs her shoulders. "Maybe." She squeaks. "Someone had to find a way to sneak him in."

Zach's eyes land on me and a million butterflies resume their dance in my stomach. My heart leaps like it wants to jump out to meet his. His eyes become misty.

"You're coming home?" he asks, voice a bit raspy.

I nod. "I am." My own voice sounds weak. "I'm recording my last album, for now"—I pause—"Hey, that's a great name for an album."

"For Now, I like that. It's not goodbye, it's see you later."

I nod. "Yeah, that's exactly it. I'm recording in New York next month. I might do a short tour after releasing it, but I'm––" My voice breaks. "I'll officially be Penny Clarke, server and bar tender trainee of Wingman's Pub. You are looking at your newest employee."

"Really?"

"Yup. Thanks to Maddie."

Over the weekend Sarina called Maddie and while we were on the phone, I was able to secure my spot at Wingman's.

Zach is quietly watching me as if he's wanting to double check he's heard everything I said. As if he doesn't believe this is real. I may return one day but right now all I want is to lead a life that makes me happy.

"Zach?"

"And your home here?"

I shake my head. "That's not home. You are."

Again, he falls silent keeping his full attention on me.

"Zach?" I laugh a little.

I touch his cheeks. "You're my home. You, Sarina, everyone at Wingman's. Larry, Petunia." I grin and he follows suit.

"You sure?"

"Never been surer of anything in my life."

He kisses me. I wrap my arms around his neck, and he grabs my waist. He attempts to pick me up and I chuckle, because my legs don't move well in this dress. His laughter tickles my lips, and he pulls away resting his head against mine.

"Okay, I know when it's time to leave. I'll take a stroll or um . . . get a burger. Yeah. Get a burger. While you two get it on." She gets to the door and turns to us. "Oh, and one other thing, the walls in our house are thin, so maybe have fun when I'm at work. Thanks."

She slips out of the room leaving us. Zach and I turn to face one another. We lean our heads together and laugh as his finger glides down my chest and between my tight cleavage. I cup his full, hard length in my hands through his slacks.

"Lift your dress," he hums into my mouth.

I do as he asks, and his hand moves to my thighs and right up. His eyes widen when he discovers something missing. He runs his fingers through my wet lips and groans. "Damn woman. You're not wearing any underwear."

I shake my head, giggle, and bite my lip. "Kind of hard to in this dress."

He leans in and presses the softest, most intimate kiss to my mouth. It's sweet and hungry all at the same time. Our tongues tangle in slow motions and he brings me closer to him so I can feel him through the fabric of his slacks.

"You're always so wet and ready for me, love."

I roll my eyes at the deep growl in his voice. A shiver goes up my spine.

"Always," I whisper. "Help me with my dress?"

"You don't even have to ask."

I turn, lifting my hair for him to get the zipper. The second I'm out of the dress I whirl back to Zach, who narrows his hungry eyes at me. He's already starting to undo his tie, and I can't help being swept up by the sight of the first few buttons of his shirt undone. My cheeks are hot, and there's an ache between my thighs. My heart races as I close the distance between us.

"Now where were we, love?"

Epilogue

ZACH

EIGHT MONTHS LATER

P enny collapses in my arms and I sink further into the fluffy black sheets of my bed. Her warm breath tickles my neck as she holds on tight and buries her face into my shoulder. We are both naked and spent. Late afternoon sunlight peeks through the window, brightening up the space. I kiss her cheek as she snuggles deeper.

"It's almost time," I say into her hair, kissing her.

She lifts her head. "I'm going to miss this room."

I chuckle. "We've made many memories here."

She bites her lip as her cheeks turn a shade of pink. I touch her face and run the pad of my thumb over her smooth skin. She sighs, closing her eyes and leaning into my touch.

With Penny's new album due out in the new year, we wanted to get our house situation taken care of beforehand. It's her last with her current label and they have only asked her to do three shows following. One in New York, Los Angeles, and the other in the UK. Which I've been able to take off to join her on the road. After that, she's decided to continue to write, maybe showcase some new music at Wingman's, but ultimately, she's going on a long hiatus.

"Larry is going to miss his bestie." She opens her eyes and her lips curve up.

"I'm sure he'll be relieved when I'm gone."

Sarina has put up with Penny and I for the last eight months. It was time to give her some space. Well, not too much space since we'll be around the block, but enough for her to have her own life. I'm grateful for her giving me a place when I struggled.

"He can always come visit his auntie Penny and uncle Zach."

I narrow my eyes at her and go in for her sides. She's most ticklish there. "I am not that cat's uncle."

Her squeals and giggles are such a turn on that I'm hard again almost instantly. She pauses, her heated gaze zeroing in on me. The sheets are now a tangled mess half on the bed half off. For a few long seconds I stare at the woman I'm going to marry. A fact she's unaware of, as the moment is happening before the end of the day.

Her bright gorgeous eyes keep me grounded. I've learned so much from her and have accepted where I am in my life. Her love for me isn't because I'm rich and famous, it's because when we're together we make each other whole again. We're like the missing piece to each other's puzzle.

"Zach," she whispers, and it comes out breathy and turned on.

She throws her naked leg over my body. She's wet and warm. I groan, my cock hard against her leg.

"You're ready to go again, aren't you?"

"Should I save some for later?"

I rest my forehead against hers. "Who says I won't be ready to go then too?"

She kisses me, her moans do me in and seconds I'm devouring her lips again, needing the friction between us. She reaches up to wrap her arms around my neck when there's a scratching at the door. We retreat from the kiss and turn our heads. Standing on his back legs with two paws against the door is Larry.

"Devil cat." I hiss.

At that comment Larry whirls around and glares at me.

"What do you want?" I ask.

Penny smacks my chest playfully. "Stop being mean. He wanted to spend our last few hours here together. I told you he was going to miss you."

"Larry and I--"

"Aha!" Her yell startles me. "You can say his name properly."

"You're such a brat," I laugh. "Maybe if we ignore him, he'll go back to wherever he came from."

"I forgot he was in here. He slept curled up next you for a few hours."

"He was not."

"He so was! I woke up around eight in the morning to pee and he was there. I thought he followed me out but apparently, he must have been in here the whole time."

"So, he heard and saw us?"

It's one thing I won't miss for sure. The cat has it out for me.

She giggles and bites her lip. "Yeah, I guess so."

I groan. "It's like having a child."

"He's still watching us," she whispers, her eyes focused on the cat.

"Ignore him."

Larry lets out a groaning meow. I reach to the side of me and cover us in the blankets. She grins.

"I like this. It's like our own little cocoon."

"I don't want Larry looking at my ass."

She snorts. "I love us."

I bring my lips to her neck "I love you, Pen."

Her breath hitches and her face softens.

"I love you, Zach. Kiss me," she says, so I do.

There's a beep from a car out front, followed by the jingle of keys and the opening and closing of the front door.

"Honey's, I'm home. God, it smells like sex and . . . is that my perfume? Ugh, anyway. Don't come out naked."

Sarina's footsteps on the stairs and voice carries into the room.

She knocks on the door. "I know you're both probably having all the sex right now, but I wanted to let you know you have twenty minutes until the agent gets to the house with your keys. Also, I'm coming to karaoke tonight. Maddie says it's a 90s theme! I'm breaking out my Spice Girls attire. Oh, and bring your ear plugs."

Without another word, her footsteps retreat.

"Of course, Maddie would spill the beans about karaoke," I say.

After months of separation, Maddie has finally started the divorce paperwork with her almost ex-husband who while he refused to work on their relationship, also didn't want to draw the papers. When she found out he was seeing someone, she filed. She and Sarina are keeping their relationship platonic, but I think they are both waiting until it's all over to make anything happen.

"We should shower and get ready."

She smiles and runs her thumb over the stubble on my jawline. I give her a quick kiss and hop out of bed to find my discarded boxers. I don't need to walk out and give Sarina a show. I round the bed to the other side and slip them on. She's watching me with her head propped up. A grin crosses her face.

"Uh, don't move and turn around slowly."

"What why?"

"The cat," she whispers. "He's watching you."

I do as she says, and cautiously turn. The cat lifts himself up off the floor and trots over happily. He smooches on my bare back and purrs as he does.

Penny giggles. "Awww . . . he does love you."

He goes in for another and I pet him. His purr is so loud it sounds like a motorboat. After a few seconds he runs towards the door and starts to scratch it.

"LARRY!" We both shout, then look at each other. Our laughter together is something I never want to not hear.

"We'll have to do a quick shower—no concert."

"It's okay. We have plenty of time now for those, don't we?" she asks.

She gets up out of the bed and walks to where I am. Just looking at her gets me all ready for another round, but there's no time for that. I lean forward and rest my forehead against hers. She closes her eyes and touches her lips to mine.

I grin. "Well, love, nothings gonna stop us now."

I keep trying to tell myself to breathe. I've always heard people saying that when they meet the person they are meant to marry, they just know. I understand it all now, because it's how I felt when my eyes first landed on Penny.

This woman standing in front of *our* new forever home is stunning in her ripped jeans, rolled at the bottom to hang just above her black doc martins. Her silver locket rests over her black cotton turtleneck. She holds open her pale green corduroy button up jacket and spins. I love how carefree she is in this moment.

The street is narrow, and the homes are hidden behind large bushes and shrubbery. Ours no different. It's a mid-size white ranch with black shutters. When Penny first saw it, it was love at first sight. I liked the privacy it offered and so did she. While we aren't hidden anymore from the media, things have calmed down since the award show and documentary release.

Daylight is fading, but there's still a hint left. The outdoor sconce above Penny illuminates the space around her. She holds her arms in up in a "ta-da" like pose and I shake my head laughing. It's quiet here. You can't even hear the cars from the main road. I love this neighborhood.

Her smile calls to me. I just have to wait a few more seconds for my plan to happen.

"Are you coming or what?" she asks, crossing her arms, playfully scowling at me.

I peek a glance over my shoulder at the freshly white concrete driveway. *Where are you, Sarina?* I'm about to turn around when a jingle stops me. My heart picks up pace. I remember a few weeks ago going to Sarina and asking to borrow Larry for this. I almost did it crouched on the chair like when we first met, but this felt

more special. This place is ours. Penny bought it for us, but together we'll make it a home. We had many conversations about my feelings towards having her buy it, but ultimately it was the right decision and I'm okay with it.

The four-legged creature comes prancing up the driveway. A bell on his collar along with the ring, which I'd given to Sarina for this purpose. She walks up the driveway with the cat leash in her hand. We lock eyes and she smiles before returning her attention back to Larry and Penny.

"Larry?" Penny asks, her voice raising.

I wasn't sure what he'd do, afraid he might run, but instead, he heads right towards his target: Penny. She crouches and calls for him. His tail sways back and forth and I step forward, walking along the red brick path up to the doorway while Larry now trudges through the colorful leaves covering the well-maintained yard.

"Hey there, buddy." She tucks a strand of hair behind her ear and pets him.

She looks up at me. "What is he doing here?"

My hands start to tremble, and I shrug with a sure smile that probably gives me away. She starts to scratch his chin and as her fingers get closer to his black collar, I suck in a breath.

She peers at the cat. "Sarina let you out to roam. Oh, you're never gonna wanna go back—" her brows crinkle and fingers stop moving when she feels something.

"What is—what is this?"

She meets my gaze and I urge her with a nod of my head. An unsure watery smile grazes her face.

"Zach?" Her voice wavers.

"Go ahead. Look."

As she focuses back on the cat, I get on my knee. She gasps, covering her mouth with one hand while her other is still on Larry's collar. I feel Sarina's presence on my right. She's getting ready to grab Larry. I reach for him and gently unhook the collar and slide the ring off, as Sarina swoops in for him and then buckles him into the harness.

"Should I stand? Or stay down here with you?" Her eyes brim with tears.

"Whatever you want to do, love," I say, softly.

She sniffles and smiles. "Okay. I should stand. Most definitely."

Her words come out a mile a minute. She takes a deep breath once she straightens herself and I take her hand in mine, while hold the ring in my other.

"Penelope Grace Clarke. You barged into my life unexpectedly and while I was vulnerable against a cat."

She laughs and wipes her face.

"There was something about the way you took charge of the situation that made me fall for you. The night at the bar when you asked to help, solidified everything for me. I had to get to know the woman who, despite what she was going through, risked being found for people she barely knew. You're beautiful inside and out. You bring joy to everyone around you. You're the only person I want to spend the rest of my life loving. I'm not as good with speeches as you, but I tried. So, Penny, in front of our new home and everyone on video chat." I point over my shoulder.

Sarina has Larry on the leash in one hand, while holding her phone in the other. On the screen is the Wingman's crew and Clarice. Penny covers her mouth with her hand and then turns back to me.

I breathe in a full breath and then out, slow and steady. From this angle with the house in view, I'm home.

"I'm asking you . . ." I pause to clear the lump in my throat. I'm not embarrassed to allow my eyes to fill with tears. Her bright smile is all I need in confirmation that she's all in. "If you'd do me the honor of being my wife?"

She nods her head. "Yes, Zach. Yes. Please."

I chuckle and slide the small silver band, with a shimmering one carat diamond in the center, onto her left ring finger. It's not flashy or big, it's a simple cut. She stares down at it with so much love in her eyes and my heart slows a little knowing how much she loves it.

"Stand up, sunshine, I wanna kiss you!"

Laughing, I get to my feet. I'm barely standing as she grabs my face and tugs me towards her. Her lips meld into mine and I wrap my arms protectively around her. My mouth parts and she slips her tongue in. Her fingers find the back of my hair and she brushes them through. I hum at the pleasure it brings me. She pulls back and we stare at each other.

"I love you, Zach."

"Love you."

"Can we say congratulations yet. I'm dying over here!" Maddie's voice rings through the phone.

I wrap my arm around her, and we turn to face Sarina. She steps forward and all their faces are squished together. They are crammed by Marks desk in the office. I look at each one of them as Penny babbles a mile a minute while flashing her ring at the screen. Mark, who I can't thank enough for trusting me with running his place when he's not there. Maddie, who I confided in about this engagement. Then Clarice. I think back to when I found out she was my mom. It hasn't been an easy road. I've had moments where I still feel betrayed, but she and I have been working towards a strong, healthy relationship. I want that with her, because I know her heart was in the right place and if I'm going to start a family with Penny one day, I want them to know what that looks like.

"Did you open the door for the first time yet?" Maddie asks.

I pull the key from my front jean pocket. I hold it up and Penny holds onto it too. We lock our eyes and then turn back. With our friends and family watching, together we unlock the door to our new life. Penny slips her hand into mine. Hers are warm and inviting and I'm never going to get tired of the feeling.

She glances up, her bright green eyes finding mine.

"On three?" she asks.

"On three," I whisper, my voice breaking.

She uses her thumb to wipe near my eye then pulls away, resting her arm back at her side.

"One, two, three," we count in unison and step over the threshold.

THE END

Acknowledgements

A special thanks to my husband. Publishing this book would have not been possible without his support and dedication. Thank you for taking this chance alongside me.

Thank you to my parents for encouraging me to keep going and to my family for continuing to support me on this journey.

A heartfelt thank you to everyone involved in the process of making this book ready for publication. This book would not be where it is now if it wasn't for your help. Beth, Kelly, and Tara. Your love and support on this new adventure means the world to me.

To all the friendships I've made in a special corner of the internet, thank you for all the love and support you've given me over the last two years. The relationships I've made will always hold a special place in my heart.

Thank you to my early readers for your support.

Finally, to all the readers who have taken a chance on my words. To the ones who have followed me since day one and to the ones who have discovered my work along the way, thank you for giving my characters a home in your imagination.

About The Author

Regina Brownell resides on Long Island, New York, between the city lights of Manhattan, and the beautiful beaches of the Hampton's. When her oldest child was born, she became a stay-at-home mom. With the support of her husband, three children, and three fur-babies, Regina spends her time balancing mom-life with her love for writing.

You can find more of Regina's books by visiting her Amazon page

Note From The Publisher

T hank you for taking a chance on this book and for supporting both the author and our publishing company. As a new
publisher, we are dedicated to delivering compelling Romance and
immersive Fantasy stories to readers like you. I extend my sincere
appreciation to those who have guided and supported us as we take
our first steps in this journey.

Your support is invaluable as we continue to grow, and we look
forward to bringing you many more stories in the future.